WHATEVER
IT
TAKES

D0359515

Also by Jessica Pack

As Wide as the Sky

Published by Kensington Publishing Corporation

WHATEVER
IT
TAKES

Jessica Pack

KENSINGTON BOOKS
www.kensingtonbooks.com

KENSINGTON BOOKS are published by

Kensington Publishing Corp.
119 West 40th Street
New York, NY 10018

Copyright © 2019 by Josi S. Kilpack

All Kensington titles, imprints, and distributed lines are available at special quantity discounts for bulk purchases for sales promotion, premiums, fund-raising, educational, or institutional use.

Special book excerpts or customized printings can also be created to fit specific needs. For details, write or phone the office of the Kensington Sales Manager: Kensington Publishing Corp., 119 West 40th Street, New York, NY 10018. Attn. Sales Department. Phone: 1-800-221-2647.

Kensington and the K logo Reg. U.S. Pat. & TM Off.

ISBN-13: 978-1-4967-1819-8 (ebook)
ISBN-10: 978-1-4967-1819-4 (ebook)
Kensington Electronic Edition: June 2019

ISBN-13: 978-1-4967-1817-4
ISBN-10: 1-4967-1817-8
First Kensington Trade Paperback Edition: June 2019

10 9 8 7 6 5 4 3 2 1

Printed in the United States of America

To my parents, Walt and Marle Schofield,
who always told us the truth, even when it wasn't pretty

Acknowledgments

This story went through many versions before the right one was found. I am so grateful to the editor, Alicia Condon, for her patience with my finding the right path to the final version. Thanks to Lane Heymont, my agent with Tobias Literary Agency, for facilitating the connection to Kensington Publishing and all the people at Kensington who brought this story to life.

Big thanks also to Jennifer Moore (*The Shipbuilder's Wife,* Covenant, 2018) and Nancy Campbell Allen (*The Lady in the Coppergate Tower,* Shadow Mountain, 2019) for their continual encouragement and brainstorming sessions that took place over the yearlong process of bringing this story together. I had to reach out to some people much smarter than me for this story; thank you to Crystal and Jairus White, Dr. Rodger S. Hansen, and Jamie McElheny for answering my questions in the attempt to make fewer mistakes on my end, though any mistakes come from my weaknesses, not theirs. Jenny Proctor (*Wrong for You,* Covenant, 2017) gave this a fast and thorough read-through before I submitted the final draft; I am so grateful to her for so many reasons.

I recently heard a quote from a female writer whose name I wish I knew that said, "That which takes me from my writing gives me something to write about." I am so deeply grateful for my family for giving me the richness of life that allows me to spend so much time in worlds of my own making and so much content to draw from. Every story I write represents a journey of my own in one way or another, and this one was no different as I explored connection and truth and finding our way both to ourselves and to the people we love. By the end, I was reminded again how lucky I am to have the family I've been blessed with and taught by. I thank my Father in Heaven for the opportunities I have had in life to learn and to give and to grow. I can only hope that I have used the gifts He's given me as He hoped I would.

1

Sienna

March

The paper sheet crinkles as I lie back on the exam table per the doctor's instructions. I stare at the fluorescent lights in the ceiling and imagine that the long breaths I am taking will pull calm over my fear like a tarpaulin over the back of Daddy's pickup.

It will be okay.

I wish someone else were saying those words to me. Holding my hand. Kissing my forehead.

"Sienna is a pretty name," Dr. Sheffield says in a coffee-shop-conversation tone. She's in her late forties, I think. I wonder if she has kids.

"Thank you."

"Wasn't there a *Seinfeld* episode about a girl named Sienna?" Dr. Sheffield pulls back the right side of the paper gown I put on five minutes ago—opening in front, per the nurse's instruction.

"Yeah."

"Lift your right arm, please."

I raise my arm, bending at the elbow. The doctor begins the breast exam while the nurse stands like a centurion in the corner of the room. To ensure propriety, I assume. I think it would be more appropriate to have fewer people looking at my half-naked self.

"Wasn't the episode about George dating a crayon?" the doctor continues.

"Yeah." Tyson and I had found the episode a few years ago after yet one more person had brought up the reference to my name. People a generation ahead of me. Dr. Sheffield fits that category just like this topic fits well into the small-talk paradigm.

"So, Sienna is a color?"

"Yeah."

"Reddish brown?"

"Yeah." Dad says it's the color of sunset in autumn, when sunlight has depth and shadows are solid. Tyson compares it to the red dirt in Hawaii, where we honeymooned a million years ago.

Dr. Sheffield's movements become slower, focusing on the upper part of my right breast and confirming that the lump isn't some macabre figment of my imagination after all.

I begin anxiously reciting the poem I memorized in the fourth grade. I need to distract myself.

> *Who has seen the wind?*
> *Neither I nor you.*
> *But when the leaves hang trembling,*
> *The wind is passing through.*

The poem always makes me think of the line of poplar trees separating the backyard from the ranch. When the wind blows, the leaves sound like a river and shimmer like thin sheets of metal. Wind is invisible, but you know it's there because of what it does.

"That's the lump?"

I nod.

"Tender?"

"A little."

"Hmm. Let me check the other side. Put your left arm over your head."

I do as I'm told, then close my eyes and picture the shimmery leaves of the poplar trees again. I recite the poem a second time and try to add other images to center myself on the far side of the swirling panic. Acres of ranch land, tight against the horizon. Tyson with his shirt off throwing bales of hay onto the trailer. I can *see* the memories but can't get lost in them the way I so desperately want to.

The doctor finishes examining my left breast and pulls the paper gown over that half of my chest. She goes back to the right side and moves more slowly for a second exam.

"Your mother had breast cancer?"

Inhale.

"Yeah."

"When?"

I do the math in my head, though I shouldn't need to.

Exhale.

"Twenty-three years ago, I guess. I was two when she died." The paperwork I had filled out in the waiting area had asked about my family medical history but not whether my mother's breast cancer had led to her death. I think that's an important oversight. I imagine my mother—a woman I don't remember, though pictures prove that I look like her—lying on a table just like this one twenty-three years ago. There is only one family photo of us, taken in the hospital on the day I was born—Dad grinning bigger than I've ever seen and Mom's freckled face flushed and sweaty. Dad calls the freckles I inherited from Mom "Cinnamon Sprinkles." Not a little smattering on my nose but rather head-to-toe coverage that gets darker when I spend time in the sun, though the parts of me that have never seen the sun are freckled too.

"Any other direct relatives with breast cancer? Aunt? Cousin? Grandmother?"

"I don't think so."

The doctor raises an eyebrow, and I answer the unasked question. "I don't know my mom's side of the family."

"They're in Canada," I continue, reapplying the effort it takes to stay in this moment. "My mom was an only child." So was Dad. So am I. I've been so sure that I would be the one to usher in a generation that would fill all six seats around a standard kitchen table. After two years of trying to start that fantasy-league family the old-fashioned way, Tyson and I went to a specialist and found ourselves in the seventh circle of modern babymaking hell. Pokes and prods turned into drillings and scrapings. Thirty-thousand dollars and multiple procedures later, we had nine viable embryos and fresh hope I find embarrassing to think about now. The first round implanted three embryos, all of which failed. Tyson wanted to take a break. At first he said it was so that my chemistries could stabilize, but then admitted that he'd started exploring some career options that wouldn't be feasible if having a baby were our first priority, which it had been for three years by then. It broke something in me. What if all our efforts had been a waste? Of time. Of money. Of marriage. Of all that stupid hope. I had been trying to recover from the fallout of all of that when Dad got sick. Now what? If this is cancer . . . what then?

"Do you know what stage your mom's cancer was when she was diagnosed?" the doctor asks, drawing me back to this moment.

"No."

"Was it a single tumor or multiple?"

"I don't know." Why don't I know?

"I'm sorry for all these sensitive questions." She is still palpating, pressing from angles I did not know existed. It hurts. Has she found a second lump?

"Do you know how long after diagnosis your mother passed away?"

Finally, a question I have an answer for. "About six months." I have outlived Mom by two years now. I am supposed to live a long, productive life to make up for her not having had the chance. I had already been failing on my course when I found the lump.

The centurion nurse holding my chart clears her throat. "Her dad is under fifty and has had prostate cancer," she says.

Her sentence should be followed by an exclamation point. Both of my parents have had cancer! One of them is dead.

I am drowning, flailing my arms in hopes of finding something to stop my descent when Dr. Sheffield asks, "When was that, Sienna?" The calm of her voice becomes the steadiness that I am looking for. I grab tight, dig my nails in, and pull myself up to where there is air to fill my lungs again.

Who has seen the wind?

Inhale.

Neither I nor you.

Exhale.

"Last fall. They caught it early, and Dad agreed to aggressive treatment. He's doing pretty good." Pretty good, but not well. Not really. I can't think about that right now if I want to hold myself together.

Dr. Sheffield nods. "Did you notice in your self-exam that the lump moves?"

"Yeah." Google said that was a bad sign.

"It's small."

"Yeah." Google said that was a *good* sign.

The doctor pulls the right side of the drape closed, sits down on her rolling stool, and puts out her hand for the chart. Paper charts—so twenty-first-century Wyoming.

"You can sit up, Sienna."

I sit up and pull the paper gown closed across my chest, trying not to feel violated. Not by the doctor—this is her job—by the lump.

Dr. Sheffield looks up from the chart, her expression sympathetic. "Thursday is your birthday?"

I shrug. I've been dreading my twenty-fifth birthday since before I found the lump. The day will end with one of the letters Mom wrote to me on her deathbed. They were a way for her to remain a part of the life of the daughter she would never see grown. I used to revel in those letters that started with "Dearest Sienna." I'd also used the advice within them the way a ship captain might map his course by the stars. According to the pattern of previous letters, this one will be full of advice about motherhood and enjoying the journey and treating my marriage as the most important relationship I'll ever have. *This is not how my life is supposed to go,* I wail in my mind with plaintive regret, frustration, and embarrassment wrapped into a ball of silent words. The keening rolls through my mind like a thunderstorm across the prairie.

Deep breath.

Hold it together.

I have the whole drive back home to fall apart.

"You've never had a mammogram," Dr. Sheffield says as she sets the chart aside.

"No." I've thought that I'm not old enough for mammograms. But I'm not a woman of average risk, am I? Why hadn't I taken that more seriously?

The doctor opens a drawer, removes a pad of paper, and starts writing. "My nurse is going to call the woman's center here in Cheyenne. If we're lucky there'll be a cancellation today. We'll need the mammogram and ultrasound before you come back here for a biopsy. Can you do all that today?"

I want to say no, I'm not ready. "Yeah."

The doctor tears off the paper and gives it to the nurse, a look passing between them before Dr. Sheffield's attention settles on me again. Her expression softens.

"This is all very routine." Dr. Sheffield smiles. "If you didn't live such a distance away, we wouldn't be moving so fast."

I appreciate her empty comfort the way a blind man might hold a sentimental photograph and force a polite smile to show acceptance of the offering. I begin to shake on the inside. This is real. It's happening. I imagine that after my mom was diagnosed, she held me and Dad and cried. Who will I hold? Who will I even tell? My family can't take this.

"The results won't be available for a few days. I don't suppose you'll be staying in Cheyenne that long, though."

"I have to head back tonight." Dad thinks I came to Cheyenne to pick up a riding saddle I want to fix up. I found the saddle listed for a reasonable price last week and convinced the buyer to hold it until today if I Venmoed him an extra twenty dollars. The saddle has a hand-tooled border and wooden stirrups but is in need of new straps and stitching. Dad agreed to pay for the saddle as my birthday gift, and I arranged pickup around this appointment. I'm going to have to think of an excuse for why I'll be hours late getting home. I don't need another saddle or another leather project as much as the ranch needs the four hundred dollars. But Dad bought the saddle because he loves me. Because he wants me to be happy. Because family is everything and I am the last branch of our family tree, barren and stark against a winter sky.

There is a tapping at the exam room door, and it opens a few inches. I can't hear what's said from the other side, but Dr. Sheffield nods in response. The door shuts again, and the doctor faces me. "We're in luck. The radiology department can see you in forty-five minutes. We'll text you with the time you can come back this afternoon for the biopsy as soon as we figure out where to fit you in. Does that work?"

My stomach begins to hurt. I hadn't expected things to be quite so efficient. "That works," I say in my big-girl voice. I want to appear confident, strong, and . . . I can't think of another word to describe the woman I have tried to be for years. I'm not that woman. Maybe I never was. Maybe I never will be.

The doctor puts the chart on the counter and rests her hands in her lap as she looks at me with a compassionate expression. Her bobbed brown hair is perfectly coiffed as though it's popped out of a Jell-O mold each morning. She doesn't look old enough to be one of those women who goes to the beauty shop once a week to have her hair set, but maybe she's older than she looks—yet young enough to appreciate *Seinfeld* and wear Dansko clogs. Or maybe she spends an hour on her hair every morning. Maybe one day I'll have a high-maintenance bob like that and stop putting my hair into a ponytail all the time. Maybe I'll be bald in a few months. Maybe I'll be dead. I swallow the bile that rises in my throat.

"I'm glad you came in, Sienna. So many women wait too long, especially when they're young. If this lump is cancerous—and I'm not saying that it is—you caught it early, and that can make all the difference." She cocks her head to the side, looking more thoughtful; sympathetic. "Are you okay?"

I look down at the textured paper drape covering my thighs so that I can hide my thoughts. No, I am not okay. I haven't been okay for a long time, and this certainly doesn't push me over the mountain range that separates me from everyone else. People who make a plan for their lives, follow it, and look back with self-assurance of a job well done. "Yeah."

"A few final questions," Dr. Sheffield says when I don't offer anything else. She picks up my chart again and glances over the paperwork.

"Your insurance is through a Tyson K. Richardson."

I pick at the drape.

"Sienna?"

"He's my husband."

"Does he know about this?"

We don't really have that kind of relationship anymore, but out loud I give the same excuse I've given everyone else these last months. "He's working in London right now." Like coming to Cheyenne for a saddle, it's true. But like this appointment I've hidden from everyone, it's not all the truth.

She waits a few seconds until she realizes I'm not offering up anything else. "But you put down Mark Chadwick as your emergency contact—that's your dad? You live with him in Lusk, right?"

I nod.

"Does he know you're here?"

I want to say that I'm not a child and I don't need my dad to hold my hand for a lady doctor appointment. Instead I shake my head. And wish Dad were here and that he *were* holding my hand.

"You and your family have been through a lot, and I'm guessing that makes it hard to talk to loved ones about difficult news, but this is a really heavy burden for you to carry alone, Sienna. Don't keep it in."

"I won't," I say.

You'd think that without much experience being dishonest in my life, telling these lies would be hard. I tell myself they're coming easy because they are kind lies. Necessary ones. Protective.

The doctor leaves. I shed the paper drape and start putting my clothes back on while I wonder who I'm really protecting. Them or me?

2

Mark

October 1993

Mark turned off the alarm on the clock radio within a nanosecond of the newest Celine Dion song blaring from the speaker on top—they loved her up here. He missed his Alan Jackson, truth be told, but when in Rome. . . . He rubbed a hand over his eyes and looked over to make sure the alarm hadn't woken Mae.

Dolly's Donuts had to be hot and ready by six in the morning Monday through Saturday, which meant the donut fryers clocked in at three a.m. He really needed to get to bed earlier, but that thought only emphasized why he continually stayed up too late. Despite the pride he'd taken in turning off the alarm before it woke her, he rolled onto his side and slid up against her smooth back, closing his eyes and loving how perfectly their bodies fit together. He nuzzled her neck, and she snuggled backward into him, a mewing kitten-like sound escaping those perfect lips. He was suddenly very awake.

"I've got to get to work," he whispered into her ear, hoping she'd convince him that he could stay in bed another ten minutes.

"Mmmmm." She didn't turn around to face him.

What he wouldn't give to stay just like this all day. Even if all they did was lie nestled together, warm in their bed: enough world for just the two of them. After another minute, he accepted the inevitable, kissed her neck, and began to pull toward his side of the bed—it would be freezing when he stepped out from under the covers. Their tiny apartment was heated by a single radiator in the living room, which meant the bedroom was left to the influence of a very cold fall. Mae rolled over to face him before he moved away, lifting her hand to trail her finger down his forehead and over the bridge of his nose. When she rested her finger on his lips, he kissed it and could just make out her responding smile in the dark. Her hair looked like mist floating around her head in the minimal light cast by the streetlight outside. "You 'ave to go?" she asked.

The accented words rolled off her tongue. "You know I do. It's a good job."

After blowing out his knee on the rodeo circuit when he was nineteen, Mark had convinced Mom that it would be worthwhile for him to get a degree in agricultural management. If generational ranching families like theirs wanted to make it into the new millennium, it wasn't enough to just know how to raise and sell cattle. The University of Wyoming, in Laramie, was close enough for him to work the ranch on weekends and come home for summers. When his final year at U of W came into view, he met with a counselor about study-abroad programs. The rest of his life was going to be spent on the ranch, and before that happened he wanted to live somewhere else. It was the only part of the world outside his home state he was ever likely to see. Mom eventually agreed to a two-semester program offered in Ontario—at least he wouldn't have to cross any oceans or learn a different language.

Mark had arrived in Hamilton, Ontario, in time for winter classes. He made friends with people from all over the world, ate his fries with gravy, and went to clubs on the weekends. He'd gone home for the summer and then arrived back in Hamilton in time for his last semester of school—he'd walk at U of W in the spring. He'd met Mae at a club his very first night back—fate, pure and simple. He'd never brought a girl home, but what he thought was going to be a one-night stand turned into a whole new life. A couple of weeks later, Mae got kicked out of her friend's apartment, but she had been pretty much staying at Mark's place anyway, and they stayed up all night, tangled up in each other and making plans. The next day Mark dropped his classes and applied for a work permit—he couldn't work on a student visa. They found a cheap apartment the same week he got the bakery job. He planned to finish up school once his permanent residency was straightened out, but for now he wanted to enjoy a life that was nothing like the one he'd lived up until now. Mom didn't know about dropping out of school yet. She knew about Mae and the new apartment, though, and had plenty to say about that. He'd bring her up to speed once he figured out how to explain it in a way that wouldn't lead to nuclear war.

"I wish I didn't have to go." He pulled Mae tightly to him. Finding a job hadn't been easy; employers were leery of immigrants, but he told himself every morning as he walked through the dark streets that he wouldn't be frying donuts forever. And going home to Mae every day more than made up for the insecurity he sometimes felt being so out of his element. Mae hadn't found work yet, but she was looking.

Mae smiled, her green eyes twinkling in the bit of light filtering around the blanket hung over the window as a makeshift curtain. "You can stay 'ere with me. I won't tell."

He leaned in and kissed her. "I'll be back at noon. Maybe we can take a nap."

"A naked nap?"

Mark had never known a woman like Mae Gérard; there certainly weren't any like her in Lusk, Wyoming. She was bold and sexy and unapologetic about both. She also had this amazing ability to live in the moment and know what she wanted. That she wanted *him,* a farm boy from Wyoming, made him feel as though he could fly. This was how the other half lived—the city people with apartments instead of acres and paychecks instead of cattle sales where the proceeds had to stretch for twelve months. He kissed her and pulled back. "I'm going to hold you to that."

She smiled at him and raised herself up on one elbow. "There is something I need to tell you, Mark. I 'ope it will make you 'appy."

"If it makes you happy, it will make me happy."

"It makes me 'appy. I tink."

He raised his eyebrows. "You're not sure?"

She didn't answer but shifted a little bit, bunching the pillow under her head. "I'm going to 'ave your baby, Mark."

Brakes and squealing tires sounded in his mind. Surely, he'd misunderstood. It had sounded as though she'd said . . . "What?"

"I'm pregnant."

They'd been together only a couple of months—the best months of his life, to be sure—but they talked about their future in vague terms because the present was so all-encompassing. And they'd been careful. *Really* careful, because getting Mae pregnant wasn't part of any of the new plans he'd been making. This changed, literally, everything.

"You're not 'appy." She started to turn away, and he took hold of her shoulder, pulling her back to him.

"I'm happy, Mae, so happy. I'm just . . . surprised. But happy surprised. Ecstatic surprised!" He smiled to prove it and kissed her freckled nose. "This is amazing, Mae. We made a baby!"

My mother is going to kill me.

3

Sienna

"So, how was Cheyenne?"

I look up from the sink, a handful of dripping silverware in my hands, and stare at Beck while my heart spins in my chest. How does she know about my appointment? "What?"

Beck pulls her perfect eyebrows together. "Didn't you pick up a saddle in Cheyenne this week?"

I exhale slowly and look away from her now-curious expression. I focus on the sink full of dishes left over from my birthday dinner, which Aunt Lottie, Beck's mom, hosted tonight. "Oh, yeah, it was good." I extol the virtues of the saddle while I put the silverware into the dishwasher. I haven't thought about the saddle even once since I put it in the barn two days ago.

"I'll have to come see it once you get it fixed up," Beck says, joining me at the sink. I volunteered for dishes because I'm all but coming out of my skin tonight. The doctor's office hasn't called with the results of my biopsy, and my anxiety is growing by the hour. Does a longer wait mean bad news? Like, they ran the tests a second time to make sure? I've been reading personal accounts of breast cancer survivors online. They are terrifying.

"I'll let you know when the saddle is ready for your shameless praise," I say, leaving out that it might be a while before I fix it up. Or never. Silence descends, and I panic a little because I can feel Beck watching me, wondering at my odd reaction and avoidance of eye contact. If anyone can break this shell I've tried to put up, it's Beck, but if I tell her it will become a wildfire out of control.

Officially, Beck and I are cousins—second, once removed—but she's also been my best friend for most of my life. Her closest sibling is seventeen years older than her, and she's only two years older than me. We've grown up together. She lived in town and I was out on the flats, but we danced in the same dance classes and joined roping club the same year. I took to heeling and goat tying in junior rodeo while she dominated barrel racing—always the more glamorous girl's event. There are more pictures of my childhood with her in them than without, and our lives were supposed to continue their parallel course after high school. Here we are, though, and she's got two kids and I've got none. She's got a marriage that's working, and I've lived apart from Tyson for almost half a year. She fits in everywhere she goes, and I fit nowhere anymore, except maybe with Daddy at the ranch. I've always belonged with Dad.

"Thank you for the cake," I say, trying to present a "free and easy" mood. I've thanked her twice already, but she doesn't remind me.

"You know I love an excuse to bake your mom's cake," she says, then knocks me with her shoulder. "And I happen to think your birthday is a pretty good thing to celebrate."

Mom's chocolate cake has been part of every birthday I can remember. Aunt Lottie made it when I was growing up, and then Beck started making it for me when we were teenagers. Two years ago, when I couldn't make it home for my usual spring visit during which we always celebrate my birthday with the family, Beck overnighted a frozen birthday cake to me in Chicago, perfectly thawed by the time it arrived. I was working full time to save up for IVF treatments and called Beck with blubbering thanks; she always knows just the thing. It took Tyson and me a week to eat the whole cake, and I didn't regret a single bite even though I was supposed to be watching my sugar preparatory to the egg harvesting we did a few weeks later. I still tell myself that one cake couldn't have made a difference, but after dissecting every move I made, it continues to be one of the things I narrow my eyes at and wonder, *Was it you?*

Beck and I chat while we fill the dishwasher and then start washing the bigger pans and dishes by hand. We can hear the other adults talking in the living room. Uncle Rich is on the city council this year and keeps us up to date on what's happening in Lusk politics, such as they are. Beck's brother—that seventeen-years-older-than-her sibling—Malachi just accepted a job offer that that will be taking him and his family to Sioux Falls next month. He'll be the third of Uncle Rich and Aunt Lottie's kids to leave Lusk. Aunt Lottie got teary when the topic came up at dinner. Used to be that Grandma Dee would be right there in the fray of these after-dinner discussions, usually offering a contrary opinion to Uncle Rich. I've been missing her lately. Not that I ever *didn't* miss her, but it's been different this last week. Maybe because I want someone to be strong for me, and if Grandma Dee was anything, it was strong. Without her, I'm the strong one in the family, and the thought makes me want to laugh and cry at the same time. Grandma Dee was always getting after me to toughen up. I wish I'd done a better job of that. If I were tough enough, then surely I wouldn't be feeling so unsteady.

I realize the kitchen has gone quiet right before Beck asks, "Are you okay?"

I smile wider and look up at her with my most innocent expression. "Yeah, just thinking about all the baby cows that will be dropping soon." This is a flimsy excuse, because we're still ten days out. We plan our gestational calendars to the day and therefore expect our first calves on the first day of April. There's always a chance of calves coming a few days early, but usually they start late if anything. Once it starts, ho boy. Hang on to your hat and hope your horse is hardy.

"How many do you expect this year?"

"Ninety-three," I say.

"It's gonna be a busy few weeks, then," Beck says.

"Yeah, but it looks like it will be good weather—at least this first week out. Thank goodness for that."

"No doubt," Beck says. Her contribution to the ranch is helping with the meals at branding, which brings out any Reynold willing and able to dig in. We brand over Memorial Day weekend, and it's the Reynold family version of a reunion. "Did you hear from Tyson today? For your birthday."

I scrub at a pan with some burnt gravy on the bottom. "Yeah, he texted," I say easily. He'd tried to call, but I'd let it go to voice mail. Then he sent a happy birthday GIF. I responded with a smiley face emoji a few hours later when I knew he'd be asleep. London is seven hours ahead of Wyoming time. I blame a lot of our difficulty communicating on time zones.

"Huh." There is something calculating in Beck's tone that causes me to give her a sideways look and wish I'd told her that I'd talked to Ty for an hour. I'm lying about so many other things that a fake phone call wouldn't be too much to add onto the heap. "Did you hear that Reggie's back in town?" Beck says.

I turn my attention to the dishes and keep my tone dry. "I hadn't."

"Just yesterday. He's doing really great on the circuit."

"That's what I've heard." Reggie is cousins with Beck's husband, which shouldn't mean that much in a town where cousins abound, but somehow it does. He's a year older than me, but we did 4-H together, roping club, and dated for a few months in high school—I was his date for his junior prom, and you'd think we'd gotten engaged that night, the way everyone just expected we'd be the next couple who had wedding photos within three years of their junior prom pictures. The summer after that junior prom, Tyson's family moved in. I'm still not sure if Reggie and I had already started to fizzle before he came, but we definitely fizzled afterward. Reggie was working his uncle's ranch outside of Cody that summer, so he wasn't around much. Tyson, on the other hand, was new and exciting and needed someone to show him around our one-horse town. Every day. For two months. I broke up with Reggie via a text message, and he started dating Courtney Miser as soon as he got home—he knew I couldn't stand Courtney Miser. But I didn't really care. No one sparkled for me the way Tyson did. Reggie could have Courtney and any other girl he wanted. Somehow at seventeen years old, I knew I had Tyson. Dad said he and Mom had fallen in love like that—love at first sight.

"We should get a group together," Beck says. "Grab some dinner one night and catch up with the old posse." Those of us who rodeoed had called ourselves the Lusk Posse back in high school. I'd forgotten about that but don't smile at the memory even though it's a happy one.

"I'm married, Beck." I rinse out the scrubbed-clean gravy pan and put it on one of the dishtowels we've laid out. Beck picks up the pan and starts to dry with one of Aunt Lottie's days-of-the-week embroidered flour sack towels. Beck and I had matching days-of-the-week underwear when we were kids—I was religious about wearing the right pair on the right day. Beck purposely wore them out of order. Such a rebel.

I expect her to backpedal and pretend she wasn't making as pointed a suggestion as my response infers. She can say, "It's only dinner" or "You've known Reggie all your life, I'm not suggesting you *date* him."

Instead she says, "Are you?"

I look up sharply, and she holds my eyes. I feel the flush in my neck and move on to the next pan. She wants me to defend myself and explain more details about my current marriage situation. I should just put down the pan and drop my defenses and tell her that I think I'm done and just need the chance to tell Tyson. But I don't tell her this because . . . well, I don't know really. I don't know why I haven't told her where things are between Tyson and me long before now, except maybe I'm not ready to admit that things are so screwed up. I'm tired of well-intentioned sympathy wrapped up in words like "In God's time" and "You just need to relax." Those comments were made every time I came back to Lusk without a baby in my arms or in my belly. If word got out that my husband and I weren't speaking to each other anymore and I literally could not remember the last time we had sex . . . I wasn't ready to field the pity.

Beck turns so that her lower back is leaning against the sink right next to me and it's harder for me to avoid eye contact, though I manage.

"It's been, what, six months?"

"Since I came back to the ranch to help Dad? Yeah." I scrub more than I need to in order to demonstrate my focus on the work at hand. Beck can't see that the pan is clean from her new position against the sink, so I really play it up.

"You know what I mean."

I know exactly what she means, but I'm not going there. Beck is a fixer, and I don't want to be her newest project. "Tyson has a one-year contract in London, and I couldn't go with him because Dad needed me at the ranch after he got sick."

"And you miss Tyson *so* much that the two of you *texted* for your birthday. Half the town thinks you're already divorced. Everyone calls you Sienna *Chadwick*."

I lock eyes with her. "Half the town simply can't remember my married name. And I'm *not* divorced, so it doesn't matter what people think." I'm not surprised that people are talking and concluding, even colluding, but it grates on me, surprise or not. I don't like being the center of attention in a room any more than the center of a conversation I'm miles away from. I've lived here most of my life, and I, literally, know every single person in this town, but they see me as Grandma Dee's granddaughter, Mark Chadwick's daughter, Beck's cousin, Aunt Lottie and Uncle Rich's niece. I'm the girl who took second at the state competition in breakaway roping my senior year of high school and then quit rodeo entirely and moved away to a big city. Oh, and I can't have babies. That about sums me up for the town I have lived in most of my life. I'm too tired to try to show something more than that.

Beck laughs—an attempt to lighten the mood? I'm quick to make myself clear before she can play whatever hand it is she's holding. "I'm not interested in hooking up with Reggie."

"Hooking up?" Beck says, raising her microbladed eyebrows, which frame her eyelash extensions. For me, the hair and makeup was something I did for rodeo events. Beck is rodeo every day: full makeup, nails, big hair, and skin-tight Wranglers. My accusation offends her, and I'm okay with that because it means she'll back off. "I'm talking about dinner with friends, Sienna, not hooking up with your ex. Forget I mentioned it."

I don't apologize for jumping to a conclusion. This pan is overscrubbed, so I finally rinse it and put it on the dishtowel. I pick up the next pan—used for the mashed potatoes, the dregs of which are now dried like concrete.

"Are you okay, CC?"

The nickname catches me off guard. I had thought "CC" was my real name until kindergarten. Even after I learned that CC was just a nickname Mom had made up when I was a baby—short for Sienna—I'd written CC on all my papers for school and it's what everyone called me. In the fourth grade, Mrs. Cole made every student use their full name. Nate became Nathan. Kenzie became McKenzie. I became Sienna, and everyone seemed to forget that I'd ever had a nickname. Except Dad and, sometimes, Beck.

I don't notice that my hands have stopped scrubbing until I feel the pressure of Beck's hand on my forearm. I look from her acrylic nails painted to look like Easter eggs to the worry line between her eyebrows. "Things seem a little . . . off with you."

The temptation to confide about my appointment strikes hard and hot in my chest. It would be such a relief not to hold this by myself, and if I told her one of my secrets I'd feel less guilty about keeping the other one, but the sensation lasts only for the time it takes me to remember that Beck doesn't need anything else to worry about. Her husband, Clint, has been out on workman's comp for three weeks after spraining his ankle at the jobsite. Beck's been picking up extra shifts at the diner, where she's worked just one shift a week since high school because she likes to see everyone and it puts cash in her pocket. Now her paycheck helps to cover bills. Their oldest son, Braeden, is five and on the autism spectrum. She's been working for a year on getting him ready for mainstream kindergarten, which will start in the fall. Calypso is two, an absolute angel, but her speech is delayed, and even though Beck hasn't said it out loud, that was the first clue with Braeden. The house Clint and Beck bought last summer needed a lot of work done on the yard, something they were waiting to tackle this spring, but with Clint's injury they have a backyard of mud and sticker weeds right now. It would be nothing but mean to add one more worry to her shoulders. Especially since I don't really know anything yet.

"I'm fine," I say.

She scowls. "You're lying to me."

I'm surprised by her boldness. She's never called me a liar before, but I *am* lying so it's hard to be offended by the accusation. She thinks what I'm hiding has to do with Tyson, hence her dangling Reggie in front of me to draw out information. She knows about the infertility and my not liking city life.

"How's Clint's ankle?" I say, changing the subject rather pointedly. "Has the doctor given him a time line yet on when he can return to work?"

Braeden starts shrieking from the living room before Beck can challenge me. If another kid shrieked that way, adults would drop everything and run. For Braeden, though, it probably means that someone is standing in front of the TV or he's waited too long to go to the bathroom.

Beck lets out a breath and hands me the dishtowel. I give her a sympathetic smile, and she smiles wanly in return—this is Braeden's third meltdown of the night. He's less and less comfortable with groups of people, and I see both the worry and the irritation in her eyes as she passes me. Everyone has their struggles, but I resist lining them up to see who has it worse. I'd give anything for Beck's life, struggles and all.

I let Dad drive home even though we brought my car. I have the only Prius in town. Dad gets crap about it on a regular basis, but he's admitted—out loud—that it's a good run-around car. Forty-seven miles to the gallon versus his truck's seventeen. When you live nine miles out of town, like we do, it makes sense to drive something efficient even if it does label you a flaming liberal around here. There's a light snow falling as we pull away from the curb, but nothing is sticking on the roads. "In like a lion and out like a lamb" means nothing in Wyoming—we'll have snow through April.

In 1988, Uncle Rich sold his portion of the Reynold family

ranch to Grandma Dee and bought a house in town with the proceeds. As a kid, I was so jealous that Beck could ride her bike to the Burger Den—on sidewalks, if she wanted to—and play with other kids in her neighborhood any time she wanted. I, on the other hand, was stuck on the ranch, where the closest neighbor was two miles away and the only cement was for foundations and feeding troughs, not driveways and flower bed curbing. It was dang hard to learn how to ride a bike on a gravel driveway. Once I was a teenager, though, I loved living out of town. I could ride whenever I wanted to in any direction I chose and practice my growing rodeo skills in the arena Dad had fixed up for me. I watched sunsets without a single roofline to interfere with the view and woke to roosters crowing and cattle lowing. Dad bought me an old Mazda pickup once I got my license, and then I could go to town and grab a strawberry shake any time I wanted.

While we drive, Dad and I talk about Uncle Rich's upcoming retirement and Malachi's move. We go over the calving schedule, which I keep on my phone, and what we need to get done before they start dropping. When the conversation dwindles, I bring up Mom—I've been trying to find the right time for two days. "I've been thinking about her today," I admit. "Birthdays kind of do that to me." I don't like that I couldn't answer Dr. Sheffield's questions about Mom's cancer. I want those answers when I get my results—which will likely happen tomorrow, since it didn't happen today. "See," I could say to Dr. Sheffield. "I'm a responsible adult and I will advocate for my health!"

Dad is quiet as he stares out the windshield, where tiny flecks of snow are beading into water on the glass. He turns on the windshield wipers. "The day you were born was the best day of our lives," he says softly. He doesn't say that the worst day of his life came two years later when Mom died, but I know he's thinking it. There is tragic beauty in how much he still loves her after all these years. He never remarried, never even dated much. Once Mom was gone, his focus became my happiness, my security, my opportunity. I appreciate it, but sometimes it feels like an awful lot of pressure.

"Do you remember what kind of cancer she had?"

"She had breast cancer, CC, you know that."

"I know she had breast cancer," I say, adding a light laugh as though Dad's teasing me. The laugh doesn't sound right, but I hope I'm the only one who notices. I adjust the heater in the car so that it's blowing more on our feet instead of our faces. I like to think my fiddling adds a casual topcoat to my questions. "But what kind of breast cancer?"

"Are there different kinds?"

I laugh again. This one sounds more natural. "You are such a *man*. There are lots of different kinds of breast cancer. Some are genetic, others aren't."

"I hope you're not worried about catching it," he says.

I swallow as he slows down for the stop sign at the turn onto Beer Can Road. God bless Wyoming.

He puts on his blinker to signal a right-hand turn. There isn't another car in sight. "Mom's cancer was a fluke, sweetheart. A one-in-a-million case. You don't have anything to worry about."

I am forced to expound my reasons with more lies I've planned out in case this very thing happened. "I was listening to a podcast about knowing your medical history, and it got me thinking that I should probably know more about mine, that's all." The only podcasts I listen to are about the beef industry . . . and that one about fixing broken marriages. "Knowing what kind Mom had, or if there were other cases of cancer in Mom's family, would be good info for me to have."

Dad turns right, and we leave the city lights of Lusk—such as they are—behind us. "Your mom wouldn't want you to worry yourself about any of that. The day she was diagnosed, we both fell apart and then she lifted her chin and wiped her eyes and said, 'Well, enough of that. We've got some time to make the most of, Mark. Let's get to it.'" He smiles wistfully.

I've heard this part of the story before, but I want more.

"How did you guys get the diagnosis?"

"What?"

I'd given permission to get my results over the phone. I couldn't go to Cheyenne to get them in person. "I mean, did you go into the doctor's office or did they, uh, call you with the results of the biopsy?" Was I there when they got the news? Did my mom look into my eyes as she learned the truth? How long was it before they knew Mom was terminal? She died so quickly after the diagnosis—what treatments were available?

"I don't remember," Dad says. "Sorry."

I turn to look at his profile. He doesn't *remember*? I'd heard him talk about where he was when 9/11 happened—driving to a stock sale—and when the *Challenger* space shuttle exploded—in Mr. Baddley's history class, watching the launch on TV. But then maybe he's blocked out the stuff surrounding Mom's diagnosis. PTSD or something.

"Do you remember what stage her cancer was? And what treatments she had?"

Dad lets out an aggravated breath, the same kind of sigh that accompanied helping me with my math homework or me arguing for a later curfew when I was in high school. "She was terminal when she was diagnosed."

"So, she didn't have *any* treatment? No chemo or anything?" A billboard on Highway 20 says 98 percent of women survive breast cancer. It would have been different twenty-three years ago, but they would have tried *something* to extend her life even if they couldn't save it. Right? Larry Shriver, the postmaster, has been on chemo for three years now, buying as much time as he can in hopes of seeing his youngest son graduate from high school in a couple of months. He is badly swollen and walks with a cane now that the cancer is in his bones, but he is going to see his boy in a cap and gown. Surely there would have been some options for Mom. I resist the idea of picturing myself with a cane like Larry—98 percent.

"I really don't think you should worry about this stuff."

"Dad," I say, with forced calm. "Both of my parents have had cancer. One of them died from it. I think it's—"

"And one of them didn't," Dad cuts in, snappy and pointed.

Heat churns up in my chest. "Are you serious? You don't think *my* medical history is something I ought to know?"

Dad's tone rises equal to my own, and I'm as surprised by his not backing down as I am about my pushing him. "Like I said, your mom's stuff was a fluke, and since you don't have a prostate, my stuff doesn't factor. Haven't we had a hard-enough year without getting into all that?"

A year that is about to get a whole lot harder, I think. "What if there's something I can do to minimize my risk, Dad?" This is disingenuous. I might have cancer right now, this minute. I picture myself telling him outright, "Dad, I might have cancer. I need to know what kind Mom had in order to get a sense of how big this could be for me."

Every potential response to saying something like that is disastrous. I can't tell him any more than I could tell Beck when she tried to figure out what I was hiding less than an hour ago. Dad didn't tell me about *his* cancer until he'd already done the first round of radiation and had decided to have the surgery—weeks after his initial diagnosis.

"I want to know about Mom's cancer," I say bluntly. "I'm sorry that's upsetting. I don't want to hurt you, but I need to know these things."

Dad leans back in his seat as if he's trying to strike a casual position. When he talks, the sharpness is gone but the tension lingers, and he can't quite evoke the softness I suspect he wants me to hear. Then again, maybe it's my own tension I'm feeling, residue left behind by the lies I've been telling and the secrets I've been keeping.

"Look, CC," Dad says, his tone still lecturing, which keeps me on edge. I'm *never* on edge with Dad; this whole conversation is so not us. "You're young and healthy and eat lots of fish. If you want to find things to worry about, try Syria or contaminated water. Or . . ." He gets excited. "Gun rights! We can always use more women in the battle for the constitutional right to bear arms." He starts telling me about an article he's just read about the bills being drafted for next year's legislative session.

I am stunned by this blatant dismissal. When I go to Dad with problems I need help with—whether it was long division, how to fix the hinge on the cattle gate, or how to tell Grandma Dee that I wasn't waiting until after my twentieth birthday to get married—he talks it out with me and then helps me. He went with me to the principal after I told him that some of the boys in my class were saying naughty things to the girls at recess. He took me prom dress shopping in Utah when Grandma Dee refused to waste her time on "frilly crap that doesn't matter a lick in the grand scheme of things." He spent hours teaching me the finer points of roping and bought me two goats the year I decided I wanted to start competing in goat roping for rodeo. Over the last few years, he's sent me links to articles on infertility, and he's the only one who knows that Tyson expected me to join him in London three months ago and I've barely talked to my husband since I told him a week before my flight that I wasn't going. I've always trusted that Dad will be there for me when I need him because he always has been. Maybe I'm misunderstanding this. Maybe all the tension is warping my interpretation of what's happening here.

The gravel crunches beneath the tires of the Prius when Dad turns onto our road, a half-mile driveway that forks at the end. Veer right to park in front of the ranch house—built by Grandpa Reynold back in the forties—or veer left and head to the outbuildings: the big barn, the little barn, the cabin where the hired hands stay, and the equipment shed I spent three full weeks reorganizing back in February. Dad goes right and stops in front of the house as he finishes his diatribe about gun control.

I'm still off balance, trying to determine whether he's acting strange or I'm interpreting it wrong, but I still need the information, so I count to three before I go back to the topic he's trying to avoid. "I get that this is hard for you, Dad, but it's really important to me. *For* me. Do you have medical records or receipts I could look through? Maybe the name of Mom's doctor or the clinic or something—a relative on Mom's side I can call to get a family medical history?" I pause to take a breath. "I only need your help to get started. Then I'll see it through on my own." Saying this out loud emphasizes how important it is. I need to know about Mom's cancer. I *deserve* to know.

Seconds tick by. Dad and I stare out the windshield from our respective seats, watching the snowflakes turn to water droplets and slide down the glass. They start small, then get pulled into another drop as though they're magnetized. Doubling their size makes them heavier, and they slide into another drop and another until the drop is so heavy it streaks down the glass, leaving a swath of drop-free glass in its wake.

> *Who has seen the wind?*
> *Neither I nor you.*

I hold my breath, literally and metaphorically, until Dad turns to look at me. I meet his eyes and exhale as normally as I can. The expression of concern on his face brings emotion up in my throat. The biopsy could come back negative and he'll never have to know how bound up I feel right now. He'll think back on this night and be uncomfortable with how pushy I'm being but not know why I'm breaking out of our usual style of communication to press him so hard about something he obviously does not want to talk about.

"I'm sorry, CC," Dad says softly. "I didn't keep any of that stuff. Between moving back here and not wanting reminders of what was *the* worst time of my life, I wasn't thinking about you needing any of it later on."

The worst time of his life.

"How about a name." I sound as if I'm ignoring the pain signals he's sending out. I guess I am. "A cousin or someone I can call."

"They don't know." Mom's mom was a drunk and her dad was already dead by the time she had me.

"If any of Mom's relatives have had breast cancer, that's important for me to know. If you give me a name, I can find them on Facebook or something." I've never actually had to find anyone before, but other people do it all the time, right?

He shakes his head and laughs without humor. "You're making too much of this, Sienna. Your mom's doctor said that Mom's cancer was a fluke."

"Twenty-three years ago," I remind him. "We know a lot more now than we did back then. What was her doctor's name?"

"I don't remember."

"The clinic?"

Dad shakes his head. "There's no one to track down, CC. Your mom was the end of her line, and her cancer doesn't have anything to do with you." He smiles, and even though I've never doubted a single smile from him in all my life, I doubt this one. Dad reaches over to tuck my hair behind my ear. "I'm sorry I don't have anything for you on this, but I guess you're just going to have to trust me. This isn't something you need to worry about, okay? Let it go." He opens the door and steps out of the car.

The tension that follows us inside the house keeps us subtly avoiding each other for the rest of the evening. Neither of us asks the other if we want to watch an episode of *NCIS,* our current Netflix binge show. Dad heads into the office; I do the dishes left in the sink from breakfast and lunch and try to think of other ways I can approach this. I've asked after family members, medical paperwork, Mom's doctor and clinic. What other means do I have to find any answers?

Once I'm ready to call it a night, I go into the office long enough to tell Dad good night and give him a quick kiss on the cheek. He says good night back without looking up from the blog he's working on about freeze branding. He's blogging three times a week now, selling ad space and steadily growing his readership. I'm impressed by his success with the ranch's online presence, but it's clear he's using it to hide from me tonight. I don't think that's fair, and yet if he really doesn't have any information for me, it's silly for me to feel mad or hurt or whatever it is I'm feeling. With so many complications in my life right now, I don't want my relationship with him to be complicated.

"Love you, Daddy," I say. "Thanks for a great birthday."

The reminder that this is my birthday breaks down the cold war that's been growing between us. He stands up and gives me a good hug, then kisses my forehead, a genuine smile on his face. "You are the greatest gift in my life, CC." He taps me on the nose. "Love you too."

I feel better to have cleared the air between us. It's not until I've brushed and flossed and pulled the covers up to my chin that I realize Dad didn't give me the twenty-fifth birthday letter I've been expecting from Mom.

A little rush of . . . *something* moves through me, leaving a tingle behind as it radiates from the center of my chest out through my fingers and toes. I've been getting birthday letters since I was eight years old—not every year, but always on the significant ones. My tenth birthday because I was now in double digits, my thirteenth because I was a teenager. I had letters on my sixteenth, eighteenth, and then twenty-first birthdays too. I was sure I'd get one this year because I'm a quarter of a century.

Did Dad not give me the letter because he's put out with me? Is he planning to give it to me tomorrow morning instead? Did he forget?

Or are the letters done?

The thought makes my heart race. I've asked Dad before how many letters there are and when I will get them. He always winks and smiles and tells me it's a surprise. Would Mom have written letters only up through my twenty-first birthday? If so, why hadn't she said, "This is the last letter, dearest Sienna."

But I'm relieved, right? I've been dreading this letter I expected to be full of advice meant for a different version of myself than who I have turned out to be. I've been bracing myself to feel ashamed and guilty for all I am not. I even imagined not opening this one at all, and instead hiding it away until I felt ready.

So why do I feel tears prick my eyes at the thought that I might never read my mom's words again? Maybe anything she says is better than nothing. Maybe I need to feel that connection to her right now more than I ever have before.

What I wouldn't give for a letter that says, "To my dearest Sienna on the day of her first cancer diagnosis."

4

Dearest Sienna,

Happy birthday!
You are eight years old today, and
this letter is my gift to you on this
special day. I've written you a lot of letters, but I chose to have them start when
you turned eight because by now you
can read them yourself—this can be our
special time together.

I remember being eight years old. My
uncle Graham took me fishing for the
first time that year. We went to Two Jack
Lake in Banff, Canada. He would bait
my hook and then clean my fish afterward, which is why I think I liked it so
much. I didn't want to do the yucky
stuff, so he did it for me. I had a pair of
bright pink flip-flops on that trip, and I
lost one in the lake. I was so sad and
then I had to wear my running shoes
for the rest of the trip—it was a good les-
son to me to take better care of my
things and make sure I cleaned up

after myself. I was in the second grade, and my favorite thing to do was art.

I wish I were there with you for real, Sienna, but I hope you know that I am looking down on you from heaven and so proud of you. Now that you're eight, it's important for you to work hard to do what's right. Listen to your dad and Grandma—they love you. Try to help Grandma with the house—she has a lot to do on the ranch. And know that people show their love in different ways. Give your dad an extra hug for me. I know he's a wonderful father to you. Always tell the truth, shower at least four times a week, go to church, and like I said before, work hard on picking up after yourself, okay? These things will help you to become a responsible and trustworthy person.

I love you, CC, and wish you a very happy birthday.

Love,
Mom

5

Sienna

At six o'clock Friday evening I come in from working outside all day and allow myself to relax. The doctor or hospital or pathologist, or whoever was supposed to call with the results of my biopsy, didn't, which means that for one more weekend I am a relatively normal twenty-five-year-old woman with both breasts and a new saddle that maybe I'll pull into the living room and work on while Dad and I watch some *NCIS*. I sit down on the boot bench just inside the back door with a heavy sigh, then roll my shoulders and neck in hopes of working out some of the tension. I've been trying to process the building anxiety by working like two men; it hasn't helped as much as I'd hoped.

I pull off my boots, hang up my coat, and step sock-footed into the kitchen, where Dad is reading the newspaper and making notes about something on the legal pad he uses like a day planner—probably stock sales he wants to make sure we get on the calendar. We have seventy-two yearlings to sell off this year, and though we usually wait for the fall, depending on price per pound, sometimes it's in our best interest to sell sooner. Dad's medical bills still make us itch, and there's no telling if the price of beef will stay up. Grandma Dee used to say that ranching is little more than legalized gambling with water and frost instead of chips and cards.

Dad didn't give me a letter from Mom this morning like I

thought he might if in fact he'd just forgotten. I could ask him about it, but after last night I don't want any more awkwardness between us. I was too pushy, and anyway, if he knew something he'd have told me. I might try to find the answers another way, though I'm not sure how. Probably Google.

"I finished up the fencing on the south side," I tell him as I fill a glass with water from the sink. We have our own well, and it is the clearest, purest water I've ever tasted.

"That's fantastic, CC," Dad says, taking off his reading glasses to smile up at me. "That was the last of the fencing, right?"

"Yep," I say, turning to rest my hips against the counter and take another drink. "We'll be ready to move the cows over tomorrow morning—Malachi and Uncle Rich still coming?"

"And Malachi's boys," Dad says. The boys are fourteen and twelve, so hardly any help, but they're good riders and they'll do what I tell them. Unlike some ranches, we own all our own land, which makes our roundups infinitely easier than it is for those who have BLM permits that end up scattering their herds over thousands of patchworked acreage. We've had the herd in our east winter pasture—eighteen hundred acres—since September. Now we need to move the cows into the calving pasture, where the prairie grass has been growing for months, and they'll be easier to monitor during calving. "Rich asked if he could use his four-wheeler. You okay with that?"

"You'll be on one too, right?" Grandma Dee didn't allow any vehicles during roundup—horses only. I prefer stock to engines too—vehicles spook some of the cattle—but Dad hasn't been on a horse since his surgery, and Uncle Rich is seventy years old. I can't do a roundup without them, and I'm certainly not going to make them get onto a horse if they aren't comfortable there.

"Well, I might start out in the saddle," Dad says in a casual tone that betrays the anxiety he's trying to hide.

My eyebrows go up.

"Just to start," he says sheepishly.

I want to argue that roundup is no time to push himself, but I don't because I know what it's like to go months between riding, and if he's feeling up to it, that's great. We'll have to take the bigger horse trailer so there's room for Kobe Giant—Dad's gelding—but that's not a big deal. "Awesome," I say. "Just don't be a hero."

He smiles and nods before putting his glasses back on and turning again to the paper. He pauses, then looks at me over the frames. "I can do dinner tonight. You've had a long day."

"I'm fine," I say. "And I'm craving fish tacos." What I mean is that I'm not craving scrambled eggs, which has been Dad's go-to "meal" all of my life. He can cook other things, but he doesn't very often. I take after Mom in that I love good food and I enjoy cooking for the people I love. Dad says that she would get up to cook him breakfast before he went to work and would be working on dinner when he got home. He felt as if it was too much work for just the two of them, but she loved to do it. I wonder where Mom learned to cook. If her mom was a deadbeat, who taught Mom to set a table and make a meal? I learned from Aunt Lottie mostly, and some from Grandma Dee. Did Mom have a grandma who helped out when she was little? Did that grandma die of breast cancer?

I exchange my work gear for a shower, then yoga pants and a county fair T-shirt left from my roping days. Dad's in his office when I start dinner. Last night unsettles me every time I think about our argument, but lucky for me there are plenty of other things to think about. I've been checking the herd here and there these last few weeks. The cows have mostly migrated west on their own, where we've been putting out hay now that the forage is low, but we'll have some stragglers we'll need to hunt for tomorrow. That's my favorite part of roundups. Dad and Uncle Rich will manage the bulk of the herd through the gates leading to the west acres while Malachi, his boys, and I go after the outliers. We'll put out fresh hay and water after we finish up on Saturday to draw out any head that we miss. When it's breeding season, we turn the bulls out with the heifers first, then keep those first-time mamas in the ranch pasture so we can keep an eye on them through the winter and make sure things go the way they should through calving. After the heifers have been served, we turn the bulls into the cow herd. This keeps the cows and heifers from calving at the same time, and we can more efficiently divide our time between the ranch and the calving pasture located forty miles away.

I'm moving through the time line for tomorrow in my head while the fish sizzles in the cast-iron pan when my phone rings on the opposite counter. Beck had texted earlier to see if I wanted to come over tonight, and I never gave her an answer because I didn't take thirty seconds to think about whether it was a feasible idea. Since I hadn't made a decision earlier, I think about it now for the time it takes me to cross to my phone. It's been a long day and my forearms are killing me from working the crimp on the fences. Tomorrow will start at sunup and, quite frankly, I'm worried that Beck will try to pick up where we left off on my birthday, and I just can't.

I wipe my hands on a dishtowel before I pick up my phone, an explanation warming up on my lips, then pause at the unfamiliar number. It's a Wyoming area code, but I can't remember the last time someone not already in my contact list called me. The energy drains out of me as I realize that it's likely the lab. I forget to breathe, then I inhale sharply and glance over my shoulder to make sure Dad is still in his office. The keys on the computer keyboard are clicking in rhythm, assuring me that he's not paying any attention to what I'm doing. I hurry toward the front porch with my phone in hand and heart thudding at the base of my throat. The wind that dogged me all day in the high pasture takes my breath away when I step outside and close the front door behind me.

"Hello?" I say, moving to the corner of the porch best protected from the wind. We've had a few days in the midfifties this week. Spring tease, we call it, but temperatures like that never hold once the sun goes down, and I am reminded that March is closer to winter than it is to summer.

"Sienna Richardson?" It sounds weird to hear Richardson as my last name since I've fallen back to using Chadwick here in Lusk. The professional voice confirms my fear that I didn't get a weekend of clemency after all. "This is she."

"This is Amy from Laramie Women's Medical Center. I'm

calling with the results of your biopsy. Dr. Sheffield said you already approved a phone call rather than an in-clinic review."

"Yes, I approved a phone call." I wrap my free arm around my waist. Tight. It doesn't protect me from the cold or make me feel strong and capable. The sky is dusty gray, only the barest glow of sunset still clinging to the top of the hills in the distant west. I focus on taking even breaths and fight off the sudden impulse to jump on Rosa and ride as far away as I can. But this phone call is a mountain lion, a predator that will eventually catch up with me and tear me from the saddle.

Amy keeps talking. "I want to preface my call with the reminder that Laramie Women's Medical Center is a leading institution in breast cancer research and treatment in the Intermountain West. We have a talented staff dedicated to addressing all the physical and emotional needs of our patients. It is our mission to—"

I use Amy's script reading to brace myself. This is it. In a matter of seconds, I'll never again *not* know. My future, which has turned blurry and vague already these last several months, is going to become even more unclear. I put a hand on my belly, the way I used to when I'd talk to the clinic in Chicago about treatments and test results that centered around my having a baby. If this is cancer, where does that leave my potential for ever conceiving?

"Um, thank you," I say when the other end of the line goes silent, though I'm not sure what I'm thanking her for. "You have my results?"

"Yes, ma'am. I'm afraid the biopsy showed some abnormalities—"

"Abnormalities?" I repeat, afraid to breathe for fear it will disrupt this new bubble of hope. Abnormalities could be a cyst or . . . something else abnormal. "Not cancer?"

"Oh, well, uh . . . cancer is an abnormality."

Exhale. Bubble of hope sufficiently popped. "So, it is cancer."

Amy says nothing for a few beats.

"I signed a paper consenting to hear my results over the phone."

"Yes, ma'am," Amy says. "I'm sorry."

"So, it is cancer then." Maybe she's apologizing for something else.

"Yes, ma'am."

I take a deep breath and then let it out slowly as the words seep through my ear, into my brain, and then go out by messenger through my nervous system to the rest of my body so that every part of me knows the identity of that cloaked figure hanging out in my breast tissue. I had expected it *would* be cancer—confirmation should not surprise me—but my insides start shaking like they did in Dr. Sheffield's office three days ago. Apparently, some part of me had placed side bets against the diagnosis. *I have cancer,* I say in my mind, attentive to the diction of the word. *Can-sir.* A bit more of the twilight disappears along the horizon, further casting the shadow of night over the prairie. It is too cold for crickets, and I can't hear the yearlings in the pasture behind the ranch from here. The silence feels punishing.

Amy finds her words and starts talking again. "Dr. Sheffield would like to see you Monday afternoon, the first of April, and took the liberty of scheduling you for a lumpectomy Tuesday morning, the second, at nine a.m. You'll need to call your insurance first thing Monday morning of this next week to make sure your authorizations are in place, but we've already sent them all of our referrals and outlines of care. If Tuesday the second doesn't work, I can help you set up a different time, but she wants you in by Friday the fifth at the very latest."

"What stage cancer do I have?"

"Without a full assessment—"

"Please." Normally I wouldn't want to make this woman uncomfortable by being insistent. But this isn't normal. My hand is still on my belly, protecting what isn't there. I think of the six remaining embryos in Chicago. Will I ever be able to try again? Is this the end of the road to motherhood that I have been staggering down for three years? The hand clenches into a fist. "What stage did Dr. Sheffield *guess*?"

The woman pauses in surrender. "It says here that the mammogram and ultrasound did not show additional tumors, which is why a lumpectomy is the prescribed course of treatment.

After the procedure, a full evaluation of the removed tissues will allow a more reliable determination, at which point additional treatments will be discussed."

"Thank you for that, but can you *please* tell me what stage the doctor believes my cancer is?" My cancer. Like "my car" and "my candy bar" and "my dad." Part of me. Belonging to.

But when the leaves hang trembling . . .

I can feel my pulse in my hand from gripping the phone too tight, but every muscle in my body is tight right now, holding me together. Keeping me in.

Amy continues. "Invasive ductal carcinoma, negative HR, HR2, and BRCA, low-grade, stage one."

I don't know what all of that means, but stage one is better than two, which is better than three. Mom had probably been stage four when she'd been diagnosed. What had it sounded like in Mom's ear when she'd been told? Had she pulled her young daughter tighter against her infected chest? Had she asked, "How long do I have?" with tears in her eyes and Dad holding her hand too tight? I hate that Dad doesn't remember that moment—he's the only person who could.

"Thank you," I say, staring at the barest glow of light now outlining the western horizon. It looks as though there is a big party taking place on the opposite side, with floodlights and a live band I can't hear. Life feels like that a lot these days, as if everyone else is living it up while I watch from the sideline. An owl hoots in the distance, and I look toward the sound. The silent flight and white underbelly of barn owls makes them look like ghosts at night. As kids, Beck and I would sleep in the backyard during the summer and count the owls as they soared above us. The most we ever counted was fifteen, though it was a faulty experiment since we had no way of identifying one owl from the next. For all we knew, it could have been the same owl over and over again. The owl I heard will be hunting tonight. Another predator on silent wings.

"So, does Tuesday the second at nine o'clock work for you?"

Amy asks. "It will be an outpatient procedure done under general anesthesia with a two- to four-day recovery time. You should be back to normal activity in two weeks."

Two weeks? In calving season with at least one more snowstorm in the forecast? Grandma Dee always said that work was good for what ailed ya, and thoughts of the ranch clear my head. For a long time, I thought she just wanted to punish me when I complained about some aspect of my life. Now the prospect of work rises up like the evening star I can just see in the eastern sky. The ranch needs me. Dad needs me. I have to be at 100 percent if I'm going to keep up, and that means I don't have time for this. Amy said it was stage one, low grade. That gives me a little time to make a plan. "I'm afraid I can't do either appointment."

"Well, we have an open slot on Friday the fifth at eight a.m., but those are the only openings we have in the week."

I can't do Wednesday or Thursday or Friday. Or any day in March. Or April. Or May either. The ranch needs me and I need some time to come to grips with this. "I'm going to have to look into a few things before I can schedule anything. Can I get your number so I can call you back when I have a better idea of what I can make work?"

"Sure thing. The scheduling department for the Laramie Women's Center is open from eight a.m. until eight p.m. Monday through Friday and nine until two on Saturdays. You can call us back at 307 . . ."

I huddle in the corner of the porch, letting each number fall to the planks of wood beneath my feet. During the summer there are sometimes moths as big as hummingbirds out here. Dad hangs our big bug zappers on the porch, Sometimes the bigger moths get stuck in the grate, and the zapper just keeps buzzing and buzzing and buzzing. Then Dad has to turn off the zapper and use a stick to pry off the carcass.

"Got it. Thank you," I say when Amy finishes giving the number a second time.

Amy repeats the mission of the Laramie Women's Medical Center. I thank her and hang up. The wind catches my hair as I step forward on the porch to grip the rail, no longer feeling the cold. I clench the rail so tight that my knuckles hurt, and I imagine the grooves and bumps of the rough-hewn pine being pressed into my skin. I let the wind slap me around a little and get funky with my hair while I attempt to make eye contact with the shifty gaze of reality.

Inside my body is a monster, tiny but fierce. Maybe my cancer is like a chicken trying to break out of its egg, or maybe it's like a spider, one hairy leg and then another stretching out from a crevice and reaching for the next space it will overtake. Or maybe it's all tied up in a box, safe and secure and willing to wait until I can take the time to confront it. I close my eyes and inhale some of that wind, wishing it could cleanse me even as I choose to believe the cancer is in a box—secure and patient.

> *The wind is passing through.*
> *Who has seen the wind?*

Stage one is good. Curable 98 percent of the time, according to that billboard that's become scripture. I've never been extraordinary at anything; certainly I wouldn't be in that 2 percent now. How many of those 98 percent lost their mothers to the same disease?

The questions Dr. Sheffield has asked loom even larger in my mind: What stage cancer *had* Mom's been? *Were* there other relatives who had also had breast cancer? Did they die from it, as she did? I feel a pop of anger that Dad won't help me find those answers, but I don't want to waste energy on being mad at him.

Invasive ductal carcinoma.

Lumpectomy.

Additional treatments.

I hear a creak and turn to see Dad standing inside the screen door.

"Everything okay, CC?"

I pull my wild hair away from my face with one hand and smile to hide whatever else might show up in my expression right now. I had promised myself I would tell him once I knew what I was dealing with, but the fact that he's blocked out so much of Mom's cancer reflects how devastating mine will be once he knows. I'm all he has left, so I force a smile. "Yeah, Dad, everything's fine."

"I took the fish off the stove, but I may have been too late."

6

Sienna

Rounding up more than one hundred head of cattle spread out over eighteen hundred acres is exactly what I need to keep the panic at bay on Saturday. I'm in the saddle for fourteen hours, then head out again Sunday afternoon and round up the last four that have wandered out of their hiding places overnight.

Dr. Sheffield's office calls Monday afternoon, but I've put the number into my phone now and I don't answer. I spend Tuesday and Wednesday finalizing our schedules, assessing each heifer and taking daily trips to the calving pasture to make sure the fence repairs are holding now that there are occupants. We stay busy all year, but everything on the ranch centers on calving. The west pasture is a few hundred acres smaller than the eastern one they've been in all winter, and sometimes they test the fences a little more, so we make sure we don't slack off with the inspections. The fizzy tension of impending calving is thick in the air, like gearing up for the first day of school or getting ready for an anticipated vacation. I think of a race, where the runners are in position, hands down and feet primed to push off at the first crack of the pistol. Tyson and I got into running for a while in Chicago. We'd run out to Navy Pier every morning. We ran a 10K race, and the energy of all those runners who had worked so hard to be there was intoxicating. I don't know why we stopped running. Probably because I became obsessed with getting pregnant.

Dr. Sheffield's office calls again on Thursday afternoon, and again I ignore it; the yearlings had found a weak spot in the east fence line, and a neighbor called to tell me he'd had a couple of visitors. It took all day to get them back and fix the fence. By Friday, we're officially ready to start welcoming the baby cows from the heifers, but the nice weather will make our mamas lazy. They are content to chew on the spring grasses, which means when tomorrow's storm rolls in, they'll likely all start dropping at once. Then the real work begins: night rounds, assessments, charts, schedules, teat checks, rejected calf care.

I make biscuits and gravy for Dad and me for breakfast Friday morning. It might be the last cooked breakfast we have for a while once the whirlwind begins. My phone rings as I'm putting the leftovers into a Tupperware container. I glance at the clock—it's not even eight a.m.—then I see that it's Dr. Sheffield's office and send it to voice mail, turning my phone over so that Dad can't see the screen even though he's still at the table. Her office has called every day this week, and it feels invasive.

"Who's calling so early?"

"Some telemarketer," I say, shaking my head as though I'm irritated. Which I am, but not for the reasons my lie implies. Dad accepts the answer, then checks his watch and quickly takes the last few bites while I put the leftover sausage gravy in the fridge. He pushes himself up from the table, already dressed in his nice Wranglers, the inky black ones, and his rattlesnake cowboy boots. He's wearing a white shirt and a bolo tie as though he's going on a date, not his six-month follow-up with his oncologist. I wonder with a start if Dr. Jefferies knows Dr. Sheffield. They're both in Cheyenne, and they both deal with cancer patients. I imagine them having lunch in an employee break room and realizing they both have patients with the last name Chadwick. "Does your Chadwick live in Lusk?" Dr. Jefferies might say.

"She does, with her father . . . who had prostate cancer last fall!"

Privacy laws don't allow for conversations like that, right?

"I'll be picking up the vaccines while I'm in the city," Dad says, keeping me in the present. "Will you make sure the barn fridge is cleared out for 'em when I get back?"

"Yep," I say while running water over the dishes. I don't have much to do today unless we start getting some baby cows, and the lack of work makes me anxious. Maybe I'll run up to the calving pasture for another look around—I'm a little worried about the north water pipe. It's a forty-five-minute drive each way, which means a trip will take half the day, but I need purpose. I need distraction. Clearing out the nasty fridge is *something*, at least.

"See ya this afternoon, CC." He gives me a sideways hug and kisses the side of my head.

I take the four-wheeler around the perimeter to check on the heifers after he leaves. I feel my phone buzz in my pocket as I'm finishing up but don't check it until I'm back inside and my boots are under the boot bench.

Tyson: **Can you give me a call?**

I stare at the message for a few seconds before putting my phone into the back pocket of my jeans. Tyson and I haven't talked on the phone for a few months now, haven't even texted since my birthday—I've been twenty-five for a full week now. His asking me to call feels like a stranger asking for a hug, but I feel a moment of vertigo as I remember running into the house on a Friday like this one during my senior year of high school— Tyson was coming to Lusk for the weekend, and I was over the moon. He'd said he was bringing my birthday present with him; I'd turned eighteen a few weeks before, but his semester had been a bear and he couldn't get away. On that day—what, seven years ago now?—I'd taken off this same pair of work boots in this same spot so that I could hurry to shower, then put on mascara before he got here. Grandma Dee had been irritated, yelling at me to put my boots under the bench so no one tripped over them. It's staggering to recognize how much things have changed.

Back then I hadn't been able to think about anything else but my boyfriend that whole weekend—Grandma Dee was ready to clobber me. Now Grandma Dee is dead, and I'm not up to talking to my husband on the phone. That eighteen-year-old girl would not have believed any of this possible. Tyson was my everything. What is he to me now? What am I to him? Who am I? How long will I be whoever I am?

My wedding album is in our storage unit in Chicago, but there's a picture of us on the wall above the couch in the living room where a hodgepodge of photos with varied frames tell the story of my family. My great-grandparents are unsmiling in their sepia-toned wedding picture—Grandma Dee said it was because back then it was seen as arrogant to smile in photographs, but I wonder if maybe they knew the truth about what life would really be like. Maybe people back then knew that life would mostly be work and disappointment and loss.

If there had ever been a wedding picture of Grandma Dee and Dad's dad—whom I've never met—it had been taken down at some point. Gregg Chadwick left them when Dad was young and pretty much disappeared from their lives after that, so a photo of him is not something to keep on a wall. There are black-and-white pictures of Grandma and her brothers, though—ice skating on the old mill pond, Grandma showing her first steer at the county fair. It took second place. There's a color photo of Dad holding up the first buckle he won in saddle bronc riding—he was pro for almost a year before he blew out his knee and decided to go to college. There's another photo of him actually in the saddle, competing in nationals down in Las Vegas—his feet are high, his hand in the air, and a fierce look of determination is on his face. He was handsome back then—still is—but it's weird to see him in such a different world than I've ever known him. In my life he's been quiet, hardworking, and . . . soft. The young man in that photo is determined and focused in ways I don't see in my dad now.

I'm moving toward my wedding photo on the far end of the collage when my eyes stop on that photo of *my* family from the day I was born—me, Mom, and Dad. I stare at my parents;

happy idiots just like Tyson and I had once been, except they at least got a baby out of their delusion before it shattered to pieces. I just have the pieces and nothing to show for it. The photo is not great quality, too orange with none of the crisp lines of a professional photograph. I imagine Dad handing over his cheap camera and asking a nurse to snap the photo. It's only a four by six, but with a thick matte it better matches the size of the other frames on the wall. Mom's freckled face is red, and small sections of her hair are stuck to the sides with sweat. Her smile is so pure that it turns her undoneness into something beautiful. My pink face, the size of an orange, is scrunched up between the faces of my parents, a balled fist on either side of my head. The two of them radiate success. A job well done. You and me and baby makes three.

Just over two years later, my mom was dead. Eight months ago, Dad was diagnosed with his cancer. Now me. Was the monster in all three of us even then? Waiting for some trigger that would start the process of individual decline? What are the odds? I don't necessarily believe in curses, but how can so many good people end up with so much bad luck? It's not fair that we didn't get a chance. It's not fair that I've believed I can make things up to all of us when I can't. When I haven't.

I finally turn my attention to the wedding photo that brought me to the wall in the first place, framed in the best eleven-by-fourteen black frame you can buy from the Walmart in Casper. Tyson is cradling me in his arms, one arm around my back and the other under my knees—I had a knee-length dress in order to show off the Tony Lama boots Dad had bought me as a wedding gift. Black with red stitching and turquoise detail. They're in the storage unit now—I haven't worn them for years. In the photo I'm holding Ty's black cowboy hat on my head with one hand while my other is wrapped around his neck. Tyson's hair is tousled, and I'm kicking my feet coquettishly. We're both laughing. *So* happy. *So* convinced that we had life figured out. I stare at my own face—freckles everywhere, bright red lipstick on my wide, openmouthed smile. Surely that isn't really me. Tyson, well, our fall hasn't bruised him as much, so he still looks like himself. Sometimes I'm grateful that he's less damaged. Sometimes I resent it. My eyes move to the picture of me and my parents the day I was born, then to my wedding day, and back again. We're all so young in these photos. I suppose it's a blessing that none of us knew what was coming, but maybe I wouldn't feel so supremely disappointed with life if I hadn't once felt so very thrilled by it.

Nostalgia's grip on me continues, and I turn my attention to the bottom shelf of the bookshelves that flank the couch, where our haphazard collection of photo albums are lined up like good little soldiers. None of them are like the fancy scrapbooked things Aunt Lottie has in matching binders; ours consist of photos held behind antistatic plastic on thick pages. The cream-colored album with green leaves printed on the cover holds my childhood. Someone had tried to take off the big, round yellow sticker with blue numbers announcing the sale price of $6.99 but only tore one edge off. I pull the album from the shelf and sit on the couch. I haven't looked through these photos in years, and I flip the antistatic pages slowly as I reacquaint myself with the life I've lived thus far, or at least through high school when the photos here end because I was a grown-up and capable of documenting my own life. It's good to be reminded that my childhood was a happy one. I had Dad, who coddled me, and Grandma Dee, who set an intense pace to keep up with. I had horses and purpose and opportunity. I'd never claim it was perfect—Did Grandma Dee have to be so hard all the time?—but I know I was lucky. Luckier than some kids whose moms didn't die when they were babies.

When I finish the last page, I go back to the start and look specifically at the photos that have my mom in them. Without noticing at first, I realize I'm counting them.

Sixteen.

Is that really all there are?

I go back to the beginning and look again. My first count was right—there are only sixteen photos of Mom in this book that chronicles my life. How have I not noticed that before?

I flip the pages back and forth, further categorizing those sixteen photos. I am in nine of the pictures; the other ones in the album are from before I was born. I stare at a photo of Mom in a lawn chair wearing a bikini top and shorts, holding a root beer toward the camera—she's not outside; rather, it's like a summer party but in the house. Maybe New Year's Eve? Her dark hair, almost black, is long and straight over freckled shoulders. Her round speckled belly jutting out over her shorts is full of me. I've imagined meeting people who knew Mom and having them blink at me and say, "You look so much like your mother." The photos confirm how true that is. Except that I've never met anyone who knew Mom other than Dad and Grandma Dee.

The plastic coverings pull back with a crackle as I take the photos of Mom out of the album. I lay them out on the couch cushion beside me, keeping them in the same order they had been in the album. Mom is noticeably pregnant in four of these photos, and I rearrange them by the length of her hair—below her shoulders and only varying an inch or so in length. In one of them her hair is up, but from the size of her belly I change the order. I do the same thing with the photos where she's holding me, from newborn to about six months. There are three pictures that I can't fit in based on the other markers I've used. One consists of a group sitting around a picnic table, smiling into the camera. Dad is one of those faces. Mom is another one. The others are strangers. Mom's hair is up and her belly is blocked by the table, so I have nothing to go on by way of a time line. Who are these other people, I wonder. Friends of Mom? Would they remember anything about her cancer? Treatments, clinic, doctor's name?

The second photo I can't line up is a close-up of Mom with her face pressed next to the face of a woman with bleached blond hair. Beck and I often do a similar pose when we take selfies. Only this photo is pre-selfie. Someone else is snapping the picture, maybe Dad. The blonde has a pierced nose, a tiny stud in the crease of her nostril that I haven't noticed before. She's smiling wide, her shoulders bare save for black spaghetti straps. Her eyes are half closed as if she blinked just as the photo was taken. I look more closely at Mom, who's also laughing but not looking into the camera. Mom's hair is up, and she's wearing a red tank top—maybe the top of a dress. I look at Mom's face in the other photos, noting how round it is when she's pregnant, and then how much it thins out after I'm born. Based on that, I put this photo second to last in my new chronology, because her face is pretty thin. I put the group around the picnic table photo before I'm born, though it's hard to tell because the quality isn't great. The last uncategorized photo, a close-up with her hair up, has a rounder face, so I put it with the pregnancy shots and look them over again, in better order this time.

The last photo in the time line is Mom holding me when I'm probably six months old. She's wearing a green jacket and baggy black pants and is standing in front of a set of cement stairs—it would have been fall, but I can't see any trees in the photo. She'd lost any weight she'd gained being pregnant with me—this is one of the few shots where I can see her entire body. She's holding me on her hip, not smiling and staring past the photographer. I have the sense she's not a willing model for this photo, and I imagine that she and Dad are going out and he's insisting that they take a photo before they go.

"Mark," she says with a whine in my imagination. "Can we just go?"

"I want to capture this moment, okay? One, two, three, chee-eese!"

Why *this* moment, though? She's not dressed up and she's standing in front of a set of concrete stairs. I look at the photo again. She definitely looks irritated, and I wonder if maybe life was heavy for Mom. These pictures are all from film, predating digital photos where you can take fifteen shots of the same pose and choose your favorite. With film, you were stuck with what you got—you couldn't even see them until they were developed. I've always assumed that she and Dad were happy together—new marriage, new baby. Dad has certainly never said otherwise, but maybe it was overwhelming to be a new mother without family to help. Maybe she hadn't felt ready—she was only twenty-one years old—or maybe she struggled with postpartum depression, or she and Dad fought about who would get up in the night. I know Dad worked at a bakery at some point—he's talked about how limited his options were as an immigrant in Canada, and he's always sympathetic to the hands we've hired in similar circumstances. Was he working the bakery before or after I was born? Or both? Is that a question I could ask him without his getting irritated? I imagine him with a hairnet and a white apron, frosting cookies with meticulous attention to detail. I've never seen him bake in real life. He's so different now from the man he was when he was younger—rodeo, baking—but Mom will always be *this*. She didn't live long enough to change into someone different. There's a pureness to that, an enviable steadiness. No comparison to make between who she was and who she is, what she lost and what she gained. She's Mable Chadwick. Frozen in time with only me to live for her now.

I glance over the line of photos again, looking closely at the belly, the hair, and the face of my mother. Then I look carefully between the last photo and the first photo. Mom is visibly pregnant in the first one—her hair is just brushing her shoulders—and I'm about six months old in the last one, when her hair is perhaps a couple of inches longer. I feel a little shiver as I realize that these photos were taken in less than a year's time. My parents had been married over three years when Mom died, and they would have dated for a while before that, right? Where are the rest of the pictures that chronicle their time together? Why aren't there any photos after Mom got sick? I would think that knowing she was dying, they would have taken lots of pictures. She went to all that trouble to write the letters for me to read—why not take some pictures for me to look at?

Mom and Dad had married at a courthouse without anyone they knew there because she wasn't close to her family and Dad didn't have anyone up there. That's why there aren't any wedding photos, but now that seems strange. *No* photos of your wedding day? Nothing but sixteen snapshots to capture the woman you loved so much that you've never even tried to fall in love again? Are there other photos somewhere? In a box that

Dad looks through when he's feeling particularly lonely? I can't imagine him not sharing those with me.

Remembering something I'd seen on TV once, I turn the pictures over. Film has to be processed in a lab, and there's a stamp of gray numbers and letters on the back. Amid the print there's a date—09-18-1999—it must be when it was processed or developed or whatever, because the date is the same on all of them. There's also a number that shows the order of the photos. I don't know how many pictures you could take with a roll of film, but the highest number here is 24, which means eight of the numbers between 1 and 24 are missing. I swap the order of two photos in the line based on the processing order, then sit back. All of these photos were from the same roll of film. That roll wasn't developed until I was five years old. Three years *after* Mom's death.

7

Sienna

April

I'm standing in the doorway to Dad's office with butterflies in my stomach. I've never gone through the ranch's filing cabinet before—there has never been something in the cabinet that I couldn't wait for him to get for me. If I were here for any other reason, I wouldn't think twice about searching on my own. But I'm going around him, and that makes me anxious. I can imagine after the difficult exchanges we've had that if I asked him, "Hey, can I look through the filing cabinet for information about Mom?" he might say no. And yet that would be a ridiculous thing for him to do, right? He doesn't want to *talk* about Mom, but he wouldn't really prevent me from learning about her. That I'm not sure is enough for me to decide not to ask. I don't want to take the chance. Repentance instead of Forgiveness, only I'm pretty sure that isn't what Jesus taught.

The file tabs are handwritten—some in Dad's handwriting and some Grandma Dee's. I stare at Grandma's familiar blocky print and wonder if I would have gone to her for help with finding this information if she were here. It's hard to know whether she would help me. She didn't know my mom very well—only met her a couple of times—and I've always sensed she was bitter about the years Dad was away from the ranch. He went to Ontario for a study abroad his final year of college, met my mom, and didn't come back until after she'd died. If Mom had lived, I don't know that he would have ever come back, though I've never thought too much about it, because Dad is the ranch to me. I can't picture him in a city, wearing sneakers and button-up shirts.

I feel both guilty and giddy as I take a breath and set to work. Work is good for what ails ya, right, Grandma?

I first look for a file with my mother's name—Mable—and quickly realize it will be in the second drawer down since the top drawer only goes to H. However, there is no file titled MABLE. She isn't under C for Chadwick or G for Gerrard, her maiden name, either. Thinking that maybe I'm wrong about the personal files being mixed in with the ranch stuff, I look up my own name. My file is in the third drawer down, S for Sienna, located between SEARS ORDERS and SLOOT PRODUCTS—an equipment company we use for rails and things. I pull out my file and lay it open on Dad's desk. Report cards, poorly done drawings, certificates of achievement, and a variety of programs for different events I'd participated in—mostly rodeo, which I'd done from nine years old through high school. I find a copy of my birth certificate and feel the thrill of success. Bingo. The copy I took with me to Chicago is in my personal files in a storage unit outside the city—I think I only used it to get an Illinois driver's license.

The relief fades as I read through the information: my name. Date of, place of, weight at, and length at birth. Everything is listed in both English and French, which I've always thought was pretty cool. There's a registration number and an official seal, but there are no parent names.

I flip the paper over to see if parent information is on the back, but it's blank save for a watermark. Isn't having your parents' names on your birth certificate kind of a big deal? I scan the document again, then go through the entire file looking for *any* document with my mother's name on it. I find nothing.

I go back to the very first file in the top drawer of the cabinet and tick off each tab with my finger as I move down the alphabet, looking for any file that might have potential information about my mom. The file titled MOM is for Grandma Dee.

There is a marriage certificate in Grandma's file, copies of deeds and contracts, and a dozen newspaper articles that feature Grandma or the ranch or both. I skim through them, then pause when I find a copy of Grandma Dee's death certificate. I remember being with Dad at the funeral home and the director explaining that Dad would need several official copies in order to settle Grandma's accounts and insurance policies. It's strange to see her reduced to the information on this form, yet I can't help wondering why my mom doesn't have a similar one.

Grandma Dee's folder has everything I expected it would hold—legal certificates and proof of the defining events in her life. Dad's dad—Gregg Chadwick—is peppered throughout Grandma's file even though he'd left them. There's a copy of his death certificate, too. From the dates, I realize he must have died when I was about ten. Dad never told me that, but there's a copy of his death certificate all the same. I find Dad's file, titled MARK. No marriage certificate. No additional photos or legal documents or love letters from Mom. Could he really have left Canada without *anything*? Wouldn't he have needed my birth certificate with his name on it to prove I was his daughter? Could that be the one I have in the storage unit in Chicago? I've never actually sat down and inspected it. Had never seen it until Dad gave it to me right before the wedding.

A strange tingly feeling crosses between my shoulder blades as I slide the last file drawer closed after having gone through every folder a second time. If someone were to go through these files, they would have no idea that my mother ever existed.

> *Who has seen the wind?*
> *Neither I nor you.*

I feel a weird panic but tell myself I'm being silly. There is nothing to *panic* over. I'm just frustrated that yet another attempt to get information about Mom's cancer has turned into grasping steam from a kettle. I'd made the decision to find what I needed to know without burdening Dad, and I'm irritated that the answers weren't available. Right? I mean, Mom's been dead for twenty-three years. It's probably unfair for me to expect any minutia to be left . . . except that she's still my mother. Part of me. The reason I'm here. It's not minutia if it matters, right? And it matters. Mortality is blinking its dark, rheumy eyes at me, and I need information. But Mom isn't in these files. It's not just her cancer that I can't find; it's her.

My phone rings from where I left it in the kitchen, and I hurry to answer—glad for the interruption—only to stop my hand an inch from it. My phone is upside down so that I can't see the caller, but I realize it's probably Dr. Sheffield's office again and feel a mixture of irritation and fear.

I have to face this.

I'm not ready.

I pick up my phone and turn it over so that I can send the call to voice mail. But it's not Dr. Sheffield's office. It's Tyson.

Why is he calling me? Maybe it's an emergency. But what emergency would he need my help with? I remember his text from earlier this morning. Whatever it was hadn't been an emergency three hours ago. And my head is so full of so much. I think of that wedding picture as I let the call go to voice mail.

I go back to Dad's office, where I spend another half an hour sifting through the piles of papers and pages in binders scattered all over the office. Mom's not there either, but by now I'm not expecting to find her. I'm worried that the only proof of her is those sixteen pictures in an old photo album from Kmart. And the letters I haven't appreciated as much as I should have. And me, I guess.

I think about a book I read in junior high about a girl who found her own face on the back of a milk carton. That was a thing they did before the Internet to get missing kids' information into the world. People must have drunk a lot more milk back then. I know that isn't my story; I wasn't stolen—I have pictures of my mom, I know her name and her hobbies and stories about her life that she's shared in those letters. But why is there a file for the antismoking campaign poster I drew in the fourth grade but nothing about my mother? Why is there a copy of my deadbeat grandfather's death certificate but not a copy of my mother's?

I catch myself putting the papers back into the same stacks I found them in. Am I covering my tracks? Not wanting Dad to know that I looked through his things?

I start working through possible ways to start a conversation I know I won't have.

"Why are there only sixteen pictures of Mom taken over the course of one year and from the same roll of film?"

"Why is there no legal proof of her connection to me or you in your files?"

"Why isn't Mom's name written anywhere in any file?"

They are questions I can't ask because they are accusatory. Dad's been evasive already, and would I even be able to trust what he tells me should I press him? I hate this feeling and wish I could wash it off or ignore it or justify it.

By the time I've looked through everything I can search, I have another idea for finding out about my mom. I sit down at Dad's computer and open a browser window. My hands hover over the keys a moment while I formulate the questions I want to ask the World Wide Web. I start by typing Mom's name into the Google search bar—Mable Gerrard Chadwick. I'm hoping for . . . I don't know what I'm hoping for. My mother isn't in this house, but she's got to be on the Internet. I start clicking links, but none of them take me to her. There's a Mable Chadwick who died six years ago in Memphis. Marble Gerrard is a man who ran for city council in New Hampshire. There are some ancestry databases, and LinkedIn profiles for similar names, but nothing for her exact name. I click on some of them anyway, read through page after page of possibilities, and then close the tab and try again. My frustration grows with every dead end. She has to be somewhere. Maybe her being Canadian is getting in the way. Do U.S. Google searches prioritize U.S. links? I go back to the search bar and add "Hamilton Ontario" to the search criteria—that's the city where I was born.

I don't get anything that's any better than what I had before.

When Dad calls my name from the kitchen, I jump. "Sienna?"

I close the page and hurry out of his office, smiling as I cross to him in hopes I don't look guilty. "Hey," I say. "You're back early."

"Am I?" He's got grocery bags in his hands, and I move to help but he shakes his head. I can tell by the set of his shoulders and the downturn of his eyes that he's exhausted. I should have gone with him to Cheyenne. I could have run the errands while he saw Dr. Jefferies.

"Did everything go okay at the appointment?"

"Everything looks fine. The blood work will take a week or so, but we don't expect any issues. You didn't clean out the fridge."

Fridge? I think to myself, glancing at the one in the kitchen. Then I remember that I'd said I would clean out the fridge in the barn.

"Sorry, I'll do it right now."

"I already unloaded the vaccines. They're on the floor by the fridge. Do you need help?"

"No, I'm good. It's a one-person job." I hope he doesn't ask what I did instead of the one job he left me with.

He puts the grocery bags on the table, cans knocking together. A can of chili rolls out, and he grabs it and looks up to give me a drawn smile. "I think I'm going to lie down, if that's all right."

He doesn't look like a man with secrets right now. He looks like a man who's struggling to keep up. I don't know how to settle everything jumbling together in my head. I smile and tell him to take a nap. I'll take care of the fridge and the vaccines, and maybe we could go to the diner for dinner tonight—Jack cooks on Fridays and he does a good job with the steaks.

"That's a good idea," he says as he shrugs out of his coat. "You take good care of me, CC."

"I hope so." I feel terrible for having negative thoughts about him. Questions. Maybe it's my diagnosis that's making me anxious and wanting to blame someone for my troubles. Dad doesn't deserve that from me. I watch him head toward his bedroom and think about what it must have been like to pack up what was left of his life in Canada and head over the border back to the ranch. I've never thought much about the fact that he'd *left* the ranch when he went to Ontario. He hadn't come back until the love of his life was dead and he had no reason to stay. Maybe I *was* all that he brought with him. Maybe I should give him a little more credit and be a bit slower to withdraw my trust. Other than this one thing, he's never done anything to make me distrust him.

I try to believe all these justifications for what I haven't found, but they sit like a chair with one leg too short.

I get the cleaner and the bucket out of the closet and head out to the barn hours after I should have. I can't sort out all this right now, but I can clean out the fridge and feel I've accomplished something.

Nothing in the files.

Nothing on Google.

Why?

8

Diane

November 1993

Diane—Dee to everybody but the bank—took a long drag off her Camel, enjoying the heat inside that contrasted with the cold of night on the outside. The leaves were off the trees now that it was November, but the first snowstorm hadn't hit yet. The cold made her shoulder ache even more, and she tried to roll out some of the stiffness in the joint. Dr. Henley said she needed surgery to fix the rotator cuff—he'd referred her to a specialist out of Cheyenne. Surgery would include six weeks in a padded sling and months of exercises to restore the full range of motion. She'd been tempted to laugh in his face, but now was probably the best time of year for her to be down, and it had been almost six years since the initial injury, caused when Jolly, her horse, was spooked by a rattler during roundup and bucked Diane into a tree. That was a shitty day top to bottom.

On the way home from the doctor's appointment, she'd bought her first pack of cigarettes in almost thirteen years. That was two weeks ago, and though the first pack had made her dizzy, she was nothing if not determined. She'd quit smoking all those years ago for Mark. After Gregg had left, he was down to one parent and she'd felt responsible for keeping that parent out of harm's way as much as possible. What did that matter now that Mark had up and left her too?

"Canada?" Rachel, Dee's best friend since Girl Scouts, had

said when Dee told her about the study-abroad thing that Mark had wanted to do almost two years ago now. "What's abroad about Canada?"

It was the only international study program Dee would agree to. And for only two semesters. How was she to know that his study abroad would turn into his studying a *broad?*

"Damn fool," Dee muttered as she exhaled the smoke into the wintery night. The herd was in the winter pastures now, heifers and yearlings close to the house. It had been a good year as far as sales went. Now she'd focus on a hundred other things she couldn't get to during the summer months. Mark had come home between his semesters in Canada and helped for the summer, but she could tell he was eager to get back to the preppy life he lived up there. It had made her sad, which of course came out in snappy orders and nitpicking. The day after he'd left to go back she'd actually cried, mad at herself for being so damn hard about everything and worried that he'd never come home again. Had the study-abroad program just been an excuse for him to get away from her? Was she that miserable a person to be around? Probably. People thought she was hard, but she was beginning to think it was just the opposite—she felt things so deeply that it terrified her. A rough exterior at least made it look as if she wasn't hurting.

So why not take up smoking again? Who cared if she got lung cancer and died? Who cared if her voice lowered and her clothes smelled? Not the ranch hands. Not the cows. Rachel would mind, but Rachel was her friend, not her mother.

The phone rang from inside the house, and Dee cursed even as she pushed herself up from the plastic lawn chair on the front porch. She dropped the almost-finished cigarette into the coffee can now serving as an ashtray and pulled open the screen door. If phones weren't a necessity, she'd have pulled it out of the wall years ago.

"This is Dee," she said into the receiver a few seconds later. Rachel had gotten a thingamabob called caller ID—a little box she plugged into her phone that told her who was calling. She thought Dee should get one too—it was a great way to screen calls so that you didn't have to talk to those annoying telemarketers. Dee didn't mind the telemarketers enough to pay the five extra dollars the phone company would tack onto her bill for the service. That added up to sixty bucks a year, just to see who was calling before you answered it anyway. The things people came up with to take your money.

"Hey, Mom."

Dee paused a moment, then smiled and felt a rush of warmth move through her. She wouldn't show it—she was still mad at him—but she doubted there was a mother in the world who didn't melt a little when she heard her child's voice from miles away. "Hey," she said evenly. "Look who's callin' me?"

He laughed, but it wasn't genuine. Nothing was between them anymore. She'd hated the idea of Mark going to school in Laramie but relented because his getting a degree in agricultural science could only be good for the ranch. She'd hated the idea of his going abroad for his senior year of college but relented because he'd reminded her that once he was back on the ranch, he'd be there forever. And it was only Canada, and Ontario at that. "So, how are things going?" he asked. "How's the herd?"

That their relationship had dwindled to the small-talk level broke her heart a little bit, but she gave him the updates and then bit her tongue when he was evasive about school and work. The college had already sent her a letter telling her that he'd dropped out of class—she'd seen it coming. As soon as that Mae woman had stepped into his life, he'd turned into a pathetic hound dog. He hadn't told her about dropping out yet. Maybe that was his reason for this call. She had already decided she would be calm and as reasonable as she could manage. "So, what's the real reason you called?" she asked when they ran out of easy topics.

He'd never asked her for money, but she kept a lecture in her back pocket just in case. No way would she make his choices easier for him right now.

"Well, I've got something to tell you," he said, anxiety as tight as a cord in his voice. "And I hope you'll be happy for me. For us."

"Okay," Dee said, steeling herself.

"I'm gonna be a dad. Mae and I, well, we're having a baby."

Dee's hand tightened on the phone, but she clamped her teeth down to keep from saying something she might regret. *Take a breath,* she told herself. And she did. *Let it out,* she instructed. And she did. *That trampy whore!*

Rachel's voice came to mind, something she'd said when her first grandbaby was born a few years ago, months *before* the scheduled wedding. "Doesn't matter how they get here, babies are magic."

Trampy whore or not, this woman was going to be the mother of Dee's grandchild.

Dee let herself remember the moment when Mark had first been placed in her arms. She'd always expected kids as a matter of course—that's what Christian women grew up to do—but she'd stared into that crumpled face and felt certain locks click into place inside her. How desperate she'd felt to do a good job. How she wished, now, that she felt better about the job she'd done. She wouldn't change becoming a Mom for the world, though. Even when Gregg left. Even when Daddy died. Even when her brothers wanted out and so she'd bought their portions of the ranch. Even when she wanted to throttle him, Mark was the best thing that had ever happened to her, and she'd do anything. Anything. Even be happy about this bastard baby.

She cleared her throat. "A baby?" she repeated, keeping her voice even.

"Yeah, in March, we think."

March. Calving season. Dee held back a joke about his heifer. She was going to have to work on her feelings toward this Mae; there was no way around it now. If only she had some idea how to cool the rage she felt for the woman who was taking her boy away from her. Now, more than ever. Rachel might have some advice on that score. She was good with people and relationships the way Dee was good with cattle and numbers.

"Congratulations," Dee said after too long a pause.

"You're happy for me, then?"

"If you're happy, I'm happy."

He didn't answer, because they both knew that wasn't a mantra she'd ever set her clock by. If Mama ain't happy, ain't nobody happy was more like it. But look where that had gotten her. Fifty-four years old, running a ranch by herself, her only child choosing to live in another country with this trampy whore who was going to be the mother of Dee's grandchild.

"I'm happy, Mom," he said, his tone softer. "I'm *really* happy."

Why did it hurt her to hear him say that? Had she truly believed that someday a woman wouldn't steal his heart?

Just because he was the most important person in her life didn't mean she was his. "Well, good then."

"If it's a boy, we're going to name him after Grandpa."

Dee swallowed the lump in her throat. She missed her dad. "And if it's a girl?" Dee asked.

"Sienna," Mark said. "Sienna Diane."

9

Sienna

I wake up Saturday morning to the smell of bacon, and I blink at the ceiling. I put on jeans, a T-shirt, and long socks, and I pull my hair back into my customary ponytail before heading into the kitchen. Uncle Rich and Aunt Lottie ended up meeting us at the diner last night, which was a relief because I'm having a hard time shaking off the thoughts I've had about Dad hiding things from me. We had a nice dinner, then Dad and I watched an episode of *NCIS,* but we both claimed we were too tired to watch a second one. I hope the fact that he's up and cooking means we'll be better company for each other today. The continuing tension between us feels as if I'm wearing my boots on the wrong feet.

"Smells fantastic," I say as I walk to the cupboard to start pulling plates and cups out.

He turns his head to smile at me. "Good," he says with a nod. "It's just about done."

I set the table, then pour myself a glass of orange juice. Dad has his Folgers French roast percolating in the coffeepot, but Tyson ruined me for cheap coffee. I'd rather not drink it at all if I can't have Gaslight's Peruvian roast. I wonder again why Tyson called yesterday. He didn't leave a message, and I should probably call him back, but the idea gives me butterflies. Tomorrow, I decide, when I feel more settled. I wish he'd just texted, but then remember that he *had* sent a text earlier and I hadn't responded.

"Two slices enough?" Dad asks as he turns from the stove with a plate in hand. I can see the creamy pile of scrambled eggs on one side of the plate. When I don't answer right away because I'm still wondering why my husband called me, he raises his eyebrows.

"Two is great," I say quickly.

He smiles and nods before turning back to the stove and putting two slices of bacon next to the eggs. A few seconds later he slides the plate in front of me. My mouth starts to water as I pick up one of the bacon slices and take a bite. The fat melts on my tongue, and the meat portion snaps. The salt makes my lips tingle.

"It's supposed to warm up this afternoon, before the storm hits," Dad says between bites. "I'm thinking if we head out to the pastures around ten, we should be good. What do you think?"

I'm anxious about being in the cab of the truck with him and start thinking over topics that will keep the conversation going—something that's never been hard for us before now. "Ten works." I reach across my plate for the pepper.

My phone rings next to my plate, and I pick it up, then suppress a groan of irritation when I see it's Dr. Sheffield's office. On a Saturday.

Not doin' it.

I send the call to voice mail and turn my phone over so Dad can't see the screen. When I look up, Dad's watching me.

"Telemarketer," I say

"Again?"

Oh, right, I've used that already. I shrug. "I bet they get paid for every dial. That's why they don't give up."

"Nope," Dad says, shaking his head while returning his attention to his plate. "I saw this on *60 Minutes*. They have fancy computer things that call hundreds of numbers at the same time.

If someone picks up, the call gets sent to one of their representatives who have nothing to do with—"

His phone rings, cutting him off. "Well, speak of the devil." Unlike me, Dad sees it as his patriotic duty to answer every call that comes to his phone. Even if it's from India.

"Hell-o," he says in his drawling country-boy voice. "Yes, this is Mark Chadwick."

I take another bite of my eggs and think about yesterday. I didn't find undelivered Mom letters in the filing cabinet. Unless there really aren't any more letters, they have to be somewhere else in the house. Would I be willing to poke around Dad's room? I can't imagine doing that. The office is one thing—it's common area—but his bedroom is something else. That room has been his all his life—Grandma Dee's is still set up like it was when she died. It's the master, so it's the only bedroom in the house with its own bathroom. It would make sense for Dad to use it, but I know he feels weird about moving into his mother's room. Instead, he stays in the smaller one across the hall from hers and uses the bathroom in the hallway there. He has the same curtains and bedspread he had in high school—I've seen pictures—and still sleeps in a twin bed. The idea of snooping through a space that is so completely and totally his is borderline repulsive to me. Which he likely knows, which is likely why that would be the place he would hide stuff about Mom. I step back from my thoughts and shake my head at all of this. It's ridiculous—that he would hide anything and that I have to plan some kind of stealth operation to find it.

"Oh," Dad says into the phone, drawing my attention back to him though I tuned out only for a second. "Do you want to talk to her? She's right here."

My eyes snap up to meet his as he hands the phone across the table. He lowers his voice as I swallow my bite of eggs and reach for his phone. "It's a doctor's office," he whispers.

A burst of fire fills my chest as I take his phone. I remember writing Mark Chadwick down as my emergency contact on those medical forms. They *called* him?

"This is Sienna," I say calmly, but my face is burning and I can feel Dad looking at me.

"Sienna, this is Dr. Sheffield."

I should probably feel flattered she's taken the time to make this call herself, but I am furious. And can't show it. "Yeah, hi," I say with fake sugar. "Can I call you back on my phone in just a minute? We're in the middle of breakfast." Because it's eight o'clock in the morning. On a Saturday!

Dr. Sheffield pauses. "*Will* you call me back?"

I bite my tongue until I'm sure I can control what comes out of my mouth when I next open it. "Of course, it will be just a few minutes."

"All right," Dr. Sheffield says. "Call this number. I'll be the one who answers it."

I hang up without saying good-bye and pass Dad's phone back to him. What if he Googles the phone number and finds out what kind of doctor's office called and asks me questions that require answers I've already lied to him about?

"Everything okay, CC?"

"Yep," I say, the end of the word sharp as a pickax. "I just need to call her back in a bit."

He's still concerned, so I add one more lie to the cabin worth of lies I've been building for the last couple of weeks. "She's a lady doctor in Cheyenne. I've got a consultation."

In our house, "lady doctor" doesn't refer to the doctor's gender; rather, it refers to her clientele. I've been seeing all kinds of "lady doctors" these last few years, and though Dad is as supportive as any girl in my situation could hope for, he's vastly uncomfortable with lady doctor stuff. He nods, and we both go back to our plates. I try not to eat too fast, but I don't taste a bite. Finally, I finish and stand up from the table, empty plate in one hand and my phone in the other. "Thanks again for breakfast, Dad. It was delicious."

"You betcha, sweetie."

I lock my bedroom door and go into the bathroom that my room shares with the guest room on the other side—the most private place in the house.

"This is Dr. Sheffield," she says when she answers after the first ring.

"You called my dad?" I seethe.

"We've been calling you for a week."

"And it's my prerogative to call back or not."

"I'm your doctor and I'm very concerned."

"I should turn you in to the bar for harassment."

"The bar is for lawyers."

Oh yeah.

"Look, Sienna, I know this is hard, I do, but you need to come in and get that tumor removed." I prefer to think of it as a lump. "When is a good day for you? There are two open appointment times at the clinic on Wednesday and Friday of next week. I've consulted with the surgeon, and she feels it will be pretty straightforward—we don't need to do an MRI or anything at this point, just get the tumor out so we can further evaluate."

I reach my free hand up behind my neck and try to massage the knots there. "I can't make any of those appointments. It's calving season on my dad's ranch, and I'm the only hand right now. My dad's been sick."

"Prostate cancer, yes, I know."

For a minute, I imagine Dr. Sheffield having gotten that information by hiding in the bushes with binoculars around her neck. Then I remember the medical history form I'd filled out before my appointment. The same one where I idiotically put Dad down as my emergency contact. "Yeah."

"I would think his illness would make you eager to come in."

She doesn't understand. No one does. No one could. "I can't get away for at least another three weeks."

"You can't wait three more weeks, Sienna, you have an *invasive* cancer. That means the cancer, which started in a mammary gland, has already spread from the ductal wall. Because it's in the surrounding tissues, you have cancer cells floating around in your body that can at any time filter down to your lymph nodes, which will send those cells everywhere." She pauses for a breath. "We are talking about the rest of your life, Sienna. If we're right about the size and grade, and assuming it hasn't already spread, you have an excellent prognosis, but you need to get the procedure done as soon as possible. Even then, we'll have to do a full pathology of the tissue to make sure we caught everything. I'm not trying to invade your privacy, but this is not something you can put off."

My head feels like it's going to explode, and I raise my hand to my temple and close my eyes. I just need a little more time to sort things out. Is that really so much to ask?

I take a breath and try to think about what she wants to hear. "I've been trying to learn about my mom's cancer," I say. "That makes a difference in how we treat this, right?"

"It *could* make a difference in long-term treatment," Dr. Sheffield confirms. "But getting that tumor *out* is what's going to be the difference between life and death. That your mom died of this disease is one more reason for all of us to take this as seriously as we possibly can."

I want learning about Mom's cancer to be the most important task at hand. I need it to matter. I need justification for the searching I've already done and the searching I need to keep doing. And yet Dr. Sheffield's words do scare me, just like she wants them to. I've outlived my mother by two years. Shouldn't I know better than anyone how serious this can be? What if I wait and the cancer does spread? I can't bring myself to tell Dad I have it; how will I tell him that I ignored it long enough for it to get worse? "I'll see if I can get some help to cover things for a few days. Let me look over my calendar."

Dr. Sheffield is quiet for a few seconds. "Next week, Sienna. You need to get in here next week. Which of these spots should I hold for you?"

I growl low in my throat but hope she can't hear me. "Friday," I say, because maybe Uncle Rich could help out over the weekend.

"Okay, I can hold that spot through Monday, but you'll have to call the scheduler to confirm it and submit your insurance information. Do you have the number for the scheduling office?"

"Yeah."

"What is it?"

Uh.

Dr. Sheffield sighs, and the edges of her tone soften. "Have you talked to *anyone* about this, Sienna? Do your friends and family members know? I can only assume you haven't told your father, but have you told your husband? Anyone?"

I say nothing. I think back to that appointment in her office when she told me that this was too heavy to carry alone. It's also too heavy to share. "There's a lot going on," I say in an attempt to explain, but the words sound stupid and I know it. My hand moves to my breast, where the monster lives. I see myself the way Dr. Sheffield does. Scared and young and not taking this as seriously as I should. I press the spot where I know the lump is—I find it every time I shower as though I'm hoping it will feel smaller. It's like a tiny seed—millet or quinoa but not precisely round—just hanging out in there. I can't feel it now through my shirt and bra, but I know it's there. Ticking like a clock? Rubbing its hands together like a cartoon villain in hopes I'll continue to put this off so it can explode into the rest of me? I think of Larry Shriver again, and his cane and his son who will have his dad in the audience when he graduates from Lusk High School but won't have his dad when he graduates college. What if Larry could have caught his cancer before it spread? Wouldn't he have done anything to have had that chance?

"Keeping this to yourself will not make it go away," Dr. Sheffield continues. "If you would rather, I can tell your family for you."

My chest prickles at the thought of handing my phone to Dad and saying, "This is the doctor who diagnosed my cancer. She wants to talk to you."

"That's ridiculous." There seems to be a subtle threat in Dr. Sheffield's offer—she has Dad's number and permission to contact him on my behalf.

"Then tell them yourself. Let them give you advice and encouragement."

"I need to get things set up so that I can leave, but I'll call and confirm on Monday."

"I'm going to text you the scheduling department's number as soon as we finish this call." Her voice is picking up speed, as though she's afraid I'll hang up. "It's a simple outpatient procedure and will take only an hour or so. A cancer foundation we work with will cover up to two nights at a local hotel for patients who live more than fifty miles away from the center. You'll need someone to drive you to and from the center—do you understand?"

"Yeah." I could take Uber to and from the . . . wait, am I doing this? The image of cancer cells floating around my body, waiting to be caught in the current of veins and arteries that will take them to the rest of me, is powerful. And probable.

In the springtime when the cottonwoods open, the fluffy seeds look like snow. Big clumps of the stuff will build up against fences and walls. If someone accidentally leaves the barn door open on a windy day, the stuff blows in and it's hell to get out because it gets in all the nooks and crannies. That's how this feels—cotton in the wind, out of my control. Can't be caught and stuffed back into the pods it came out of.

"Sienna?"

I blink quickly. "I-I'm here."

"Call first thing Monday. Let me help to save your life. Please."

"I'll call," I say.

I hang up and stare at the tile floor. I'd helped Dad lay it about eight years ago. It's pretty good, for a couple of novices who watched a few YouTube videos and decided it wasn't rocket science. We're used to doing things ourselves—I can't remember the last repairman we called. We don't care if the hinges in the kitchen match or the pipes chug when we turn on the outside hose. I used to see that independence as something we did together, but is it the same part of me that's trying to do this by myself?

I want to go back to bed. I want to cry. I want to run away and pretend none of this is happening.

When my phone rings in my hand, I jump, concluding that it's Dr. Sheffield having forgotten to tell me something. I'm irritated all over again as I raise the phone to answer it. But it's not Dr. Sheffield. It's Tyson. Again.

Dr. Sheffield's worn me down and I've run out of irritation or excuses. What's worse than the call I just got off? I might as well get it over with.

"Hi, Tyson," I say into the phone, leaning against the tub and feeling exhausted even though it's not even nine o'clock in the morning.

He pauses, as though surprised I answered. "Hi," he finally responds.

We both sit there, and I think back to that wedding picture in the living room. Those kids could never have imagined that they would be on opposite ends of a phone call on opposite sides of the world and not know how to start a conversation.

After a few seconds, he clears his throat. "So, I've gotten a bunch of e-mails from the insurance company over the last few days. Looks like things are pretty bad."

My eyes drift closed and my chin falls to my chest. So much for secrets.

10

Sienna

I do my best to minimize the situation as I tell him about the lump and going to Cheyenne and the diagnosis as though I'm updating him about beef prices as of last month. It's the first time I've put words to everything that's happened, but I can't tell if I'm relieved or made more anxious by hearing it all out loud. His listening is interspersed with "Oh, Sienna," and "Wow" and what could be called gasps, but that's not very masculine so I don't categorize them that way. I'm tempted to give in to the obvious emotion of what I'm saying, but I don't. That would be inviting him in, and even amid all this I can't do that. It wouldn't be fair.

"How is your dad handling this?"

I'm quiet long enough that I hear him let out a breath—definitely an exasperated sigh rather than a gasp.

"You haven't told him?"

"I can't," I say, and explain how Dad's still recovering and it'll be too much and he'll want to come with me and we need him at the ranch. The coincidence of having committed to the lumpectomy right before Ty's call is uncanny. That I can talk to him as easily as this is equally strange. I guess his having been my confidant for so many years is a hard habit to break.

"Isn't hiding all this a whole lot harder than telling him? I mean, he's gonna know eventually and then he'll know you didn't tell him."

I must be feeling brave today. "There are other reasons I don't want to tell Dad—stuff I'm trying to make sense of." I pause like a golfer watching in absolute stillness as her ball rolls across the green.

"Stuff?"

I haven't talked to Ty in three months and haven't shared details of my life in longer than that. It's his distance from all of this that makes him a good confidant. So I tell him about the pictures, the files, Dad evading my questions. I realize how very conspiracy theory it all sounds and expect Tyson to try to convince me to tell Dad. He doesn't. "So, anyway, it's all twisted up together. I can't bring Dad into this when there are these unanswered questions but I can't put off this lumpectomy any longer either."

I wait for him to tell me that it will be impossible to keep this from my dad and I'm going to have to find some way to tell him. "What about Beck? Can you talk to her?"

"If I tell Beck she'll tell her mom, and Dad will find out and . . . I'm just not ready to lose control of it that way."

"She might not tell."

"But she probably will, and Clint's been down with his ankle, and there's just so much on her plate already."

"You really think you can go have surgery without help?'

I tell him about the hotel room the nonprofit pays for and Uber and . . . boy, does it sound stupid. But it's all I've got. I brace to defend myself against whatever he says next.

"I could come help out."

For a few seconds I'm confused, thinking he means that he can come out and help with the ranch. Then I realize he's not talking about calving, he's talking about the procedure. It confuses me. I'm tempted to explain that this whole cancer thing is going to pass—98 percent of women survive it—but surviving this won't fix him and me. In fact, it will make the hard things harder between us because who knows where I'll be in the whole infertility continuum when all of this is done. "You're in London, Tyson."

"I can get a week off."

I laugh because this has to be a joke. "Take a week off just like that and fly to the other side of the world?" I couldn't get him to take an *afternoon* off back in Chicago—even after work at home he was taking calls and sending documents. That was *before* he'd said he wanted to take this London job and have us put the baby-making on hold.

"They've offered me an extension of my contract," Tyson says. "If I accept the extension, I'm sure I can put a week off into the deal. They really like me here."

The initial offer to go to London had come last summer. The implantation had failed two weeks earlier. I was back at work but went to bed as soon as I got home each day. "They've asked me to transfer to London for a year, and I'm thinking it might be exactly what we need. You can get stable, we can have some adventures, and I can add a nice credential to my résumé." I didn't want adventures, and I didn't care about credentials. I wanted a baby, and the last two years of my life had been so devoted to that goal that nothing else mattered. I didn't like city living, never mind a cosmopolitan city like London. Tyson had assured me it would be one year—just one.

"When were you going to tell me?" I say this as though he owes me personal updates, which he doesn't. He's been wanting me to come to London from the start, almost didn't go when Dad got sick and I ran back to the ranch last October, a month before he was supposed to leave. I assured him I'd join him after Christmas and that he might as well be in London if I would be in Wyoming during that time anyway. But I didn't go to London after Christmas, and he was mad—accused me of planning it from the start. Of giving up on us. I texted him that I was sorry he felt that way. Then didn't respond to his follow-up texts for almost a week.

"The offer came on your birthday, and ever since then I've been trying to figure out how to get us to a place where we can talk about it."

I guess this was that place.

"And I guess you want to take the extension," I say, my tone flat. Am I disappointed? Relieved? Both? Neither?

"Can you think of any reason why I shouldn't?"

"Would you be coming back here because you think we can fix us?"

"No, it's so that when we look back on this time, neither of us can hate me."

We're both quiet, but I feel something let go inside me. When we look back. But not together. This is his peace offering, and it's all I can do not to accept it too enthusiastically.

"So, I guess my cancer showed up just in time, then. You get to swoop in and be the hero and kick the dust off your shoes when you finish up."

I expect him to be offended, but he's very calm when he speaks next. "Do you want me to come or don't you? I'm not trying to be a hero. I haven't been able to save you for a really long time. But I can help if you need it, and it sounds like you need it. I want more than this, Sienna. I want to meet new people with different stories and work toward a future I can be excited about. I don't see how you and I are going to build that when you're never going to come to London and I'm never going back to Lusk."

A wave of envy takes me off guard. A future to be excited about. New people. Different stories. I wonder if new people includes a new woman—someone whom he walks through Hyde Park with and reads *Harry Potter* out loud to. I take a few beats to poke around in my heart and head to see how I feel. I should be angry and grieving and maybe even beg him to give me another chance, but what I feel instead is relief. Not a waterfall of it. Not a fall-onto-my-knees-and-kiss-the-floor kind of relief, just the gentle "it is what it is" sort of feeling that I used to feel after getting a bad hook in a roping competition. The way I felt when I stopped doing rodeo because I knew I had no future in it. Without Tyson's wagon hitched to mine, there will be one less person to feel responsible for failing.

I lean my head back against the tub and close my eyes. "You want a divorce?"

He pauses, lets out a breath. I imagine him sitting on the window seat of the London flat that came with the job—he'd sent me pictures after he first arrived. The window looks over the financial district, and at night the view is beautiful. He'll be dressed in tailored trousers and a button-up shirt with the top few buttons undone. He's probably bought half a dozen new pairs of shoes since arriving there—he loves nice shoes. That image is the Tyson I have watched him moving toward for years without realizing it was happening. Through all the hard stuff, I turned inside myself and he reached outside, grabbing ideas and experiences, and now he was on his way to finding a different happiness. "We'll get your stuff out of the way first, but I think we're both worn out. These last months have been hell, Sienna."

"These last years have been hell," I say, and open my eyes. Things were good until we started trying to have a baby, but it's been downhill since then. It's not hard to see that what we loved most about each other is what the other person could give us. When we couldn't give each other those things, the foundation rotted out. He needed to succeed with something, and I didn't care. About anything. Do I even love him anymore? Maybe the fact that I want him to be happy even if it's without me means that I *do* love him. Or maybe the fact that I can so easily see the end of our road means that I don't.

"We could meet with a divorce lawyer while you're here," I say.

"Uh, let's just deal with your stuff. We can do the rest of it later."

"But you'll be *here*. We could get a lot done and save—" I feel an eagerness to do something. Anything.

"Stop it, Sienna," Tyson says. "I hadn't planned on saying anything about that stuff. I just didn't want you to think I was coming for some kind of reconciliation, that's all. I need to talk to my office and make sure this will work, but I'll let you know as soon as I have things in place, okay? When is the procedure—next Friday?"

"Yeah, they want me to confirm on Monday that I'll be there." I pause and take a breath. "You'll really come out here to help me with this?"

"I still care about you, Sienna, and this . . . this is shitty. I want to help, and I'm pretty sure I can pull it off."

"Okay," I say, staring at the tile floor again. It's almost romantic, his running to my aid, but romance isn't enough. Heroics aren't enough. Wanting something different isn't enough. Like he said, we're both worn out. I need to get this surgery and work out the stuff about Dad and Mom. He needs to work toward an exciting future in London. "Thanks for doing this, Tyson."

He pauses, lets out a breath. "You're welcome."

11

Sienna

Dad looks at me across the table Tuesday morning, a turkey sausage link speared on his fork and paused halfway to his mouth. He lowers it and blinks. "You're going out of town *now*?"

"I know the timing isn't great," I say, peppering my eggs and not looking at him. My stomach is in knots. "But I called Manny, and he's able to come back early with a cousin of his in tow, and the heifers are doing great." The calving had started Sunday. We have eight baby cows so far.

Manny has helped us on the ranch here and there for ten years, but he works the orange groves in Florida for the winters. It had been a gamble whether he could accommodate coming to us a month early, but it seems his contract there only had a week left and he was able to make adjustments. He'll be here tomorrow morning and stay through the September stock sales. His cousin can stay only until his position in Montana is ready for him next month, but the two of them will make up for my being gone. If I still believed in fate, I would think all this was meant to be. But accepting Manny's availability as a blessing means having to see something of value in the cancer and my marriage ending and my dad's evasions. I can't follow the line that far.

"We've still got, what, twenty heifers and then the seventy cows that need to deliver?" Dad asks, not doing a very good job of hiding his concern about my leaving.

Twenty-three heifers and sixty-two cows, I correct in my mind but don't say out loud. "It's probably my last chance to make this thing with Tyson work, Dad. He's coming from London."

He continues to look at me, and I don't break eye contact even though I'm terrified he can see the lies twisting me up inside. Telling Tyson about the cancer makes it feel more possible to tell Dad, but at the very least he'll be upset I didn't tell him sooner and want to come with me. Dad can't work the herd much, but he's a priceless resource for Manny and the new hand. We both can't leave the ranch this time of year, and I can't really address all the Mom stuff until the cancer is out of the way. My secrets need to stay secrets a little bit longer just like his do.

"Do you want this *thing* with Tyson to work, honey? I've kind of gotten the impression that you aren't missing him too much."

I trail my fork through the puddle of syrup on my plate, the grooves filling almost immediately. "I don't know what I want to happen with Tyson, but I feel like I need this time with him right now. Maybe it will push me over the fence and I can finally move on." More lies—I'm clearer on where I stand with my husband than I have been in a very long time, though. I keep thinking of him with a lovely English rose who has an unblemished past and a bright future. I want that for him. Tyson has become part of that other life, the fantasy one. I've scheduled a meeting with a divorce attorney in Cheyenne before my preoperative appointment on Thursday. I haven't told Tyson, because he'll insist on not doing it, but why not kill two birds with one stone? Divorce and lumpectomy, bing, bam, boom.

Dad bites off one end of his sausage. I suspect that he's upset with me for making all these plans without him. I'm going over his head. It's emasculating and inconsiderate, as he's the official owner of the ranch and my father. But working as hard as I have for all these months has earned me a weekend off when my husband comes from the UK to see me, and we both know Dad won't argue. I see the change when he pushes aside his frustration and accepts things as they are.

"So, you'll leave Thursday, then?" Dad asks when he finishes chewing.

"Yeah, Tyson flies into Cheyenne that afternoon. I'll have the cabin ready for the hands by tomorrow and all the schedules up-to-date before I go."

Dad reaches his hand across the table, palm up. I hesitate a minute before I put my hand on his. He wraps his big, strong fingers around my smaller but just as strong ones. He has hands like Great-Grandpa—Grandma Dee always said so—while my hands are more like Grandma Dee's. Delicate, almost, but strong. I wonder what my mom's hands were like.

I try to absorb Dad's strength and optimism and goodness, and I hope he can't feel my fear and guilt and weakness. "If you need to go, CC, then go. We'll make it work here. I . . . I just don't want you to be more hurt than you already have been. That's my concern, not the ranch."

"Tyson didn't *hurt* me, Dad." Truth.

He gives my hand a squeeze and lets go so both of us can finish eating. When we're done, he takes the plates to the sink. "Sorry I questioned you, sweetie. This weekend must be pretty important for you to have gone to all the trouble of making the arrangements. You've also been working like two men these last months. I wish I could pay for you and Tyson to go to the Bahamas for a week to show my thanks."

"I don't want to go to the Bahamas." I don't want to go to Cheyenne, either. "I'll be working with the guys until I leave, but they know what they're doing, and when I get back we can talk about how we'll figure out the new budget to work in paying them a few extra weeks—I'm really sorry about that part."

"Don't be," Dad says while he rinses off his plate. "We'll figure it out. If the guys are doing the heavy stuff, I can at the very least bark out some instructions. It'll be good for me to dig in a little. I've left way too much of the work up to you."

Dad still naps most days and takes the side-by-side when he has to get around the ranch—he only managed an hour on horseback during roundup. When he was receiving his treatments, he picked up some bug every other week, and it sent him flat to bed every time. Even after the treatments were over and his hair grew back steely gray instead of the salt-and-pepper it had been before, he never seemed fully recovered. He doesn't know that I know about the adult diapers he's bought online and hides in his room. Dad refuses to admit he's ever been sweet on the choir director at church, but I suspect the reason he hasn't pursued a romantic relationship isn't the kind of thing he'd talk to his daughter about. It's one more thing I'll never ask.

"Just promise me you won't overdo it," I say.

"I'll mostly just drive out with them so I stay in the know and can update the schedule," Dad says, then raises his hand as though he's in a court of law. "I promise I won't overdo it."

"Cross your heart?" I run my fingers through hair still wet from the shower I took before we sat down to eat.

"And eat your pie," Dad finishes for me with an added wink at the end.

I hadn't known until I was nine that the real idiom ended with "hope to die." I like our version better. Especially now.

I braid my hair to keep it out of my face and secure it with the hairband I have on my wrist. Grandma Dee would tell me I'd catch cold going outside with my hair wet, but there isn't time to pull out a hair dryer. "All right, I'm out to play with the baby cows for a little while." Thank goodness I have things to keep me busy for the next couple of days. The ranch. The calves. Purpose and responsibility.

Invasive ductal carcinoma.

Meeting Tyson to start divorce proceedings as though we're just selling a car together.

Lumpectomy.

Breathe.

12

Sienna

The Cheyenne Regional Airport is located in central Cheyenne—
an example of the many frontier towns that grew out from a central point. First there's a store. Then a bank next to it. Then a
blacksmith. Eventually there's a Chili's and a bus depot, and by
then the airport, which used to be on the edge of town, is now
in the middle. It's a single terminal airport with free parking and
a coffee shop inside. I don't think they have more than a dozen
passenger flights in and out a day. O'Hare has something like
twelve hundred. The only time I've ever flown through Cheyenne
was when Grandma Dee had her stroke and I had to get here fast.

Today I'm waiting in the front parking lot for Tyson, whose
plane I watched land about ten minutes ago. My palms are
sweaty on the steering wheel of my faithful Prius when I see
him. My stomach flips, and I feel a little betrayed by the reaction. He's wearing charcoal slacks and a white button-down
shirt, rolled up to the elbows. His hair is short, his jaw square,
and he's wearing leather shoes I suspect are Italian and not for
sale anywhere in the state of Wyoming. He looks like a model—
London has been good for him.

He spots me and smiles like a guy in a rental car commercial.
I smile back, but my anxiety is popping like corn in a kettle. I
get out to open the hatchback so he can put his carry-on inside.
He pulls the hatch down and turns to me. I wonder if he's going

to kiss me hello and then he does it before I can prepare myself. I'm stiff, and he doesn't let the kiss linger, then pulls back and smiles at me. "You're looking really good, Sienna," he says, making me wonder what he expected me to look like.

"My hair won't fall out until chemo."

His smile falls. I turn away, saving him from a response, and head to the driver's side door I'd left open. He goes to the passenger side. Among some older couples in Lusk, the woman never drives if her husband is in the car—I think Uncle Rich and Aunt Lottie are one of those couples. I've wondered if it's because he likes to be in charge or she likes to feel taken care of. Tyson and I have never been like that, and pretty soon we won't know if we ever would have. We put on our seat belts, and I wind our way out of the airport parking area toward the attorney's office he still doesn't know about.

I ask him about his flight, and he answers me, direct to Salt Lake, then the commuter flight to Cheyenne. He slept on the first flight and feels pretty good, though he expects the jet lag will set in around four o'clock mountain time. This is the kind of talk that would be shared between strangers at one of the cocktail parties in Chicago that he liked and I tolerated. I stopped participating in that part of his life after the first couple of years. I was uncomfortable, and he was uncomfortable with my discomfort. "How are you feeling about tomorrow," he asks me. "Nervous?"

"A little." I've worked really hard not to think about tomorrow; there's nothing my worry can improve about it, so I've kept myself busy with other stuff. I put on my blinker and turn left into an office building parking lot.

"What's this?" he says, looking over the sign that gives the different names of the companies located in the building. Nothing about the all-glass building says doctor's office, which is what he's expecting.

"I made an appointment with a divorce attorney, Roland K. Johnson—he had a good website." I turn off the car, grab my purse from the middle console as though we're running into a fast-food place to grab a couple hamburgers, and get out before

Tyson formulates an argument. He has no choice but to get out of his side, but he keeps his door open and looks at me across the top of the car while I adjust my purse strap on my shoulder. My purse is turquoise suede, with six-inch tassels that hang from the bottom. I've owned it since I got my Justin Boots with the turquoise trim—pair these accessories with a black sheath dress and a denim jacket and you're killin' it at the local bar. Not that I ever did that scene; I knew I was going to marry Tyson before I graduated from high school and then all we had to do was wait the year that Grandma Dee insisted we needed to be sure. Maybe we should have waited two. I started using the purse a couple of months ago when the strap broke on the crossbody bag I bought in Chicago. I could fix the crossbody, but there's nothing special about it except that it prevents a girl from getting mugged quite so easily.

"I said I didn't want to work on divorce stuff," he says in an even tone.

"Who knows when you'll be back here, Tyson." I lift my hands in a gesture of futility and let them fall to my sides. "We'll just talk to him about the best way to go about a noncontentious divorce. I don't think it will be too complicated since we don't have a lot of assets to split and no . . . kids." I *almost* keep the bitterness out of my voice when I say this. Last night when I couldn't sleep, I compared my situation to my mom's. She had a child and knew she was going to die. Did that make her fight harder? Did she take advantage of every possible treatment she could because she had someone to live for and every day counted? Was there anyone alive who knows those kinds of details? It should be Dad, but he isn't talking.

Who do I have to live for other than Dad? Would I have approached this differently if I had a child? I think I'd have made the appointment as soon as I found the lump instead of waiting two weeks to find a doctor in Cheyenne. I wouldn't be hiding it from anyone either.

I go back to the topic at hand before I get too lost in these thoughts, which, really, are a waste of time. Fact is, I don't have kids to live for and soon I won't have a husband to worry about anymore. "We were married in Wyoming, which makes the divorce simpler in that way too."

"I don't want to do this," he says, shaking his head.

"You said you were tired of living this way," I remind him, looping my hand through the air as though I'm casting a net over the two of us. "When will we have a better opportunity? Besides, I already made the appointment and we can't just not show up."

Tyson steps forward and rests his arms on the top of the Prius, not looking away from my face, which does nothing for my rising anxiety. The sun that was just enough to take the edge off the cold goes behind the clouds, and a breeze whips my ponytail. His hair barely moves. His voice is harder when he speaks next. "You've got a pre-op appointment for surgery in, what, an hour? This is crazy, Sienna."

"This is *efficient*," I clarify. "You're ready to move on, and it will be way more convenient to take care of it here than it will when you're halfway around the world."

"I think we should wait until we get you through the treatments."

"We?" I say, lifting my hands and shrugging my shoulders. "By next week you'll be back in London and I will be dealing with whatever comes next. I appreciate your being here—I still can't believe you came—but the cancer really has nothing to do with *us,* Tyson."

He furrows his brow, and the tension is growing. Emotion is rising in my chest due to the power of speaking the truth out loud after having told so many lies these last few weeks. I have no reason not to say everything, because I do not think I will ever see him again after these next few days.

I take a breath meant to infuse me with determination to see this through. "When you said on that phone call that you were fed up, I felt the most hope I've felt in a really long time."

"Hope?" he asks in confusion.

"Yeah, hope, because if we go our separate ways, I don't have to feel guilty for failing you anymore."

His expression turns sympathetic, and I hurry to speak

again—sympathy hadn't been what I was going for. "I've failed you and Dad and Grandma Dee and those three embryos that couldn't plant themselves inside me despite all the work to create the perfect environment for them to do what millions of embryos do without the coaching. Everything I've ever wanted is so much more out of reach than it's been before, and I can't stand seeing that reflected in the people around me." My voice cracks, and I try to swallow the emotion because I don't want to seem as though I'm pulling it out to manipulate him. "Yeah, I have cancer, but it's my thing, okay? And I'll be able to better focus on it and what it means for *me* if I don't feel as if I'm dragging you down with me. We've both moved on with our lives; why should we pretend that we haven't?"

He stares at me, and although part of me wishes I knew what was going on behind those deep brown eyes, part of me is terrified he'll say it out loud, because then I'm responsible again. A car pulls into the space one place away from Tyson's side of the Prius. He closes the door before coming around to my side and stops about a yard away. He shoves his hands into his pockets.

"We'll go to the appointment and find out what we need to do, but we don't file yet, okay? We wait until you're through this surgery and whatever follows, until your head is clear and this stuff with your dad is worked out. Then we decide how we want to move forward."

I don't hate it.

"Deal," I say.

We hold each other's stare. If I thought we could go back to who we were in that wedding photo on the living room wall of the ranch house, I think I would do whatever it took to get there, but I feel silly for ever thinking that kind of happiness was real.

Tyson puts out his hand, and I think he wants us to shake on our agreement, so I put mine forward too. Instead he takes hold of my hand, turns toward the building, and leads me toward the entrance. We're holding hands as we walk into the divorce lawyer's office. How sick is that?

13

To my dearest Sienna on her wedding day,
    Thinking about you on your wedding
day makes me smile as I sit here by the
window of our apartment and listen to
you sleeping in the cradle beside me.
I'm sure your wedding day is very
different from mine, but even though it
was only a courthouse ceremony and
your dad and I didn't have anyone to
celebrate with us, we felt God watching
over us and we meant every word of the
vows we said to each other. After the ceremony we splurged on some Chinese
food and talked about where we would
go on our honeymoon one day.
    Marrying your father was the best de-
cision I ever made, CC, and it makes my
heart happy to think of you pledging
your life to a man you love the way I
love your dad. He's lucky indeed to have
you. I encourage you to go into this
union with your whole heart—don't let
the small annoyances of life get in the
way of growing together, and never

miss the opportunity to be together. The most beautiful part of marriage is the way two people make the world a better place through the children they bring into the world. Every child deserves to come to a family who loves them, like you did, and I promise you that nothing will make you happier than holding a child who is part of you and part of him. Never take a moment for granted.

You know better than most people that there are no guarantees in life, so I advise you to live every day to its fullest, and when things get hard, which they will, think about the fact that you're not just living for yourself. You're living for your children, your husband, and me and your dad too. You are our legacy, and even though I have not been there, I know that your dad and your grandma have given you every bit of good they could to help you on your way.

Be faithful to your husband. Bless your home with a happy heart and a willing spirit. Think of the good of the whole more than the good of the individual, and know how many people are counting on you, praying for you, and watching you with glad hearts.

I love you, my dear girl, and have no doubt you'll make the prettiest bride Wyoming has ever seen.

Go with love,

Mom

14

Sienna

"There have been nine calves born since I left," I say out loud while I text Dad back with only my left hand. I've managed to prop my right arm up in such a way that it's not aching at the moment. "One of the heifers had some trouble." I make a face, not needing to explain that Dad had to put her down—Tyson knows how this stuff works. I've never had to be the one to take down a distressed animal, though I would if faced with the decision. It's mercy; I know that.

Tyson looks up from his laptop, set on the little round table by the window of the motel where we've been for two nights now. "Did the calf make it?"

"Yeah, one of the cows took it in. That's lucky." The dressings on my right armpit and breast incision are held in place by an Ace bandage that wraps all the way around my chest like a bulky halter top. I'm lucky that I didn't need a drain. In a few days I'll be able to trade the Ace bandage for a sports bra; I found two that fasten in the front for $9.99 at Walmart after my pre-op appointment on Thursday. I'm due for another pain pill in half an hour; Tyson has an alarm set on his watch to make sure we don't miss any. The post-op instructions were adamant that we not chase the pain, especially these first three days. So far we've stayed on top of it, but that means my brain is fuzzy, I can't account for time properly, and I feel slightly sick to my stomach all the time. The only reason I can coherently text Dad is because we're on the tail end of the last pill. It takes forever with just one hand, though, and I feel bad when Dad asks how things are going and I write, "Great."

Tyson continues to watch me as if he's got something else to say, but I keep my focus on my phone. He's been a great nurse: keeping me on schedule with the medications, helping me get dressed, taking me for walks around the parking lot of the motel, and making sure I get all the sleep I need. My body is starting to ache from being in bed so much.

"I don't think you should go back to the ranch yet."

I glance at him over knees covered in cheap motel bedspread and upon which my phone is propped. "I don't really have a choice," I say. "Dad hasn't said it outright, but this is more than he can handle. Even with the guys. I need to get back."

"And do what?" Tyson says, waving toward my chest. I'm wearing a button-up pajama top, but the bulky bandage is still obvious. "You act as though you'll jump on Rosa and work like you've always done."

I know I'm not up to that, but I can do some things. I finish the text to Dad and toss my phone on the empty side of the double bed. Tyson has been sleeping in the other bed. "I have to get back, Tyson. It's not worth discussing alternatives."

"And how are you going to explain that to your dad?" He waves toward my chest again. "They said it will be two weeks before you can resume normal activities, and they mean sitting at a desk and washing your own dishes, not managing a ranch."

"I going to tell him I caught something this weekend—a flu or something. I'll put myself on light duty." The fact that I'm decades younger than most lumpectomy patients has reassured me that the recovery time line I've been given is much longer than I'll need.

"Which means, what?" Tyson asks. "Taking a four-wheeler instead of a horse and only working ten hours a day?" He sounds perturbed but I'm not being difficult, I'm being realistic.

"I have no choice, Tyson." I'm snappy now, too, because I'm right and he's wrong and the meds make me irritable.

"What if you tell your dad that we're turning the weekend into a week. We can find an Airbnb that will be more comfortable than this, and you can continue getting the rest you won't get if you go back there."

I'm shaking my head before he finishes, but I soften the answer because I know that his concern is genuine. I'm lucky to have anyone helping me right now, let alone him. "I wish I could do that, Tyson, but I can't."

He sighs in frustration and runs his hand through his hair as he leans back in his chair. He crosses his arms over his chest and thinks something through for a few seconds while he stares at me. "Then maybe I should go back to the ranch with you. I can make sure you don't overdo things and I'll help where I can."

I smile at this. Not because Tyson doesn't know his way around the ranch—he's helped with calving almost every year and isn't afraid to get his hands dirty. But he doesn't enjoy ranch work, and he's more willing than he is skilled. Beyond that, if I bring my husband home with me, Dad will think we're getting back together. I don't know how I can keep the details of my limitations a secret *and* pretend that Tyson and I are making progress in our relationship at the same time. "That won't work either," I say. "You're supposed to be back in London by Thursday, right?"

"I could probably get a few more days if I need to. I think every day you set aside for recovery will make a world of difference."

"It was hard enough on everyone for me to leave when I did."

"You're going to overdo it, Sienna." He's getting angry. "You won't be able to help it. What if you pull out your stitches or get an infection or something?"

"I won't." I pick up my phone, more to give me something else to focus on than for any other reason. "I promise to take care of myself, okay?"

Tyson growls and goes back to his laptop. I try to play Words with Friends but give up after a couple of games because a thought that has been chasing through my brain the last several days is no longer so far below the other things taking precedence. Tyson has gone back to work on his computer, his eyebrows pulled together as he types.

"Why haven't you told me to just tell Dad?"

He looks up at me over his computer, and the anxious look on his face causes something to flash through me, like when sun glints off metal in a place where it shouldn't. I sit up a little straighter, using my feet to push me up in bed and grimacing at the ache that starts up again. "You're coming up with all these solutions but haven't said even once this whole weekend that I should just tell Dad." Come to think of it, he didn't suggest telling Dad when we talked on the phone, either. In the parking lot of the attorney's office on Thursday he'd said something about waiting for the divorce until I'd worked out my stuff with Dad. "Tyson," I say in a serious tone.

He takes a breath and continues to stare at me, but I sense an internal battle taking place in that handsome head of his. "Telling your dad is the obvious choice," he says with such diplomacy that I'm even more suspect.

"But you don't think I should."

He leans back in the chair. "You said on the phone that you had a bunch of questions about your mom and that you felt weird toward your dad because of them."

"I don't think I said I felt weird toward Dad." I can't remember for sure whether I said it or not. And I *do* feel weird toward him but that's not the point. "I said I didn't want to worry him and that he'd want to leave the ranch to support me through the surgery, which isn't possible since one of us has to be there." I pause a moment, thinking back to my initial phone conversation with Tyson a week ago. "And then you offered to fly to London instead of telling me to just tell him what I'm going to have to tell him eventually. That makes no sense." The irony of my spelling this out so clearly is not lost on me.

He holds my eyes, looking caught, but also maybe a little . . . relieved? Resigned?

"I've been meaning to ask if you got a Mom Letter for your birthday—the big two-five."

A Mom Letter? It takes a moment for my brain to shift to

what feels like a new and unrelated topic. What does a letter from Mom have to do with any of this? Tyson's looking at me intently. "I didn't get a letter. I think they're done." I never asked Dad about not getting one. "It was a relief, really. I was waiting for the biopsy results at the time and wasn't up to a letter." Tyson knows the letters have sometimes been more negative than positive for me.

"Can you tell me again what had you upset about your mom when we talked last week?"

I feel like I'm being interviewed, but I tell him, again. Dad evading my questions about Mom's cancer. Nothing in his files. The short-form birth certificate. Sixteen photos taken over a few months' time. "What does that have to do with the letters?"

He shifts in his chair and crosses his arms over his chest again. "I'm going to tell you something, and I don't want you to get mad, okay?"

"O-kay," I say, but I'm already mad because whatever it is he is about to tell me is probably something he should have told me before now.

"I don't think your mom wrote those letters."

15

Sienna

Oddly, I am not infuriated by his suggestion that my mother didn't write these letters but I feel I'm floating above it all, somehow, waiting to see how I'll feel when I better understand what he means. Maybe it's my meds. Why would he make something like this up and tell me now, a day after breast cancer surgery?

From my place of emotional suspension, I replay all the letter giving—mostly birthdays but also significant events. Dad knocking on my door, handing me a letter, saying that he would give Mom and me some time to ourselves, as though she might pop out of the envelope and sit on the edge of the bed for a visit.

Tyson is the only person I've ever let read the letters. They are the most private and personal things I own, and I'd shared them a few months before we got married because I had wanted him to feel my mother the way I felt my mother. He's also the only person who knows that sometimes they make me feel guilty for not being the person she'd expected me to be. Tyson had held me after that confession—we'd been married about a year—kissed my forehead, and made no judgment. Had he already believed Mom didn't write them when he'd comforted me? I imagine shadows moving behind a curtain, watching my life, fabricating my reality. And Tyson watching the shadows, sharing a quick nod of conspiracy while I was trying to be gracious about such a gift.

He holds my eyes, then lets out a breath I suspect he's been holding as he's watched my thoughts play out on my face. "I started to suspect after the wedding letter."

It wasn't hard to recall the wedding day letter. I had been curling my hair the morning of the wedding—no one was helping me—and my stomach was in knots because of time lines and rain during the night and the fear of sweating through my dress. I was thinking that maybe I should wear my Levi's jacket over the dress. It would go with the cowboy boots, and only Tyson's family would think it weird for the bride to have denim over her knee-length dress, but I hated covering up the pretty lace. Dad had knocked on my bedroom door and come in before I told him he could. What if I'd still been getting dressed? I had bitten back the impulse to take my frustrations out on him and instead met his eyes in the bathroom mirror with a forced smile.

"Wow, sweetie. You look amazing."

I softened a bit—I'm such a girl sometimes. "Thanks, Dad." I had to move my attention back to the curling iron, which was why I didn't see the letter until he put it on the counter, between my Cover Girl mascara—waterproof just in case I cried, though I didn't think I would—and my Wet n Wild blush. Thank goodness I'd put the K-Y Jelly in my bag a few minutes ago. I stared at the letter, hating the way my stomach dropped at the sight and wishing I could ask Dad to take it back. I glanced from the letter to Dad's face to the strip of mahogany-colored hair—Clairol 113—wrapped around the curling iron and smoking as the hair spray burned.

Once I read the letter half an hour later, I felt bad for being so hesitant. It was sweet and encouraging and made me feel that I was on track to meet my mom's expectations of me. That it made me cry a little because my mom wasn't there to share the day was overshadowed by all the good things. I told myself that a lot of brides cry on their wedding day; my tears were just for a different reason than most, and I very well might have cried about Mom not being there without the letter reminding me. I slipped it into my purse so that it would go with me to my new life in Chicago.

In the present, I swallow, still looking at Tyson and hovering over this scene. "The wedding day letter?"

Tyson nods. "During one of our hotel stays, while you were getting ready." He smiled like that nervous groom he'd been—the reminder makes me blush, but I refuse the temptation to indulge in memories of that night. "Anyway, a bunch of wedding cards and things fell out of your purse, and I was straightening up and saw the letter. You'd already told me about it, and I didn't think you would mind my reading it, so I read it and . . . it just sounded weird."

"Weird, how?"

"Well, it said something about you being the prettiest bride in the state of Wyoming."

I nod. It hadn't stood out to me. "So?"

"Well, how would your mom know you would get married in Wyoming?"

"My dad is from here and he's always known he'd inherit the ranch. It wasn't rocket science for her to assume we'd come back." Because Mom had written the letters when she was *dying*. As a final gift to the daughter she would never know at any of the crossroads ahead. Surely, Mom and Dad had talked about Dad bringing me back to the ranch, right? Dad has told me that they all would have come back if Mom hadn't gotten sick. I've never wondered why they hadn't come back sooner. I'm coming down from where I've been apart from this conversation. Defensiveness is prickling through my extremities.

"It was just so certain, that's all." Tyson shrugged. "I mean, what if you'd been married on a beach in Hawaii or what if your Dad had stayed in Canada? And then all the letters had things that just sounded so old-fashioned. One of the letters talked about her looking at you in a cradle while she wrote the letter, and the advice about being subservient to your husband. It assumed you wouldn't want a career, assumed you wanted a big family, and put all this pressure on you living out some legacy for your mom and dad, even Grandma Dee." He pauses, and his eyes tighten as though he's afraid he's said too much. "And it's not like I *knew* she hadn't written it because of that, I just thought it was weird. So I flipped over the stationery and read the date, and then you came out of the bathroom and I flung it to the side and threw my arms open." He throws his arms open to demonstrate, and I'm taken back to that exact moment—I had opened the bathroom door of the Holiday Inn wearing a pink lace nightie one of my high school friends had given me at my bridal shower. Tyson was in bed with the covers pulled up to his chest as if he were in an episode of *I Love Lucy*. As soon as he saw me, he threw his arms open. In that moment, I had been his whole world and nothing existed but us. I blush again to remember it, embarrassed to have been that girl with so many stars in her eyes. Now he is watching my reaction, and I am embarrassed by that, too.

The memory hangs in the air like a fly strip in August. Do I remember a flash of green stationery flying to the side? He'd known almost five years ago that the letters weren't what I thought they were and he'd never told me? Never even hinted. Not even when I'd told him how the sixteenth birthday letter sounded like it could have been written by . . . Grandma Dee. I finish the fall and am back in my body, looking at Tyson and trying to make sense of this. He has proof.

"What was the date on the back of the stationery?"

"2000."

I was six years old in 2000. My mother had been dead for four years. The letters had always parroted Grandma, but I'd assumed it was because she and Mom wanted the same things for me. A slow, hot burn starts in my belly, and I cross my arms over my chest as best I can with the bandages. My breathing is coming faster. I can't swallow.

"You never told me you suspected anything." My voice is low, showing the hurt. "All these years."

"I should have, and I'm sorry. I just . . . I just didn't want to ruin it for you. Didn't want to cast a shadow on your dad."

Dad had facilitated the deception even if it hadn't been his idea. I am such an idiot. I hadn't liked the letters and yet I'd not once thought to check for a date on the stationery. I should have looked into every detail of the paper, envelopes, looping Ls, and slanted Ys. Why hadn't I figured this out before Tyson did?

The room spins slightly, and I feel as if I'm going to slide off the bed. Thoughts poke at me like pins.

"Sienna?"

I open my eyes. When had I closed them? Tyson has stood up from the cheap little table he's been using as a desk and is now waiting next to my bed.

"Are you okay? You're looking pale." The look of sympathy on his face disgusts me.

I glare at him, and suddenly it's so easy to be mad at him for this. "Oh, am I looking *pale*? My apologies."

He stays where he is and pulls his eyebrows together. "Uh, I wasn't being critical."

He reaches out and touches my shoulder. I wrench it away from him, sending a jolt of pain all the way through my right side. I put a hand to my head, which is suddenly throbbing, and wish I could stand up and stomp out of this motel room. It occurs to me that every time I feel overwhelmed by something, I want to run away. My eyes are stinging, and I don't want him to see me fall apart. "I need you to go." My voice is shaky.

"It's almost time for your pain pill."

"I don't need a pain pill, and I don't need you!" I scream. I feel a splitting off again as though the tired, hurting, and scared part of me takes a giant step to the left and the angry, defensive, confused part stays here in this bed and tries to make herself big and loud like a grizzly bear. "Can you just go?"

His jaw tightens, and he looks as if he's going to say something but thinks better of it.

He puts up both hands in surrender. "Okay, I'll go grab us something to eat. I just—"

"Go!" I scream louder than either of us expects. He startles, then turns toward the door. I imagine him going through it and then me throwing all the furniture in front of the door the way they do in cartoons, so he can't come back in. He shouldn't have told me this. Not now. But then he *should* have told me a long time ago. And Dad . . . *Dad*. As one truth after another has crumbled, I've tried to put off judgment and remind myself of all the good he's done for me. But *this*? How can I justify *this*? My chin starts to quiver, and I cover my face with my left hand. The door closes behind Tyson.

Who has seen the wind?

In the solitude I completely fall apart.
Dad lied to me?
Lied.
To me.
My whole life.
Mom didn't write the letters.
Dad pretended that she did.
Tyson knew it.
He didn't tell me either.
Someone else wrote the letters.
Tricked me.
Who?

16

Sienna

By the time Tyson comes back with sushi—how long has it been since I've had sushi?—I've finished crying and taken a pain pill that further mellows my mood. I apologize for being angry—it was the easiest feeling to feel. He nods his understanding and takes the plastic top off the takeout container. We're quiet while we eat. The meds make the sushi taste tinny, so I eat only three pieces before letting him have the rest. He helps me change into a clean set of pajamas and then makes me take another walk around the parking lot even though it's only fifty degrees outside. I'm shivering by the time we return. Neither of us talks about the letters or Dad or the fact that Tyson knew about the letters. He's known since our honeymoon that Dad was lying to me about something. I'm the only person who is surprised.

The pills make me sleepy and apathetic. Who cares about the stupid letters? I'm probably going to die like my mother did anyway. Tyson helps tuck me in, then turns off the lights so I can sleep even though I suspect he'll be up for another couple of hours, working by the light of his computer. I've always been a side sleeper, but lying on my right side is out of the question, and when I try to lie on my left side, gravity pulls on the right. So I lie on my back and stare at the ceiling, reviewing the day and trying to plan ahead even though it's hard to think.

"Will you come back to the ranch with me?" I ask before I let myself fall asleep. I'd made the decision once I was on the tail end of the freak-out.

"If you want me to," he says.

"I was thinking maybe we could tell Dad that we went hiking or rented some mountain bikes or something. The weather's been nice enough. I fell and hurt my shoulder." The bandaging doesn't include my shoulder—it's tight around my chest and under my arm—but a shoulder injury seems like the best fit.

"If that's what you want."

It's a very neutral acceptance.

"Do you think I should tell him?"

Tyson is quiet for a minute. "I think between what you didn't find in your dad's files, the letters, and his not answering questions about your mom's cancer, there's a lot to deal with." He pauses as though letting that sink in. "And you may not be in the best place to deal with it. You just had a tumor removed, things have been hard for you and me for a really long time, and you're in pain. I mean, if you feel like you should tell him, I'll support you, but there's no real downside to waiting a bit longer, ya know?"

"That makes sense," I say, and I'm relieved to hear someone else support the hesitation I've felt to confront Dad. A hesitation that's only increased as one thing after another has risen up to block my way. It's going to be even harder for me to be around Dad now, knowing all this stuff and wanting answers but not being ready to ask the questions, or trust what he might say if I do. I remind myself how much I love him and how much he loves me. That helps some, but it also intensifies the betrayal.

It's getting harder for me to keep my eyes open, and my thoughts are getting fuzzy around the edges, so I hurry to finish what I need to say. "You're right that I can't work the ranch yet, but I'll be more active if I'm home, and that will help me heal. And my bed is better, so maybe I'll recover faster. If you can help, then I won't feel so bad. . . ."

"I can stay until Friday," Tyson says.

"Thanks for all this, Thyson." My words are starting to slur. "I'm sorry I was so mean."

"It's okay, Sienna." He sounds far away. "And you're welcome. I do love you, ya know."

I let my eyes flutter closed and the fuzz moves in, shutting out the world and the words and leaving me floating for a little while.

17

Sienna

Dad flaps around me like a mama hen when we get to the ranch Sunday afternoon. I feel tight as a guitar string standing there in the kitchen as Tyson explains what happened on our "hike." Tyson went to the Walgreens in Cheyenne this morning and bought me a sling to keep up the ruse. Then he redid the bandaging before we left the hotel, incorporating my shoulder and making it look more natural under my top. Dad wants to rewrap my shoulder—he has a lot of experience with injuries on the ranch—but Tyson convinces him to let it be for a little while. He tells Dad we went to a clinic and they gave us instructions. I've made Tyson a liar.

For dinner, we eat chili from a can and corn pones that Dad must have bought from the diner yesterday. After Grandma Dee died, he ate out a lot and gained thirty pounds. It wasn't good for him, and I don't like thinking about him not taking care of himself when I'm not here. Tyson manages the dinner conversation with an expert's touch, and I'm relieved that Dad's worry about my shoulder injury eases through the course of the meal.

Every time I look at Dad, I think about the letters. Imagine him planning them out. Finding someone to write them. Lying to me about them. Lying to me *in* them? I can see two possibilities regarding the contents of the letters—either they reflect what my mother would have said or they are pure fiction. Maybe the truth is somewhere in the middle, but every possible explanation is still a betrayal. Each time Dad tapped on my door and gave me a letter, he was perpetuating the lie. I think of the letters I got when I was younger and how I would tell him all about them. Because of course I thought he didn't know what the letters said. He would smile and nod and add some detail about a story Mom had mentioned in my letter. Lies. Betrayal. As the meal moves forward I begin to feel as if I am held together with paper clips.

Dad takes us out on the side-by-side to check on the calves after dinner—two more born that morning—and I go along because I miss the work. Dad and I talk over the schedules and the ways Tyson can help out and argue over whether I should go to the chiropractor in the morning. When we finally get back to the house, I excuse myself and retreat to my room because the chain of paper clips is beginning to pull out of shape. I also want to look at the letters. I keep them in an old shoebox under my bed. I want to see the print date for myself and reread the letters and try to identify the handwriting. I quickly realize, however, that I can't get the box of letters out from under my bed by myself and nearly scream in frustration that I have to wait for Tyson to come help me. Determined to prove myself capable of something, I decide to change into my pajamas. It takes a full ten minutes and I'm sweating and on the brink of tears by the time I finish. This is the third day since my surgery, but since I had expected to heal twice as fast as most patients, I am doubly irritated by how long this is taking. I pull myself together before Tyson comes in.

"Nice job—you got changed by yourself." He smiles at my amazing accomplishment. "But let me fix your ponytail."

That's something I can't do with one hand, and so I sit on the edge of my bed and he works on getting my hair back in the elastic. It will have lumps, and I can already tell the elastic isn't tight enough to hold for very long. "Beauti-mus," he says the way his nephew, Sterling, said beautiful when he was little. I always loved watching Tyson with his sister's kids and realize that I might never see those kids again.

Enough.

"Can you get the box of letters out from under the bed?" I point helpfully to the bed I'm sitting on. He gets on his hands and knees, and I look at the ceiling instead of his backside pushed up in the air as he reaches under the bed to pull out the box.

> *Neither I nor you.*
> *But when the leaves hang trembling . . .*

"Here you go," he says a moment before he plops the box on the bed in front of me. I move too fast, hurting my shoulder, then keep my right arm into my chest as I try again with only my left hand. I pry off the lid with my thumb and push it to the side—the smell of old paper and peanut butter cups breathes out of the box. I used to hide the best of my Halloween and Christmas candy in this box so that Dad wouldn't steal any. I'm tempted to ask Tyson to leave, but it feels mean to cut him out of something he's a part of now.

Soon, ten sea-green sheets of paper with blue birds across the top are laid out on my bed in chronological order: eighth birthday, tenth, twelfth, the day I started my period, fourteenth, sixteenth, eighteenth, high school graduation, wedding day, twenty-first birthday. I've never gone four years between letters, which is why I expected one on my twenty-fifth birthday. I've also expected one when I had a baby of my own.

Tyson and I are kneeling on the bedroom floor, looking over the grid-scape of letters. My chest is killing me, and I hold my arm tight against my middle as if I have a tummy ache. My thoughts are already mush and a pain pill will make it worse, so I'm putting it off. At some point, though, the pain will become as mind-numbing as the medication. I was planning to read each of them, but I don't want to do that with Tyson here. For now, it's enough to just look them over.

"It's all the same handwriting," I say for no reason at all, because it's quite obvious and writing fake letters in multiple hands would be a pretty big tip-off. I stare at the way the cursive words curve and curl together; it's pretty. When I was thirteen

I'd taped one of the letters—the one from my twelfth birthday, I think—to the window and then held a piece of paper over the top so I could trace the letters. I had wanted my unremarkable handwriting to look like hers. It seemed to help. By ninth grade, my handwriting looked more feminine. More like Mom's . . . except it wasn't Mom's.

"Here's what tipped me off." Tyson picks up a random letter and turns it over. The tiny manufacturing information printed on the bottom of the sheet is barely visible. I have to squint to make out the words but sure enough WALLERTON PAPER STUFF ® 2000 is printed in green ink only a shade darker than the paper itself. I didn't even know stationery came with print days. Did all stationery do that?

"My mom died in '96," I say.

"But you didn't get your first letter until, what, 2002?"

I pick up one of the other letters lying on the bed and squint at the print on the back again: WALLERTON PAPER STUFF ® 2000. Scampering panic moves back and forth in my chest like that mouse Beck and I caught in a shoebox one time. It ran back and forth and back and forth for hours until it was exhausted. After Beck went home I felt bad, so I let it out in the barn, forgetting about Jinx until the orange cat jumped down from the shelf where she liked to perch, promptly caught the mouse, and bit its head off. I went crying into the house, and Grandma Dee told me to get over it. It was just a mouse. "Life ain't pretty," she said. I went to my room and cried by myself after that.

I sit back on my knees and hold my right arm tighter against my stomach. I don't know why that feels better, something about the pressure it puts on my chest, I guess.

"You okay, Enna?"

The sadness I feel, knowing that I've been tricked, is prickly in my head and sharp in my chest. I don't know what to do with it. Tyson doesn't try to touch me the way he did in the hotel, and I'm glad. I feel I might shatter at the slightest brush of his fingers.

I nod in response to his question and stand up, using the bed to help get to my feet. I start slowly, gathering the letters with my left hand, not caring about the order they're in and wondering if I should just throw them away. I imagine putting them in the newspaper bin we keep next to the wood-burning stove. The next time Dad went to start a fire he would find all of Mom's letters waiting to be burned. Would he bring them to me and say there must be some kind of mistake? Then I could confront him, and he'd tell me the truth in a burst of regret and shame. Even though I'd still be mad, I'd understand, and we would end up closer than we were before because there were no longer any secrets between us. Like a Hallmark movie.

I pull open the top drawer of my dresser, full of socks and underwear, and put the letters on top. If I decide to read them, they'll be easier to access than the box tucked under my bed. I can't look at them anymore tonight. I'm sick and sad and scared and really tired.

"I think I need to take a pain pill and go to bed." It's only seven-thirty, but Tyson doesn't argue and goes to my duffel bag, which isn't unpacked yet. He sets out gauze and the aftercare instructions and the bottles of pills—oxycodone and amoxicillin—before turning to face me.

"We should put a new dressing on," he says carefully, probably expecting me to protest.

"Okay."

He helps me out of my button-up pajama top, and the Ace bandage so that he can remove the gauze. I look at a spot over his head while he gently cleans up the incision areas. There's nothing intimate about his ministrations and certainly nothing about my body in this condition that could be remotely attractive. I keep thinking about the letters and the times I was irritated by the way Mom's advice backed up Grandma Dee's. If Grandma Dee were alive, I think I would confront her. Then again, I never confronted her on the other stuff that now seems meaner and colder and blunter. I struggle to think of a single time she was warm. Why was she so mean? Did she even like me?

It probably takes twenty minutes, start to finish, for Tyson to put the new dressing on and get me back into my pajamas.

There's a tapping at the door within seconds of his doing up the last button of my top. Tyson and I exchange a look, and I nod. Everything's covered up.

"Come on in, Mark," Tyson says. I walk toward the bed, avoiding eye contact with my dad as I've been doing all day.

"I wondered if you guys wanted some ice cream." I sit on the edge of the bed and try not to think of that pile of letters in the drawer. I could grab them right now, shove them in his face, and demand he tell me who wrote them and why he did this to me and how am I supposed to trust him with anything now?

"None for me, thanks," I say instead, holding what I feel tight inside my chest. In the motel room Tyson said it would be best to wait until I'm ready. My thoughts are fuzzy right now, and I feel so incredibly sad. Definitely not ready.

"I'll join you in a minute, Mark," Tyson says. "Sienna's down for the count, so let me just get her tucked in."

"She's, uh, sleeping in here?" Dad asks.

The guest room on the other side of the shared bathroom has a queen bed. It's where Tyson and I usually sleep when we come to the ranch together. Grandma Dee's old sewing machine is in there, along with a blue dresser that was mine when I was little and a collection of laundry baskets and gift-wrapping supplies and extra coats on mismatched hangers in the closet.

"I kept him up last night with this stupid shoulder," I say, nodding toward my injured side. I don't have the sling on, so I'm holding my right arm with my left hand. "I think we'll both sleep better tonight if I'm in here."

Dad nods, his expression so sympathetic it hurts because I *know* the compassion is real. I *know* he loves me. I *know* he wants me to come to him for help. And now I *know* he tricked me. "Can I do anything for you, CC?"

Tell me the truth, I think, but I don't even want to ask the questions about Mom anymore. I couldn't trust what he told me. "Nah, I'm good. Nurse Tyson is surprisingly good at this."

"Surprisingly?" Tyson says in mock offense, putting a hand to his chest.

Dad laughs. I manage a wavy smile and look between these

two men. I love them in different ways. Trust them in different ways. Or used to. Neither of them is the safe harbor I once depended on, and where does that leave me? Drifting. Alone. Lost.

I close my eyes as a wave of regret and exhaustion nearly topples me. I can't do this. I can't recover from this surgery *and* deal with Tyson's presence *and* wonder about all the things Dad hasn't told me. So I won't. I never liked getting the letters anyway. I should feel validated to know they were a scam; released from the guilt I felt all these years for my lack of grace. Maybe I *had* sensed something all along. Maybe that's why I struggled to appreciate the letters the way I thought I should.

I lift my left hand to my forehead and close my eyes as I take a deep, shaky breath. "I'm really not feeling well," I say. "I can get myself in bed. You guys go enjoy your ice cream."

Instead they fuss over me, as they are both apt to do, but I can't help feeling that both of them are motivated at least as much by guilt as they are by love. Dad kisses me good night on the forehead, and I blink back tears. Tyson leans in to kiss me on the lips, and I resist the urge to reach my left arm around his neck and ask him to stay with me, wrap me in his arms, and remind me that life wasn't always this heavy.

They turn off the light on their way out, and I lie there in the dark wondering how Tyson can stand to shoot the breeze with my dad over ice cream. Then again, Tyson has known about this for years. Maybe I can also just let the lies be a thing that happened. Maybe I can love Dad exactly the same as I used to. The Bible tells us to forgive; can I do that when I don't know everything I'm forgiving him for?

When I close my eyes, tears leak from the corners. I have to get a grip. I have to get my priorities in order, which are to get better and get back to work so my mind will stop looping through all this garbage that makes me feel small and scared.

Figuring out the letters won't pay the hands or ease the demands of calving season or keep the equipment running. It won't restore Dad to a stronger version of himself I might not be so hesitant to confront or bring back Grandma Dee, who makes less sense to me than ever. It won't lower the walls Tyson and I have built up. In the grand scheme of things, the letters are silly. Stupid. A waste of energy.

I still have to recover from surgery. Mom is still dead. Dad still loves me with his whole, big heart. I still won't get the future I want. Tyson is still too good for me.

Maybe next year, or the year after, I'll return to these letters and try to puzzle their mystery out. But not now. *So* not now.

18

Sienna

By Thursday I'm ready to lose my ever-living mind. My back hurts from too much time in bed, and I am frustrated beyond belief that I haven't healed as fast as I had expected. In Chicago that first year, Tyson and I bought gym memberships and went a few evenings a week. I had never had to "work out" before, and standing in front of a mirror lifting dumbbells up and down and up and down and up and down annoyed me. Energy output should be accomplishing something, like getting bales of hay out of the field, or feeding livestock, or riding a horse. I would look at the other people working out—some sleek, some just desperately hoping to become sleek—and want to tell them, "You can do actual physical work instead of paying this place to let you pretend to do work!" But then, I was there too. The soreness in my chest now feels as if I had a good workout on just that one side and didn't stretch afterward.

Other than the gym, the most physical exertion daily life required in Chicago was taking groceries up the stairs a couple of times a week. Meanwhile Dad was home on the ranch working fourteen-hour days for five months out of the year and eight-hour days all the others. He broke a sweat, wore out ropers, and kept toned because he did something that mattered. Every night he could look over the hours behind him and see specific tasks he'd accomplished. I, on the other hand, paid money to isolate my triceps so they looked good in a sleeveless dress. I didn't renew my membership the next year and stopped taking the L unless I absolutely couldn't cover the distance on my feet, which wasn't that often. Walking miles every day kept me in shape well enough, but after six months back on the farm my muscles were toned up and I felt as if I'd earned the right to fit in my size 6 Big Star jeans again.

When Dad and Tyson go up to the winter pasture after lunch—scrambled eggs yet again—I take a full shower for the first time since the surgery, keeping my back to the water. Afterward, I pat myself dry, which takes forever, and then keep my back to the mirror while I pull out the gauze and things I need to replace the dressing. That's when I realize I won't be able to put the bandaging back on without looking in the mirror. I argue the point in my head, but it's useless—I'm going to have to look sometime; it might as well be now. I take a breath and turn to see my post-op body for the first time. From the front, the incision looks like a shaky half circle across the top of my right breast. There's some bruising and redness that contrasts with the pink of the incision scar, but it's not as bad as I've imagined. From the side, I can see where the tissue is missing, though. The sloping curve of my breast is indented like an inverted speed bump. *It won't get better,* I tell myself. For the rest of my life, I'll have this divot in my breast, and I wonder if it will remind me of all that's going on right now—Tyson, Dad, questions about my mother. I feel the emotion rising but shake my head and stare at the ceiling until it passes. It doesn't matter. It's fine. What did I need that tissue for anyway?

I lift my arm like a chicken wing so that I can get a better view of the underarm incision. They told me before I left the hospital that the sentinel nodes they removed were clear—they look at them right there in the operating room, I guess. The two-inch scar, like a stretched-out letter S, runs from the center of my armpit to the front edge of my chest. I can't see it when I put my arm at my side. It hurts more than the breast incision does. It's redder too, irritated by movement, I assume. They shaved my armpit before the surgery, which was nice of them, but I wonder when I'll ever dare shave it again. Already there's stubble growing in. Maybe I'll have to go au naturel for a while; the thought leads me to wonder if women in Europe still don't shave their armpits. I can't imagine Tyson could go for a girl like that, but if she's nice and makes him happy and can give him cute babies, maybe armpit hair doesn't matter so much. I dab some of the antibiotic ointment on the length of both incisions and pull the instructions out of the drawer where Tyson put them so that I can read up on what I'm supposed to be doing for wound care six days in. Six days and I have not done a damn thing around the ranch.

The post-op instructions say I can leave the incisions open to the air now, but it makes me nervous to leave these angry marks so exposed. My attempts to wrap myself back up, albeit loosely, don't work, however, so I give up and carefully put on the sports bra that fastens in the front. It takes me forever to get it on, and by the time I finish I'm as exhausted as I was after fixing a hundred feet of fence two weeks ago. I read a blog about a cyclist who was back on her bike three days after her surgery. All I did was shower and put on a bra and I need a nap.

I make myself some toast so that I have food in my stomach for the ibuprofen and antibiotic and practice keeping my arm at my side instead of scrunched into my chest like a broken wing. Keeping my arm at my side pulls at my armpit incision, and I find myself drawing my right arm across my stomach without even noticing.

I've just put my paper towel in the garbage when my phone rings. It's Dr. Sheffield's office, and I take a breath before I answer the call that will certainly be about the results of my lumpectomy.

"Dr. Sheffield wants you to know she is very pleased with the results—clear margins, so no additional surgery will be necessary. The pathology confirms that the tumor was only in stage one. Everything has been best-case scenario so far," the woman on the phone says. "Dr. Sheffield wondered if you've learned more about your mother's cancer."

"I haven't. Sorry."

"That's fine," the nurse says cheerily. "It doesn't necessarily change anything. We just worry when there's a family history but not BRCA. There might be another gene in play. It won't interfere with your treatment plan for now, however. When you come in next week for your post-op, the doctor will go over treatment options in more detail, and one of our patient reps will take you on a tour of the radiology department. You can even talk to other patients if you would find it helpful to know more about their experiences."

I remember Dad telling me that radiation is easier on the body than chemo, and I've read that chemo may damage my ovaries.

"Dr. Sheffield suggests that you write down any questions that arise between now and then so that she can answer as many as possible. How about Thursday, a week from today?"

I've reached my bedroom by now and sit down on the side of my bed. "I don't know. I'll need to check the calendar and call you back." I hope to be back in the saddle by then, and I'm not sure I'll manage to leave the ranch *again*.

The nurse pauses. "Dr. Sheffield thought you might say that. She insisted I stay on the phone with you until you committed to an appointment time."

I grit my teeth but then put the nurse on speaker so I can go to my calendar on my phone even though I know there's nothing scheduled because it's calving season and we don't schedule appointments this time of year. We end the call a minute later, with plans for me to be in Dr. Sheffield's office next Thursday at nine-thirty a.m. The sutures should be dissolved by then, but she'll need to check the incision sites and make sure things are healing the way they should. I set my phone aside and lie down, feeling as though I've been awake for two days and wondering how I'll hide that appointment, or the radiation treatments, from Dad. It makes my breathing come faster to think I might have to tell him before the week is out. I close my eyes and focus on taking long, calming breaths. I want to tell him when I'm ready, but I'm starting to worry that I might not know when that moment comes.

I startle awake when Tyson sits on the side of my bed.

"Sorry," he says.

I roll onto my back to look up at him, which is how I realize that I slept on my left side. That's a good sign. "It's okay," I say groggily, and carefully sit up, then scoot back against the headboard and pull my arm into my chest.

"Your dad invited the Reynolds over."

I blink again and focus on his face. "What?"

Tyson shrugs and shakes his head at the same time. "He wanted everyone to have a chance to see me before I left." He smiles awkwardly, and I think of the worksheets the attorney gave us to fill out. He needs the information in order to write up the initial complaint, which he'll hang on to until we're ready to file.

"Great," I say dryly. "I'm *so* in the mood for a family visit. He's already sent out the texts?"

"He sent them out as soon as we had service—I was driving. I tried to talk him out of it."

"It's fine," I say. "At least seeing you will get Beck off my back." I swing my feet carefully over the side of the bed and wave off Tyson's attempts to help me stand. I need to get used to doing things myself. I roll my shoulder once I'm on my feet, grateful it hasn't seized up too much.

"Off your back about what?"

"She wants to set me up with Reggie."

Tyson visibly startles, staring up at me from where he's still sitting on the bed.

I hurry to offer reassurance. "I told her I'm not interested."

"Um, we're still *married*."

I'm only wearing the sports bra with my joggers, so I head to my closet to find a shirt. The hurt in his voice makes me wince inside, and yet we both need to come to terms with where things are for us. "I think she suggested it just so I'd divulge all our secrets."

"You haven't already done that?"

I move hangers across the closet rod, assessing each button-up shirt as I go. "I don't know how to explain it, so I just . . . don't." I choose a navy-and-white-checked flannel because it has snaps instead of buttons. I struggle to get my arm into the sleeve, and then Tyson is there, guiding my arm as if I'm a child. "Thank you," I say.

He takes a step back and watches me snap the snaps. I feel shy but don't want to show it, so I don't turn away.

"Maybe we should have tried harder."

Past tense. He's coming to accept the inevitable. I hold his eyes and snap the last snap. "Maybe we did the best we could."

He puts his hands in his pockets and looks at the section of carpet between us. One moment stretches into several. I've always loved his thick dark hair, which always used to be in need of a haircut. Over the last few years he's been more attentive, getting trims every four weeks and using gels and pastes and special conditioners that keep it manageable . . . and boring. He's still got a bit of a baby face, but I note that he's lost weight in London and it's made his face lean. I miss those cheeks and the scruff of a beard he used to wear before his job required a clean-cut appearance. Life has changed him in other ways than it's changed me. Would it have been different if we'd had a child together? I want to think that it would—he wouldn't have had to work so hard and so much to pay for infertility treatments and make sure we had amazing health insurance, and I wouldn't have struggled with depression and feelings of failure. A baby would have given him a reason to come home and given me purpose. But maybe that's as much a fantasy as our plans to have a family were. Maybe we'd have had kids and found ourselves in this exact same place of distance and differences. Five years from now. Ten. We'll never know, I guess. I meant what I said about not wanting to feel responsible for his happiness anymore. I wish that meant I didn't love him, want him, long for him—or for the us we used to be anyway. I watch him until he looks up at me again.

"So, how are we playing this tonight?" he says, his tone back to business. "Are we pretending everything is great so that they're surprised when we split up in a few months, or should we give the impression that there's strain?"

"I think we act like we're . . . friends." Before now he's seemed resistant to accepting that we are going to legally dissolve the last thing holding us together. I'm relieved by the fact that this is changing, I tell myself, but I'm sad, too. "We *are* friends, aren't we?" I ask him.

Tyson doesn't smile. "Yeah, I guess that's what we are."

I look away first.

Uncle Rich, Aunt Lottie, Malachi and his kids, as well as Beck and her family, show up with a strawberry rhubarb pie and a pan of brownies even though they were told not to bring anything. Manny and Carlos join us, and we eat every bit, with root beer floats to boot. Tyson talks and visits and explains what he's doing in London half a dozen times. He's hugged and coddled, and I can see the concern my family has had about me and my marriage fade from their expressions. Except Beck, who keeps that air of mild suspicion in place. I try to blend in, which isn't hard since Tyson is the center of attention—they haven't seen him for a year. I keep feeling Beck's eyes on me, so I'm extra attentive to my movements, making sure I'm consistent. Eventually I stack three people's plates carefully together and pick them up with my left hand, holding the forks in my right so as to look as normal as possible. It's stupid not to expect Beck to follow me, but I'm only thinking of escape until she's next to me at the sink with a stack of plates twice as big as mine.

"You okay?" she asks, taking me right back to our conversation in Aunt Lottie's kitchen a few weeks ago.

"I'm fine," I say. "It's just this shoulder." I lift my right shoulder for emphasis and don't even have to fake a wince when something pulls in my armpit incision. "It kinda wiped me out."

"Stuff like that is the worst," she commiserates. "And what lousy timing too, with Tyson in town and calves every couple of hours. Not quite the second honeymoon you were hoping for, huh?"

I laugh because a romantic weekend hasn't crossed my mind. I think maybe that part of our marriage ended when the sex became scheduled—I kept a sex journal that I would take with me to appointments. Tyson was humiliated when he learned about it. I told him that it was no big deal; sex was work for us now, not playtime. I probably shouldn't have said that. "He's been a big help around here. The ranch has barely noticed I'm out of commission."

"I don't believe that for a second," Beck says, running plates under the water before putting them in the dishwasher. "But I'm glad he came." She turns her head to the side to look at me, trying to read me like she always does. Drives me nuts. "So, things are good with you guys, then?"

"Yeah."

"You didn't even tell me he was coming." The lightness in her tone doesn't cover the hurt. I haven't thought about the fact that not telling her would seem suspect, but then there's a lot I'm not telling her these days. I turn the faucet to my side of the sink with my right hand because my left would be awkward and think about Tyson's prediction that I won't be able to take it easy once he leaves. Does turning a faucet count as overdoing it?

"It all came together so fast," I explain. Every time I actually tell the truth I feel like I should write it down somewhere.

"Are you going to move to London now that he's extending his contract another year?"

I think about my answer, trying to construct the most believable option. "I'll stay at the ranch through the summer at least." I'll be undergoing treatments pretty soon, which means everyone will know. I glance at Beck, wondering if I can trust her to keep it a secret if I tell her now. I get butterflies at the thought and decide against it. Maybe after Tyson's left.

"I think it would be fun to live in London for a while," Beck muses. "I read a lot of novels set there, you know. It's a cool city."

"Romance novels?"

"Something wrong with that?" She swivels her head when she says this, and I laugh. It feels good to laugh.

"London is even more city living than Chicago."

"Yeah, but it's got history and so many parks."

"Well, like I said, I'm thinking about it." Which I'm not.

"Are things okay with you and your dad?"

I turn to look at her with eyebrows up. "What do you mean?"

"I don't know," she says, shrugging her shoulders. "You just seem like you're . . . avoiding him tonight or something."

I do? I keep my expression in a place of neutral surprise. "Nah, things are fine with Dad and me." If Beck's noticed, has Dad noticed? That makes me even more anxious. "Did you hear that there were nine calves born while I was in Cheyenne? And every one of them was a bull. Isn't that weird?"

"All bulls?" she says, pulling her eyebrows together. "That, like, never happens."

"I know," I say easily enough, my mind racing to the next topic of conversation to keep her focus anywhere but on me and the men in my life. "I've been meaning to ask you what you're planning with your yard. I know it got derailed when Clint got hurt, but I was thinking that if the whole family set aside a day to come over, we could get a bunch of it banged out. Malachi could rent a trencher, and he and his boys could lay out the sprinkler system in a few hours, I bet—Clint would be able to do the timer portion, right?"

We spend fifteen minutes talking over the idea, which gets Beck excited and, most important, distracted. Aunt Lottie could manage lunch for all the helpers, and Dad would help where he could. Depending on what the day is like on the ranch, Manny and Carlos could come for a couple of hours too. By the time everyone is standing to leave, Beck's down to choosing a day for it—one of the Saturdays in May that isn't already crammed with end-of-school-year stuff. Toward the end of calving, if at all possible, but before Memorial Day weekend, when we still plan to brand. Memorial Day is five weeks from now—will all these people know about my cancer by then?

Everyone gives me careful hugs good-bye, and as soon as they're gone, I announce myself plumb tuckered out.

Tyson excuses himself too and follows me to my room, where I tell him I don't need his help getting ready for bed.

"You've pushed yourself today, Enna." I wish he'd stop calling me that, because I melt a little bit every time he says the name he made up just for me a long time ago.

"Maybe a little." My armpit is throbbing. I shouldn't have let the ibuprofen wear off. "It felt good to be doing something." I realize that I haven't told him about the pathology report, so I do that while he sits on the edge of the tub, watching me get ready for bed without his help. His Cubs T-shirt, which I wear as a nightshirt sometimes, is hanging on the back of the bathroom door, and I wonder if he notices it. I don't want to get dressed in front of him, so when I finish washing my face and brushing my teeth, I turn to face him, leaning against the counter.

"It's such a relief that they got it all," he says.

"Yeah," I agree. "So I'll have my post-op next week, and we'll outline a treatment schedule." Easy-peasy is the tone I'm going for.

"Are you going to try to hide your treatments from your dad?"

"I think I'll have a better idea of when to tell him after my appointment next week."

Tyson stands up, and the narrow distance between the tub—behind him—and the counter—behind me—forces us to be close to each other in a way we haven't been. He takes a step toward me, and even though we've talked to a divorce attorney and I'm recovering from surgery and he's leaving tomorrow, I feel a smooth shiver of heat move through my body. I don't take my eyes away from his as his hands come to rest loosely on my hips. I haven't felt this during his whole visit, and I don't want to feel it now. It's too complicated. I ease to the side, and he drops his hands and lets me move away. I'm both grateful and disappointed that he gives up so easily. I lean my left shoulder against the door frame to face him.

"What time is your flight tomorrow?"

"Two," he says, staying where he is and looking at me with regret in his expression.

"And you've got the shuttle to Cheyenne all set up?"

"Yeah, it'll be here around nine."

I nod. "That's good. Sorry I can't drive you."

"It's fine." He looks away and catches his reflection in the mirror. He leans forward and finger-combs his hair. Then he stands and looks back at me. "Anyway, I guess we'd better turn in. I'll be doing morning rounds with your dad, but I think he's planning to check on the cows in the afternoon. He'll probably ask you to go with him." He turns to look at me, crossing his arms over his chest and showing off his shoulders in the process. They must have gyms in London.

I'm glad for the warning of Dad's plans so that I can arrange for one of the hands to take my place. "Okay, I'll figure it out."

"You'll be careful after I leave?" he says, his chocolate eyes worried.

"I promise," I say.

"And you won't file without telling me first."

I shake my head. "I'll do my worksheets next week, though. You'll do yours too?"

"Yeah," he says, then turns toward the door that leads to the guest room where he'll sleep one last time. Alone. In just his boxers, assuming he still sleeps only in his boxers like he used to. I remember the feel of his hand on my hip in the middle of the night as if making sure I'm still there. Does he still reach out sometimes? Does he blink in the dark when he realizes he's alone? I feel that shiver again and wonder if slow and careful lovemaking would violate my post-op instructions.

> *When the leaves hang trembling.*
> *Trembling.*
> *Trembling.*

I spare the thought only that half a second. Then I turn away from him and head into my room, closing the door resolutely behind me.

19

Sienna

I'm out of the shower, wrapping a towel around myself, when Tyson taps on the bathroom door from the guest room. I finish covering myself in time for him to open the door. He looks me over, long and slow, and I use every bit of strength to push away how his look makes me feel. He's leaving in two hours. Maybe forever. This is what I want.

"How'd you sleep?" he asks.

I can't tuck the towel in on my right side, and it's awkward to tuck on my left. I end up just holding the towel in place by keeping my arms wrapped around myself. "Pretty good," I don't feel tired as soon as I wake up the way I have since the surgery, and I dare to hope I've turned the corner. "You?"

"Like rubbish," he says, and runs a hand through his hair. He comes into the room and sits on the tub like he did last night when I told him the pathology results. He's wearing a white T-shirt and plaid pajama bottoms, and I wonder if he wore them to bed or put them on over his boxers before coming to talk to me. "What if we tell your dad before I leave?"

My heart speeds up at the unexpected suggestion. "You're the one who said I should wait."

He shakes his head and braces his elbows on his knees. "I know, but last night all I could think about is that you're going to have to tell him by yourself and manage these treatments and . . . all of it." He looks up at me with sympathy in his expression. "It's a lot."

"It won't be less today than it will be in a week or a month."

"You'll probably be starting radiation treatments in a month."

The thought of everything lying ahead of me will make me dizzy if I think about it too much. "I'll tell him when I'm ready."

"And you'll be alone."

I want to say, "I've been alone for months." But that was more my decision than his. What I actually say is, "If we tell him right now, two hours before you leave, then I'll still be alone to deal with the fallout." I shake my head. "I'm not ready to tell him, and I really need to get dressed."

He lets out a sound that's part groan and part sigh—frustration seeping out around the edges.

I go into my room, closing the bathroom door behind me. I've managed to put on my sports bra—in under three minutes this time—and pull on a pair of jeans for the first time since the surgery before Tyson taps on my bathroom door and lets himself in again.

"What if you come to London with me."

I blink at him and my hands stop in the process of doing up the button of my jeans. "What?"

He nods. "Tell Dad you're coming with me for a couple of weeks and take that time to relax and recover and get your bearings."

"I have a follow-up appointment next week." Which I may or may not go to. "And . . . and there's no way I can just go to London. My life is here. The ranch needs me." I watch his face fall and let my mood soften with it. He really is worried about me. "But I appreciate your concern, Tyson. You've taken good care of me this last week, and I can't thank you enough for that."

He shakes his head and glances at the wall before he looks back. "Then I think you need to tell Beck."

Did he make a list or something with A, B, C, and D options? "No," I say, shaking my head and turning to my closet.

"Sienna, please."

"No," I say again, sharper. "I'm not ready."

"If you tell her not to tell anyone, she won't. You're not in junior high anymore, and she's your best friend." In junior high, when I was in seventh grade and Beck was in ninth, I confided in her that I liked Reggie, and by the end of the day everyone knew it. Here I am more than ten years later and people still have this image of Reggie and me in their heads and I'm still holding Beck to blame, even though I had gone on to date him and dump him for Tyson. But I know what he means—this isn't junior high. And Beck might not tell anyone, but confiding in her makes me queasy. I need more time, even if it's only days. Besides, how much do I tell her? Just about the cancer, or do I include the divorce attorney? What about the letters and the empty files and the sixteen pictures?

I pull an old roping club T-shirt off a hanger and put it on by sliding my right arm through the sleeve first, then carefully putting my head through the neck and then putting my left arm through. It's not graceful or fast but it works, and I want to celebrate the success. I turn to face him. "I know I can't hide it forever, but I want to be fully recovered and know what I'll be asking from everyone when I do tell them. I want to look for information about my mom for a little longer, too—maybe see if I can get the long-form version of my birth certificate. Telling anyone right now would interfere with all of that."

"I don't feel right about leaving you with no one who knows what you're facing."

"I'm done talking about this," I say on my way to the door. "You better get packed. Time is short."

"Sienna," Tyson says, in almost a bark. I have my hand on the doorknob when I turn back to look at him, hardening in response to his hardness. "I think you're going about this the wrong way. You're trying to do it alone when you shouldn't."

"I *am* alone, Tyson, and this is *my* thing. My cancer. My dad. My story, in which you are no longer a key player, so let it go and pack your bags. You don't want to miss your flight back to that rosy future you're so excited about."

I let myself out of my room and slam the door shut as the punctuation to what I've said. I stride down the hall and into the kitchen area. "I'm going to do the loop," I tell Dad without stopping for conversation. I grab a coat from the rack with my left hand and let myself out into the cold morning air, which feels invigorating. The tingle in my nose and cheeks helps me leave the argument behind me as I gingerly put the coat on. Then I walk through the break in the poplar tree boughs tinkling in the wind and into the ranch space. I step into the side-by-side and take myself as far from the house as I can so I can count cows and calves and think about something else.

I'm avoiding going inside and seeing Tyson again by puttering around in the barn, trying to pretend I'm busy, when I hear tires on the gravel driveway and come out of the barn to see the black-and-white shuttle pull to a stop in front of the house. A quick check of my phone confirms that it's early—twenty minutes early. I tell the driver to wait and then hurry inside to find that Tyson is just out of the shower. The morning's argument is forgotten as I help make sure he hasn't missed anything while he shoves things into the suitcase—a far cry from his usual meticulous packing. His hair is still wet when Dad and I walk him out to the van, our breath clouding in front of us thanks to the cold front. The driver takes Tyson's carry-on, and Tyson turns back to us for the inevitable good-byes.

I put on my big pasty smile, ignoring the lump in my throat. "Safe travels," I say.

"I wish I could stay."

I just smile wider, faker.

"It's sure been great having you, Tyson," Dad says, stepping forward to share one of those handshake-leading-to-back-patting-hug exchanges men do.

"It was great to be here," Tyson says. He comes to me and wraps me in a gentle hug that I could stay in all day if there was any wisdom in doing so. Because there isn't any wisdom in it, I push away first and then give him a quick peck on the lips. *For Dad's sake,* I tell myself. Tyson holds my eyes an extra second, then gets into the back of the shuttle, and thirty seconds later he's disappeared down the drive. That's that. I refuse to consider how I feel about his leaving, refuse to even identify the emotion welling up. I've been lucky to have him as long as I did.

Manny goes with Dad to check on the cows, and I move my puttering indoors. I do the noon rounds with Carlos in the side-by-side without any complications. When we do the two o'clock rounds, however, one of the last of the heifers is on her side, bellowing in pain. I do an outside the body assessment and quickly determine that the calf is turned, meaning its back is to the birth canal, which will never work. I can reach inside and turn a calf nine times out of ten, but not with my current limitations. I try to talk Carlos through it, instead, which frustrates both of us, since I don't speak Spanish and he doesn't speak much English. In the end I reach up with my left hand. I'm awkward with that arm and can't make it work. I'm swearing when Carlos asks to have another try. This time it works, and the calf finally slithers onto the ground, breathing and strong. Mama takes over by licking the calf while Carlos and I stay on our knees and recover. I would pat him on the back except I'm covered in manure just like he is. Turning calves is not a pretty job.

"Well done, Carlos," I tell him. He's typically a picker, working farms, not livestock. For a novice with a language barrier, he did a great job, and I know I could not have done it without him.

"*Gracias,* ma'am."

"Don't call me ma'am," I say as I struggle to my feet. "Call me Sienna."

"*Gracias,* Sienna," he says. He looks at my right arm, which I'm holding tight to my chest because, even though I'd reached in with my left arm, the stretch went all the way through me. "You hurt."

"I overdid it, yes," I say, particular about the distinction. He knows I hurt my shoulder last weekend. I gave up the sling only a few days ago.

"I do afternoon," he says in his broken English, pointing me toward the house. "You rest. I come get you if I need help."

I do not argue, but I thank him and make my way into the house. Getting up to my shoulder inside a cow is not in accordance with my recovery plan, and I hear Tyson's voice saying that he's worried I'll overdo it. I didn't even make it four hours.

Since no one's home, I strip in the laundry room and throw everything I have on in the "ranch" washer, as opposed to the household washer located on the other side of the kitchen. The household washer is for clothing without manure, oil, or blood on it. The ranch washer is for the gross stuff. I take a good long shower, cleaning myself up as carefully as possible. My armpit is burning from the inside out, and I lift my arm slowly and cautiously, afraid I'll see the incision has popped open. It looks the same as it did this morning, but it feels like my second-day postop. I'm forced to take a pain pill, which forces me to take a nap—neither of which were on my agenda for the day. It's after six when I wake up. I get dressed in a clean T-shirt and yoga pants, telling myself that my armpit isn't as bad as I thought. I'm just tired, so it feels worse.

I am determined to further prove myself recovered by making dinner. There's spaghetti and canned sauce in the cupboard—I can whip up dinner in half an hour, and I'll make enough for Manny and Carlos so that I can put off one-on-one time with Dad a little bit longer. I bend down to get the stock pot out of the cupboard, moving other pans out of the way since it's in the back. I knock another pan forward when I pull on the handle of the pot I want and automatically catch the dislodged pan with my right hand. I cry out as bright white pain shoots through my shoulder and down my side. Both pans clatter to the floor, and I hold my right side with my left hand while trying to take a full breath. I sit on the floor and curse my situation while leaning my back against the cabinet to recover. I resist the tears of frustration threatening—I can't put energy into anything but getting better.

I finally stand and move more slowly and with more caution, my right arm in the broken wing position again. I can do this. I need to get dinner going. I just need to be more careful.

Half an hour later I've managed to set the table and am staring at the pan of boiling pasta on the stove—how am I going to drain the noodles with one arm? I am so frustrated I want to scream. I piss and moan to myself and then Grandma Dee the situation by just digging in. I fish the noodles from the pan with a fork, making an equal pile on each plate before I cover them with sauce so that the noodles won't dry out. I text Dad that dinner is ready and to bring the hands with him, then realize I can't eat spaghetti with one hand. *Dammit!*

I stand in the middle of the floor and take three deep breaths, knowing I need to be calm and clearheaded to work through this. I need to take some ibuprofen so that I'm not so distracted by the pain. Surely Carlos has told Dad about the birthing this afternoon; I can say I tweaked my shoulder again. I get myself a glass of water and am on my way to my room and the huge bottle of ibuprofen that Tyson bought me at the Cheyenne Walgreens when I hear the back door open. Dad must have already been on his way in when he got my text. I paste a smile on my face as I turn toward him. It will take two minutes to assure him I'm fine.

Instead of Dad stomping off his boots, however, I hear a female voice call out. "Knock, knock?"

Beck's voice.

Oh, hell.

Beck appears from the boot room, her perfectly coifed blond hair glinting beneath the fluorescent light of the kitchen. "Hey there," she says, chipper as a magpie. "Sure smells good in here." But her eyes go to the arm held against my stomach, and the concern in her eyes is heavy when she meets my gaze again.

"Thanks," I say, the false brightness of my tone chipping badly. I want to ask her what she's doing here but instead settle on, "What's up?" It's dinner time, and Beck has two kids and a husband at home. Plus, the ranch is ten miles out of town; no one just drops in because they're on their way to somewhere else.

"Oh, nothin' much," Beck says. She starts shrugging out of her jacket as she walks into the kitchen as though she's going to stay awhile. What's going on here? "I had hoped I could help with dinner."

"It's done already," I say. "I just called Dad and the hands in to eat, but I'm going to go lie down. I, uh, tweaked my shoulder again helping with a calf this afternoon."

Beck holds my eyes. "Yeah, Tyson told me something like that might happen."

The room flips upside down and then back to right-side up. When would Tyson have said that? They hadn't talked last night when the family was over as far as I saw. Beck speaks again before I have a chance to work out the significance of what she's said.

"You go on and lay yerself down," Beck says, gesturing me toward my room. "I'll get some dinner in these boys and do the dishes. Then we'll talk, okay?"

Not okay. Beck starts filling up the water glasses I'd already set on the counter. I watch for a few seconds, wondering what, exactly, Tyson said and if there's any way I can undo it. Then Beck turns away from the sink and looks up at me, blinking quickly. "Don't make me cry yet, CC," she says in a throaty whisper. "I'm gonna try to hold it together for your dad just like you've been doing, but you better go lay yerself down before I lose my grip."

20

Sienna Chadwick
September 16, 2007
Larson 4th Hour
7th grade
first memory in present tense essay

My cousin Beck and I are stacking cans on green
carpet. I am wearing a pink nightgown even though
I think it's afternoon. I think I am three years old.
Beck is two years older and bossing me around, so
she must be five. It smells funny. We stack the cans
and then knock them over and laugh at the sound
they make. Beck is blaming me for the cans having
dents and I don't know what she means cause they
all look the same to me. In real life Beck has brown
eyes but in my memory she has blue eyes like mine
and I kind of like that I remember it wrong because I
have always wanted Beck to be my sister and in this
memory it seems like she is. I don't know where we
are. Neither of our houses have green carpet back as
far as I can remember. Beck keeps calling it grass. It's
cold so it must be winter and it must be a Saturday
because when I was three Beck started all day kindergarten and I missed playing with her during the
week. And this is two hundred words so I'm done.

21

Sienna

The ibuprofen takes the edge off the throbbing but not as much as I'd hoped. I lie on my back and stare at the ceiling and curse Tyson for telling Beck. And Beck for . . . I don't know, listening to Tyson, I guess. And cancer most of all for what it did to Mom and what it's doing to me. And Dad because I can't talk to him about anything right now. I can't trust anyone.

There's a knock at my door, and Beck comes in with a bowl of spaghetti, cut up like she does for her kids. I sit up, gritting my teeth through the pain of it and hoping she can't tell. But she probably can because she's Beck. "Thank you, but I'm not hungry."

"You should eat anyway," she says, and hands me the bowl before turning to get the chair from my desk. She brings the chair over to the bed while I set the bowl in my lap. I stare into the food as the silence stretches between us. I feel like a child expecting a reprimand.

Beck sniffles, and I look up to see tears running down her cheeks. "I'm so sorry, CC," she says, her voice wobbling as she tries to dab at her eyes with the napkin she brought with dinner. She sniffles again, then squares her shoulders and gives me a watery smile. "Now, what can I do to help, and if you say 'nothing,' I swear I'm going to lose every bit of decency I've ever had all over you."

So I tell her, taking a few bites of the now-cold spaghetti as a way to keep from looking into her face, which shows her fear way too much for my peace of mind. I only mean to tell her about the cancer, but I can't explain why I'm keeping it from Dad without explaining everything I've found—or, rather, not found—about Mom. While I'm talking I try to imagine what it's like to hear all of this. Beck loves Dad and tried real hard to make him part of her family when I was living in Chicago. He went to Sunday dinner at Aunt Lottie's every week, and Beck would stop in at the ranch every few days with a casserole or something. Her surprise at Dad's odd behavior and the missing information mirrors my own and warms me up to the topic. I end with the truth about the letters, and then silence descends like the collapse of the blanket forts we made as kids.

"I just can't believe this," she says, shock and something near to reverence in her voice. "I mean, why not answer your questions? Why wouldn't there be anything in the files?"

"I don't know," I say with a shrug of my left shoulder. I set the bowl on the nightstand, hoping she doesn't tell me to take one more bite for every year of my age, like she does with her kids. Like Dad used to do with me. "I mean, he's got to be hiding something about Mom from me, right?" It sounds like such an understatement.

"Or maybe he's just trying to back up the letters."

"How do you mean?"

Beck leans forward in her chair, resting her elbows on her knees. She's wearing lipstick and earrings, and her hair is piled up on her head in a bundle of perfect curls. I can't remember the last time I was that dressed up. "Well, let's assume you're right about Grandma Dee being behind the letters. It starts out innocent and kind of snowballs, and they realize that the letters put some limitations on other stuff—like they can't have anything around with your mom's real handwriting, right? And getting rid of any of that stuff just . . . sort . . . of . . ." She stops, seeing the same circle I see. "Yeah, that's not a good-enough reason. There should be something typed somewhere with info. A marriage certificate or *something*."

Beck suddenly puts a hand on my knee. "Oh my gosh, what if she's not dead?"

This thought has not occurred to me, and I gasp at the possibility, then shake my head. "He couldn't be lying about that." But the stakes seem bigger now. "I Googled her and couldn't find an obituary or death notice or anything."

Beck slumps slightly. "But your breast cancer kind of confirms that she must be, right? I mean, she had it and now you have it."

Had it, I want to clarify. They cut it out last week, but I don't interrupt her train of thought. "Yeah, maybe," I say. "But what was it that he wanted to hide?"

Beck shakes her head. "Something embarrassing?"

"But why hide that from *me*? What would the point of that be?"

"I-I don't know."

We both sit there in silence for a few minutes.

"So, what are you going to do?" Beck asks.

"Get better and get hold of my long-form birth certificate," I say for lack of anything else coming to mind. "I started looking into ordering it online after Tyson left this morning, so I just need to finish that, or it might be the birth certificate in storage in Chicago. Maybe I could go get it." I shrug as if that would be easy.

"I just need to find a starting point to get information from a resource other than Dad, then use that info to get more."

"And after you get all the info you want, then you'll tell your dad?"

"I don't know," I say, hoping Beck knows that the frustration in my voice isn't directed at her. "He's still not as strong as he was before his own cancer. Covering for me has taken even more out of him. I think about all this stuff with Mom, and I'm so mad I think I want to leave and not see him or talk to him for however long it takes for me to sort it out. And then I do see him, and I soften and know he loves me. I mean, I'm all he has."

"You're his world," Beck says, not making anything easier by stating that truth. "Always have been. I remember him telling Mom once that you were the best work he'd ever done."

I hadn't heard that before, and it makes a lump rise in my throat. How could that man be the same person who lied to me about letters from my dead mother? "There's been this weird tension between us since I asked those first questions about Mom's cancer. Confronting him with *all of this* will make it worse, and then I wonder what I would really gain by confronting him. Am I trying to pin him down and get answers? How can I trust anything he has to say now that I know how much of what he's already said isn't true?"

"You can't trust what he tells you," Beck confirms.

I nod.

"Which means you've got to go to Canada."

I laugh and wave my left hand through the air. "Right, just head on over the border and clear everything up."

"Well, yeah. The short form says where you were born, so you know your mom was in Hamilton as of 1994, right?"

"Go to Canada," I say again. "Just like that?" Ironically, Chicago is pretty much on the way to Ontario. What if I went to the storage unit, got my birth certificate, and continued on? How much farther is it from Chicago to Ontario?

Beck shifts in her chair, a wriggling kind of movement that shows she's getting excited, though that makes it sound as if this is something fun, and it's not. "I had to get Clint a copy of his birth certificate for some insurance thing. I drove to Cheyenne and had it in a couple of hours."

I shake my head even as the idea begins taking root. It would be doing something. I'd be in the city where I was born. I could find more than just the official certificates—I could . . . I don't know. Maybe get a death certificate and find out where my mother lived back then. Would there be neighbors who remember her? Dr. Sheffield still wants to know if there is a family history of breast cancer. I could track down Mom's medical records. Dad couldn't get in my way and then instead of confronting Dad *for* information, I'd be confronting him *with* information. I would be in control, and after the last several months—maybe years—of my life, the thought of being in charge is intoxicating. I am Mable Chadwick's daughter. I have an official birth certificate I can use as proof in the city of my birth to get additional information. "When would I go?"

"You'll have to be all healed up," Beck says, frowning. "Dang, I wish I could go with you, but I don't have a passport. . . . Could I get one in time, do you think?"

I make a face—it takes a few weeks to get a passport.

Beck's phone dings, and she picks it up and frowns. "Looks like the natives are getting restless—I'm helping with the city Easter egg hunt in the morning." She types back a response, then looks up at me regretfully. "I'm sorry."

I choose to believe she's apologizing for the whole big everything going on in my life right now. I smile and reach out my left hand. She takes it and gives it a squeeze. "When it rains it pours, right?"

"And then you get dunked in a river."

She smiles sadly at my attempt at humor, then lets go of my hand, stands up, and takes the chair back to the desk. She turns to face me. "So, what can I do to help?"

"I don't know."

"If you think of anything, you'll let me know, though, right?"

I nod.

She turns her head so that she's looking sideways at me like a chicken. "Promise?"

"Promise," I say, making an X over my heart. "Cross my heart and hope for pie."

She laughs but sobers quickly. "Any way you'd let me borrow one of those Mom letters?"

My hesitation prompts her to explain. "Mama's got handwritten recipe cards from near every woman in this county," Beck explains. "I can't imagine that Aunt Dee sent away to have those letters written, do you?"

"No, I figure it's got to be someone she knew." I'd even checked a letter Aunt Lottie had given me when I graduated from high school because she was the first person who came to mind when I thought of who Grandma Dee would go to for help. It was a relief that the handwriting didn't match.

"If you don't mind letting me borrow one, I'll see if I can make a match."

"You can't tell your mom." Bless her heart, but Aunt Lottie was a worse gossip than Beck. If she learned what was going on, the whole town would know by Sunday. "You can't tell anyone."

"Are you kidding me? Telling Mom would be like pouring gas on a fire you're trying to put out." She shakes her head while I stand up from the bed to get a letter. "I'll tell her I want to copy some of her recipes and borrow her box. That's all. And I won't tell anyone." She lifts her eyebrows. "Tyson told me that you thought I wouldn't be able to keep my mouth shut."

I feel the flush in my cheeks while I add that to my list of grievances against my husband. But I don't apologize to Beck for having said it, because it's a fair concern on my part. After a minute Beck lowers her eyebrows. "I won't tell," she says. "I just want to help."

I open the drawer and look at the stack of letters I stuffed inside. I pull out the one from my tenth birthday, remembering that it talks about being honest and making good friends. I was so excited to receive that letter. I took it to show-and-tell at school on the last Friday of the month. I turn and hand it to her. She folds it up and puts it in her back pocket. Then she gives me a careful hug.

"You call me if you need anything at all. Otherwise I'll see you when I bring dinner round 'bout five tomorrow. You read up on that long-form certificate, and we'll talk about Canada, all right?"

I go with her to the kitchen where Dad and Carlos are finishing dinner. Manny's plate is in the sink—he must have taken the evening rounds himself. Beck puts her bright and bubbly back on to say good-bye to Dad and tells him that I'm a hard man to keep down. He agrees and walks her to the back door while I start loading the dishwasher, slow and careful. On her way out she's telling him that she's bringing over meatloaf tomorrow night and not to argue with her and that he's to call her if I step out of line. I roll my eyes—meaning it more than she thinks I do. When she's gone I turn, surprised to see Dad standing watching me. I'm struck with something close to pity. I want to say I don't know him now that I've learned how he's lied all these years, but the man in front of me is still my dad. He's still the man who has always been there, and I love him so much. Carlos clears his throat and I turn my eyes toward him, I hadn't noticed him having stood from the table. He nods and thanks me for dinner while handing me his dirty plate. I take it and wish him a good night.

"You doin' okay, CC?" Dad asks when we're alone.

"I'm hanging in there," I say, turning away to rinse the plate because it's hard to hold his gaze.

"Wanna watch some *NCIS* with me?"

It's been a while since we've watched our show together. I'm tired and I want solitude, but I say yes. His whole face lights up. "Fantastic. I've been worried about Gibbs since we saw that last one. I'll get some popcorn and meet you in the living room in five."

It's nice to sit and watch TV with him, and I'm convinced I'm the only one who feels the strain. We call out guesses of who done it and what each clue means, then laugh when we're wrong. One episode leads to two before we both call uncle. In the process I almost forget that this man sharing a bowl of popcorn is also the man who handed me those fake letters.

Manny and Carlos are taking care of the midnight rounds, which is a relief because Dad's got bags under his eyes and tries to hide a yawn as he stands up. He looks tired and fragile. "That was fun, CC," he says with a smile. He holds out the empty popcorn bowl. "I think I ate more than my share, though." He puts a hand to his stomach.

"Good night, Dad," I say, and give him a hug. He kisses my forehead. It's not enough to settle the bubbling betrayal in my gut. I meet his eyes again and say good night a second time. I think about the wind in the leaves of that poem I have been reciting in my head so often these last weeks. It has to be wind in the trees because there's no other explanation for the leaves' movement. Does that mean Dad's motivation has to be love because there's no other explanation? I can't accept that.

When the leaves hang trembling . . .

When I get into my room I notice my phone on the night-stand. I pick it up to see that there's a text message from Beck.

Beck: **Rachel Jensen wrote those letters. Meet me at her house at 8. She says she'll talk.**

22

Diane

February 2002

"You should take some of these brownies home, Dee." Rachel nodded toward the plate of perfect two-inch squares of chocolate heaven sitting on the counter.

Dee shook her head and put the last of the smaller plates on the counter next to the sink where Rachel was rinsing everything off. "If I take them home, I'll eat them."

"And if you leave them, then *I'll* eat them, and I have a grandmother-of-the-bride dress to fit into next month."

Rachel had six children and fourteen grandchildren, while Dee had just one of each. Dee wasn't envious; what did she care about grandmother-of-the-bride dresses and big family dinners at the holidays? Sometimes, though, she felt as if she'd screwed everything up by being so determined to outwork her brothers and prove herself over and over again. The women her age in town were baking cookies and going to Cancun. Dee wore dresses only for church and funerals these days, and there were more and more of those every year. But, then, she didn't like to bake, and traveling had never really appealed to her. She liked to work. She was good at it, but she'd had to trade some of the traditional parts of being a woman to do it. She hadn't let Gregg run things, for one, and only had one child because she couldn't risk being too distracted. She didn't regret anything, though. That was a waste of time.

Dee went back into the living room for the drinking glasses the other book group ladies had put down during their discussion. When she returned to the kitchen, Rachel was rinsing the last plate before putting it into the state-of-the-art dishwasher she'd bought from Murphy's two months ago. Rachel had taken out a whole cabinet in order to fit the ugly thing into her counter. A little dish soap and hot water never hurt anyone. Plus, the washer had cost four hundred dollars! That was two months' worth of groceries.

"This is the last of 'em," Diane said, putting the glasses next to the sink and grabbing the rag so she could wipe down the counters.

When Rachel had first asked Dee to come to a book group, Dee hadn't even known what she was talking about. Rachel had explained that she'd gotten the idea from *The Oprah Winfrey Show* and begged Dee to help her get it going. Dee had given in—best friends were best friends, after all—then actually liked it once Nadine Thayla quit coming. That woman could find some measure of liberal rhetoric in every single book they read. Not that Diane didn't still think it was weird to read books and then talk about them, but she liked the routine of reading a chapter or two of that month's book before bed each night—at least in the wintertime. She hadn't read novels since those required in high school. She'd even gotten a library card and checked out additional books. Reading never interfered with her work—some of these ladies would talk about being so captivated they stayed up until two o'clock in the morning reading. Not on your life!

This month the group had read a romance by a new author, Nicholas Sparks—a guy writing romance? Diane had hated the sappy thing. The ladies let her speak her mind before gushing about how lovely the words were. Rachel's famous brownies had bridged the gap in opinion. Book group was about the only social thing Diane did these days. She liked it more than she'd admit.

"So how are things with Sienna?" Rachel asked while putting the cups into the top tray of the dishwasher. Dee knew for a fact that dishwashers left spots that sink washing never did. More often than not, the way things had been done were the best way to do them.

"The same, I guess." Dee didn't really know what it meant to be a regular grandma, so mostly she taught the girl to work the ranch—everyone needed to know how to work. Sienna was shaping up to be a pretty good worker, for a seven-year-old. Dee was proud of that. But over the past six months or so, the girl had begun making up stories about her mother, and it was getting on Dee's nerves. Sienna told her Sunday School teacher that her mother had been in the Twin Towers when those crazy A-rabs had flown into them on September 11th of last year. Then she'd told a friend at school that her mom had been kidnapped, and the child's mother had called Mark to find out if it was true. Sienna had been told her mother had died of cancer. She knew she was lying when she made up these other explanations. The fanciful stories had caused some tension at home when Dee thought Sienna ought to be punished and Mark refused. He was so soft on Sienna. When Dee had told Rachel about the made-up stories a couple of months ago, her friend had made that "poor dear" face that most people made when referencing Sienna's motherless circumstance.

Rachel didn't have that expression on her face now, though. "Well, I've been thinking," Rachel said in an offhand tone that didn't fool Dee for a moment. Dee had known Rachel all her life and could read her like a feed schedule.

Diane scrubbed at the stove but knew that without some Ajax she'd never get the burnt-on crud off. Anyone who cooked as much as Rachel should have a gas range; these electric coil ones were impossible to clean without tearing the damn foil or scratching the finish. A gas range would have been a much more sensible purchase than the dishwasher. You could always wash dishes by hand, but you couldn't boil potatoes.

Rachel took a minute to put soap in the machine and start the cycle. The sound of a shower in a tin can filled the room. What a cacophony.

Rachel waved toward the living room and, after depositing

the rag in the sink, Dee followed her. She sat on one of Rachel's pink velvet chairs and rested her elbows on her knees. She was eager to get home.

"Well, I was thinking about when Carl had his first heart attack, back in 1991."

Dee nodded to show she remembered, though she had no idea what this had to do with Sienna making up stories about her mother.

"It took all of us off guard, of course, and he was worried about something happening before he had a chance to see all the kids. Darryl was in Iraq for Desert Storm, and Lauren was finishing up her last semester in Salt Lake. We just didn't know what would happen, so I got some note cards at the hospital gift shop and Darryl wrote them each a card that said all those things you wished people had said before they're gone. Ya know, 'I'm so proud of you' and 'Be sure to call your mama.' " She smiled wistfully and adjusted the doily on the arm of her chair, held in place by T-pins. Dee didn't have a single doily in her house. Rachel had at least a dozen. "It was very sweet, and it made Carl feel better to say—or I guess, write—his final words in case he didn't make it through. Then, the shunt surgery went well and he *did* make it through—praise the heavens. I didn't really think about those cards until . . . well, after he passed in '97. I dug those cards out of his nightstand drawer, and do you know that sometime over those last years he'd written a letter to me and one for each of the kids, even those who had been around when he was in the hospital that first time. We all opened our letters a couple of weeks after the funeral, and it turned out that the stuff he'd written six years earlier hadn't changed much." She shrugged her shoulders but looked at the family portrait on the wall. Almost eight years old now, but the last photo they'd had before Carl died. She'd had six more grandkids since then and a great-granddaughter to boot. Dee had never had a formal picture taken of her family, such as it was. "I wonder if letters like that would help Sienna," Rachel continued.

Dee shifted slightly in her chair. "Well, I'm sure a letter would be helpful, except that her mama didn't write a letter." She hated talking about Sienna's mother. Mark had put together a photo album, and sometimes Sienna would sit on his lap and Mark would tell her stories about the woman in the photos. It always made Diane uncomfortable when he did that. The look on his face, the wistfulness in his tone. And she doubted that some of what he talked about was even true—how would he know so much about that woman's history?

Rachel wriggled forward a little in her chair, and her eyes twinkled in a way that made Dee nervous. It was the kind of twinkle that was followed by things like "Let's get you a new dress" or "Wouldn't you like to be a brunette again? These Clairol home color kits are very popular." Dresses Dee would never wear and two dye jobs she had to have fixed at a salon—for fifty dollars each—had made Dee wary of this particular aspect of her best friend. "I know her mama didn't write any letters, Dee—she was young and sick, poor dear—but, well, Sienna wouldn't know they weren't from her mama. I mean, does she have anything with her mama's handwriting that would give it away? I remember you saying that Mark came back with Sienna and heartache and not much else." Rachel sat back in her chair and pulled her penciled eyebrows together. "Maybe you were being metaphoric."

Diane scrunched her eyebrows together, trying to puzzle out what exactly Rachel was getting to. "What are you talking about?"

"Well, maybe Sienna's making up these stories because she hasn't really connected with the reality of what happened to her mom. And maybe she hasn't connected with the reality because she doesn't really know *her*, ya know? Some letters might make Mable seem more real, and then Sienna wouldn't have to be making stuff up. It would be different from Mark just telling her things. It would be . . . I don't know, being remembered, I guess. Personal. If she's struggling to come up with a persona for her mother at seven years old, where will she be when she hits fourteen? You might could nip some of the future angst in the bud with some motherly wisdom, if you know what I mean." Rachel crossed one leg over the other, a satisfied smile on her bright pink lips

"You think fake letters from her dead mother would help her stop being a liar?"

Rachel frowned at Diane's summation, then stood and laughed awkwardly. "I just feel for that little girl, that's all, and know you worry about her more than you let on. Those letters Carl left for us were precious, so I was thinking how her mama probably would have written letters like that if she'd have thought of it. Breaks my heart for all three of them that things ended like they did." She started heading back to the kitchen. "Anyway, forget I said anything. It was a silly little idea I came up with—you know how I get. Now, come back into the kitchen. You are not leaving this house without some brownies!"

23

Sienna

"Don't be mad at your dad or your grandma, Sienna," Rachel Jensen says from where she sits in a pink velvet chair with her back straight and her wrinkled hands layered on her knee. Her fingernails are painted a light pink, with some design in white drawn on both thumbs. Her posture is both confident and anxious. "Like I said, it was my idea, and I'm the one who wrote the letters."

Beck squeezes my hand, silent encouragement that I need like I need air. I'm trying to sit as normally as I can, despite my shoulder aching and unshed tears stinging my sinuses. That it was Rachel's idea doesn't vindicate Grandma Dee or Dad. It just makes me feel more betrayed.

"So, how did it all work?" Beck asks in her soothing mom voice. The kids are home with Clint getting ready for the Easter egg hunt; she has to meet them at in thirty-seven minutes. She'd explained before we went inside that she'd had to tell him last night. "I mean, he's my husband," she'd said. I knew it was only a matter of time before everyone else knew, even though Beck really did want to respect her promise not to tell *anyone*. "We're not angry with anybody, are we, Sienna?" Beck says to Rachel. "We just want to make sense of things. Tell us how the letters came together, if you would."

I *am* angry, but I don't say so because Rachel hasn't told us everything yet.

Rachel shifts slightly, as though hoping she can find a more comfortable position. Her tone is casual, as if she's recounting combined efforts toward a display at the county fair. "Mark would tell Dee things that she would write into a letter, then I would copy it so that you wouldn't recognize the handwriting." She shrugged. "It was meant to make your mama real for you, Sienna. Not to hurt ya. Never that."

But it had hurt me.

I try to think of something else to say, but my silence seems to make Rachel nervous, so she fills it in. "My daughter lives in Boston. There's a cute little paper store in Cambridge, and she'd sent me a package of that stationery for my birthday." She looks at her hands layered on her knee, giving me the sense that she's more embarrassed about using her daughter's gift for the deception than she is about the deception itself. "Blues and greens really aren't my colors."

So, if Rachel's daughter had sent pink stationery that Rachel had wanted to use for herself, would this have happened? I imagine Rachel frowning at the green paper and going through her options for getting some use out of it. "Oh, I know. What if I offer to write fake letters to Dee's granddaughter?"

I take a breath and let it out before speaking, trying to keep my questions as objective as possible. I don't want to shut Rachel down by being accusatory, and yet I still can't believe that sweet old Rachel Jensen would play a part in such fraud. Never mind my "honesty is the best policy" grandmother. "Did you write them all at once?"

Rachel shifted again. "To start we came up with eight pinnacle events, which included a few different birthdays, high school graduation—that sort of thing. But then, well, Dee thought of some other things that it would be good for us to tell you as time went on. I still had the stationery, so we worked on a few more."

"My sixteenth birthday was one you did later, wasn't it?" In the months prior to turning sixteen, I had been coming up with excuses to skip church, mostly because it started at nine o'clock in the morning. I didn't hate the letters yet, but I was anxious about getting one for my sixteenth birthday—I hadn't received one since I was twelve. I'd asked Dad when I could expect the letters a half-dozen times, and he always told me to let it be a surprise. When Dad tapped on my bedroom door the night of my sixteenth birthday, I sprang up from my bed and ran to the door with my heart racing. I wasn't able to open that letter fast enough.

Then the letter said all the same things Grandma Dee was always telling me—about staying away from boys, knowing myself before I started dating, and going to church so I would know how to do right. I had thought Grandma Dee was unreasonable, but here was Mom advising me in the exact same way, with an air of subtle disappointment that seemed to say she'd known all along I wouldn't measure up. It emphasized the pressure I felt to make up for what Mom and Dad and Grandma hadn't had in their lives. Dad wasn't intense like Grandma Dee with his soft-spoken advice and worried eyes, but he didn't stick up for me with her either.

"Sienna, dear."

I look up into the lined face and bright eyes of my grandmother's best friend. In recent years, Rachel had finally stopped coloring her hair, and it bloomed like dandelion fluff around her face, the morning light from the windows filtering through the gossamer strands of fluffy. There were pastel Easter decorations all over the house—toll painted bunnies and plastic Easter eggs hanging on the ends of her curtain rods. She'd probably have a houseful of kids and grandkids over tomorrow for an Easter egg hunt in the backyard and a leg of lamb for Easter dinner. She wore a full face of makeup even this early in the morning and looked like the kind of grandmother you would see in a Hallmark commercial. Rachel smiled, bringing on more wrinkles, and cocked her head to the side. "I got the idea of the letters because you were making up stories about your mother, how she died and things like that. Dee was worried about it. I thought the letters would make your mother more . . . alive, I guess. My Carl had written letters to our kids when he had his first heart attack, and it meant the world to them after he died. If your mother had thought about it, I'm sure she'd have written those letters herself, dear. We did it because we love you and wanted you to have that connection."

I shake my head, and Beck tightens her grip on my hand again to try to remind me to be nice. Fair. Kind. Would Rachel have orchestrated letters like that for one of her own grandchildren? "It was the wrong thing," I say in a whisper as diplomatic as I can manage right now. Rachel's face falls, and Beck squeezes my hand harder. I hate that she wants me to put politeness first. As though Rachel's willingness to tell us the truth now makes up for years of lies. I pull my hand out of Beck's grip and stare hard at the old woman who helped betray me. Alongside Grandma Dee. Alongside Dad. "You twisted who my mother was to fit your own agendas."

Rachel smiles sweetly and shakes her head. "No, dear, we made her real for you. Everything in those letters was true."

"*You* couldn't make her *real* for me by pretending to be her and pretending that the advice she would give me would be the exact same as Grandma Dee was cramming down my throat." I lean forward, and Rachel pulls back slightly, though her back stays perfectly straight. "I deserved to know my mother, and *you* cannot give that to me." I stand and leave because I really don't want to lose my crap on this old woman. I also don't know what else to say. I let myself into the passenger seat of Beck's minivan, which perpetually smells like French fries, and pull the door shut with my left hand, pressing my right arm across my chest to try to contain the throbbing. I forgot to take ibuprofen in my anxiety to get out of the house this morning.

With my eyes closed, I take deep breaths and try to calm myself down even as tears leak out the corner of my eyes. I am swiping at them with my left hand when I hear the driver side door open. Beck slides into the seat, and the door shuts.

"Sienna, I—"

"Don't tell me that I shouldn't be mad," I say. "You *knew*

your mother." It's petty. But also true. Right now "truth" feels more important than any other virtue.

Beck is quiet. Several seconds pass in virtual silence. Beck's phone chimes with a text message, but she doesn't check it.

"The only person in my life who actually knew my mother is Dad, and he chose to play along with this." I open my eyes and stare at the orange brick of Rachel Jensen's rectangular house in front of us. There are three brightly painted, wooden Easter eggs connected to dowels and pushed into the flower bed that lines up with the front of her house—the tulips haven't yet bloomed.

"But your Dad gave the info for the letters," Beck told her. "I think he did put in the things he thought your mother would say."

I shake my head. "My parents were together for only three years. How would Dad know what Mom would have told me when I started my period or the names of her best friends in high school who liked boys too much? Can I really believe they talked about those things and Dad remembered it years later? I have no way of knowing what's real and what isn't, and the fact that they lied about it makes everything suspect."

Beck is silent for a few seconds. "Rachel asked if you had talked to your dad yet, and I told her that you hadn't, and we would appreciate it if she didn't give him a head's up."

"She'll tell him," I say, because why not? She knows I'm upset and she's been worried about Dad since Grandma Dee died, always asking Aunt Lottie how he's doing, taking him a batch of her pralines at Christmas like she used to when Grandma Dee was alive. I can't put off talking to Dad because he might learn about it before I get the chance if I hesitate much longer. The idea makes me shrivel inside like last year's pumpkins.

The conversation Beck and I had last night when I laid it all at her feet comes back to me. "Unless I go to Canada and find those details for myself."

"I'm not sure you have time."

"I'll go now. Today."

Beck's eyes go wide. "Now? You had surgery last week."

I lower my arm into my lap in an attempt to show that I'm more recovered than I actually am. My shoulder burns, but I blame it on the tension brought on by sitting across from Rachel and holding myself in check. "I can't stay here, Beck." I think of the credit card in my wallet, linked to the joint account with Tyson. It doesn't expire until October, and although I haven't used it since he went to London and we decided to pay our own expenses separately while we were apart, there's money there and I think he'd let me use it. I hate the idea of asking him, but I hate facing Dad even more.

Beck opens her mouth but then closes it without voicing the concern written all over her face. Instead she takes my left hand in hers. "I'm so sorry, CC."

A lump rises in my throat, and the tears come back. The only time I don't feel like crying is when I'm angry.

"What can I do to help?"

"Come with me to tell Dad I'm going to Chicago, back me up, and help me get out of there as quickly as I can."

24

Sienna

"I'm not back to full functioning anyway, Dad, and I'm worried I'll hurt myself if I push it. I've already done too much, and my shoulder hurts as much as it did my third day after the fall." Parts of this are true, sort of like parts of the letters were true. Maybe. There is a war taking place in my head. On one side, I know he's not well enough to manage the ranch without me, and he can surely sense there is something bigger going on than what I'm telling him. On the other side of the battlefield is everything else. And that is what's winning.

"You're already coming over for Easter dinner tomorrow," Beck says, smiling in a way I hope looks natural to Dad. She asked Clint to cover for her at the Easter egg hunt, which I know wasn't easy for any of them. "And I'll bring something by on Monday."

"I don't need dinners," Dad says, a bit more sharply than either of us expects. He shakes his head. "Going through a storage unit can't be easier than helping supervise things around here. Why do you have to go do that now?"

"Tyson was planning to do it but then came to the ranch instead. I feel well enough to make the drive, and we need to get it taken care of before the end of the month." I don't feel bad about lying anymore. Apparently lies and deception are the foundation of our relationship.

Dad lets out a breath and runs a hand through his hair, causing it to spike up. "The timing . . ."

"Is bad, I know. But I need to go. I'm sorry." It's a cold response and yet it's as warm as I can manage. Eagerness to get out of here and do something has been growing like bindweed in my head, taking over everything else. I've been played for a fool, twisted and manipulated and powerless in my ignorance.

Dad stands up from the table and heads to the back door, a familiar response to conflict like this. All my life, that's how he dealt with things, going outside to find something productive to do and keep from saying something he'd regret later. "All right, then. Good luck."

The door closes behind him, and I turn to look at Beck.

"That was awful," Beck said.

I nod and look around the house I grew up in, exactly the same now as it was twenty years ago. Orange and brown furniture, pine-paneled walls, brass light fixtures, and faux marble countertops. All the happy times and contentedness I used to feel slides through my fingers, and all I can see are the times Grandma chewed me out for this thing or that and the times Dad left the room instead of defending me. Was my childhood a happy one? Were the good times as big a lie as the letters were?

"You're sure you're up to this?" Beck asks as I stand and roll my shoulder.

"Yep." I have to be. I can't stay here a minute longer.

25

Sienna

June 2014

"Smells good, Sweetie," Dad said as Sienna set down the bowl of mashed potatoes.

"Sure does," Grandma Dee said, smiling at Sienna in that "You done good, girl" way of hers. It was about as much praise as Grandma Dee ever gave for anything. Sometimes Sienna wanted to point out that in just five more weeks she wouldn't be doing the cooking anymore and maybe Grandma could muster up a little more appreciation in the meantime. But Sienna would never say anything like that and felt guilty every time she thought about Dad and Grandma Dee eating scrambled eggs or frozen burritos every night. Aunt Lottie had said she'd invite them over for Sunday dinners every week instead of once a month. At least they would get a home-cooked meal one night out of every seven.

"Let's hope it tastes as good as it smells," Sienna said as she took her place at the table.

"If it doesn't, I'm giving it to the chickens," Grandma Dee said.

Sienna rolled her eyes, the expected response to Grandma Dee's expected comment. Not that it wasn't true. On those times when Sienna overcooked the chicken or forgot the sugar in the cornbread, Dad would smile and tell Sienna it was fine. Grandma Dee, on the other hand, would take a couple of bites, then dump the plate into the chicken can—a ceramic canister kept next to the sink where they collected leftovers—and make herself a sandwich. She would go about it with that air of disappointment that was as much a part of Grandma Dee as the steely gray hair that she French braided every day and the absolute knowledge that if there was work to be done, Grandma Dee would be there. Sienna and Grandma Dee's relationship hadn't ever been easy, but Sienna had come to love what Grandma Dee was more than hate what she wasn't and to take Grandma's rough edges with a grain of salt. Her grandmother hadn't had an easy life, after all.

Dad prayed over the food—slow-cooked pot roast and gravy from the full side of beef they had dressed in the fall and kept in the deep freeze, mashed potatoes, peas from the garden, and rolls from frozen dough bought at the store. Dessert would be apple crumble with fresh cream—they kept one dairy cow amid the two hundred or so beefs. It was one of Sienna's jobs to milk Gwen twice a day come hell or high water. Sienna felt bad every time she thought about Dad and Grandma having to do it once she'd left.

"So, what's on your agenda this week?" Dad asked after taking a few bites.

"Ugh, don't ask," Sienna groaned. "I've been telling myself that wedding stuff doesn't start until tomorrow morning." Sienna had never done anything like this. Beck was helping where she could, but she'd had her first baby a few months ago. Sienna had never seen Beck overwhelmed by anything, but little Braeden had her beat.

"Well, the Sabbath *should* be a day of rest," Grandma Dee said, looking up from her plate to wink at Sienna and give a partial smile.

"Right?" Sienna said, enjoying the moment of banter. Then she shrugged. "This week's to-do list isn't that bad. I need to finalize the menu and guests for the rehearsal BBQ and work on invitations—that's tomorrow. Tuesday, we're cutting hay. Wednesday, I'm going to Cheyenne with Beck and Tracy for my dress fitting. On Thursday Tyson's coming so we can get the engagement photos and our wedding license . . . Oh—" She looked up, flushed with excitement all over again as she remembered this next part. "Since we don't have time for an official honeymoon before class starts, Tyson's folks are sending us on a cruise at Christmas— part honeymoon, part Christmas gift." She sensed that she was smiling too hard, so she forced her expression to relax and kept her focus on her weekly to-do list. "Apparently, I need a pass- port and it can take a while, so I guess I need to get it started this week." She waggled her eyebrows at how fancy that sounded—a passport! "We'll work on that when we get the wedding license since I guess the same office does both. The recorder's office or something downtown."

"Oh, wow, a passport," Grandma Dee said in a neutral voice. "Highbrow."

The way Grandma Dee said it deflated Sienna's excitement and made her feel . . . stuck up, as if she thought she was better than people who will never go on a cruise and wouldn't even want to. Sienna had gotten pretty good at knowing how to pre- sent things so as not to draw out Grandma Dee's cynical side, but apparently she'd gotten sloppy. At the same time, she didn't think it would hurt Grandma Dee to be happy for her.

"How does a passport work for her, Mark?" Grandma asked. "I mean, she's Canadian *and* American, right? Which passport does she get?"

"Oh, well, I don't know," Dad said, keeping his eyes on his plate. He poked at his potatoes, seeming uncomfortable. Have I hurt his feelings too? Sienna wondered. He wasn't as sensitive as Grandma Dee, which meant making him feel bad was worse.

"I live in the U.S., so I think I just get a U.S. one," Sienna said, trying to be helpful. She'd never thought of herself as Canadian and didn't like the separate feeling of having a differ- ent nationality from the rest of her family. She hadn't even real- ized until a sociology class in high school that she had dual citizenship. "I'll just need my birth certificate and Social Secu- rity card, I think."

Sienna looked up to see that Grandma Dee was looking at Dad. Sienna looked at him too. Dad looked up and noticed he was the center of attention. He swallowed and took a drink of his milk—he always had milk with dinner.

"I can look into it," he said with a nod. "I'll run by the recorder's office and see what they need; then I'll make sure all the paperwork is in order for when Tyson gets in to town. Easy-peasy."

"Your dad will go with you guys to get the license too," Grandma Dee decided. "Just to make sure it all comes together."

Sienna wanted to argue that since she was getting married and all, she needed to start doing these kinds of things herself. Sometimes she felt pushed to be more independent than she wanted to be—like going to the doctor herself and picking up ranch orders in Cheyenne. Other times they treated her like a baby—Dad filling out the paperwork for her driver's license and going with her up to the desk at the DMV. He didn't let her get a phone until her junior year of high school and a Facebook account until she was almost seventeen; then made sure she had the highest privacy settings possible. But, then again, there was still so much to do to get ready for the wedding. Maybe it would be nice to have some help.

"With a little luck on your part, Sienna," Grandma continued, "your dad will get everything filled out and all you'll have to do is sign a paper."

"That would be great."

Dad smiled at her, and she let more of her irritation go. Sometimes Sienna wished there could be a way for her and Tyson to live here. If not at the ranch, then in Lusk, at least. But Tyson was majoring in international marketing—Lusk didn't have any jobs like that. Sienna looked between Dad and Grandma Dee. Once she married Tyson, she wouldn't work side by side with Dad anymore. She wouldn't bicker with Grandma Dee and wish she'd just give her a hug now and then. She wouldn't sit at this table in this house and have dinner with them on a Sunday. But she'd still come back to the ranch sometimes, and they would have dinner together then, with Tyson, and share all the new things happening at the ranch and in Chicago. Sienna further reassured herself with the knowledge that one day she'd be bringing babies with her to fill up the seats around this table—it would feel so good. Maybe once Sienna was gone, Grandma Dee would appreciate the fact that she'd been doing the cooking in this house for most of her life. Maybe they would learn how to make their own lasagna. *That would be good for all of us,* she told herself. So, yeah, changes were coming, but change wasn't necessarily bad any more than it was necessarily good. Just different.

"Sienna," Grandma Dee said, drawing Sienna's attention back to her. Grandma winked. "Good job on dinner. Those poor chickens are just gonna have to do with their scratch tonight."

26

Sienna

I text Tyson right before I leave my bedroom, with Beck carrying my duffel bag for me. I packed light. He should have been back in London for several hours by that time, but he doesn't return my call until I'm well into Nebraska and five chapters into the Liane Moriarty audiobook Beck said I would just love. My Prius connects his call to my stereo via Bluetooth, so I don't have to try and hold the phone and drive at the same time.

"There is no way you can make that drive by yourself, Sienna." I imagine him pacing.

"I'm fine," I say. "I've got the sling, and I'm taking the pain pills only at night."

"That you're taking the pain pills at all is reason enough for you not to do this."

"I've already left."

He swears.

"I'll stay in Omaha tonight and then finish up tomorrow. I'll be going to the storage unit to see if my long-form birth certificate is there first. Can you send me the gate code and the lock combination for our unit?"

"You can't go pawing around in the storage unit." His voice is getting louder.

I raise my voice too. "The filing cabinet is right there toward the front. Remember how you said we'd want it there in case we needed to get anything?"

"This is crazy."

"This is what I'm doing. I'll pay back whatever I use from the joint account."

"How?"

I'm taken aback by both the heat in his voice and the accusation, but he doesn't give me a chance to respond. "You're not getting paid to work the ranch, and I'll be surprised if you have more than a hundred dollars left in your personal account from your last paycheck."

I'm actually down to eighty-seven dollars, but I'm not about to tell him that. "I'll figure it out."

"No, Sienna, you *won't* figure it out, because you *can't* figure it out. You'll do whatever the hell you want to do and not give a damn what I think." The line goes quiet, and I blink at the windshield and endless ribbon of highway ahead of me. My phone beeps to indicate that the call is ended. For a second I think I simply lost signal and then realize he hung up on me. Tyson?

I wait for him to text me an apology or explanation or something. He texts me the address, gate code, and combination for number 348 instead. I wonder if he filled out the divorce worksheets on the flight. I wonder if he spent those twelve hours listing all the reasons why he was done with me and I just handed him the final straw he'd been looking for. I don't let myself mourn our marriage and instead adjust my position and start my book up again. When I unfold myself from the car in Omaha, I feel the way I imagine an eighty-year-old woman feels. My joints are stiff, my head hurts, and my shoulder is almost immovable. I've limbered up enough by the time I'm in my room to pull off a phone call to Beck.

"What did Tyson say about using the credit card?"

"He's mad and . . . sick of this, I think." But I *know* he's sick of this. Sick of us. Sick of me.

"*This* as in . . . the two of you?"

Funny how it's easier to divulge the truth over the phone than it is face-to-face. I stare at the ceiling. "Neither of us have gotten what we wanted or expected from this marriage. It's been a long descent." The swirling plaster of the ceiling begins to turn into shapes. An elephant, a man's face that's melted on one side.

"It's only been five years."

Only? Five years feels like forever. "He wants this corporate life where he travels and makes big things happen." I don't mean to sound like I'm blaming him, but I don't take back my words either.

"And what do you want? The ranch?"

I think about that as though I haven't thought about it so many times before. "I honestly don't know what I want, Beck. Especially now. Maybe I just want . . . life."

"Yeah." The word is hard and dry.

"I always thought I would live my mom's life, or the life she didn't get to live, ya know? Fall in love, have a family, build a future. I imagined anniversary trips and grandkids and, well, everything's different and I don't know how to envision my future anymore, but I'm okay if I have to do it alone."

"Oh, don't say that." Beck sniffed, betraying that she is crying on her end of the phone. "You deserve to be loved, Sienna. Wanted and adored."

"Maybe," I say. "But Tyson deserves that too, and neither of us has been doing a very good job of it for each other." I push myself up from the bed, wincing at the effort it takes, and brighten my voice to take the edge off. "Anyway, it will all work out, right? My doctor says I have an excellent prognosis. I just need to get this Mom stuff taken care of so that I know where to put my feet."

"Foundation." Her tone is reverent.

I nod even though she can't see me. "For so many years I have been living in the future, then I was trying to keep my balance in the present, and now the past is pulling me in. Maybe I'll find a piece of myself in each place and come out with a wholeness I haven't had before. That's what I'm hoping for, but there's work to do before I can get there. Does that make sense?"

"It does," Beck says. "And I'm praying for you, Sienna. To find that wholeness, to find your . . . place."

I imagine her prayers going to heaven and God turning to look down on the person Beck is petitioning for. I wonder if He knows me, if He knows my story, if He'll help me put it together. Or maybe I'm just one person in a sea of faces and I don't warrant any special treatment. I've never been sure, but I know Beck is sure and that means something.

When I wake up the next morning, gritty and sore, there's a text from Tyson.

Tyson: **At least fly to Toronto from Chicago.**

I text him back to tell him thanks, and he doesn't reply. I think about his suggestion over breakfast with my arm in a sling and my lower back aching and decide to take his advice. Before I check out of the hotel, I've booked a flight for that night at four o'clock. It gives me butterflies when I read the confirmation e-mail. I'm going to Canada!

The drive to Chicago seems twice as long as the drive to Omaha, even though the distance is about the same. I can't find a comfortable position for my shoulder and have to stop for a Coke twice because I'm so tired, my vision blurs. The road is long and boring, and my anxiety is increasing with every mile, making it hard to focus on the book. I finally trade it out for a classic rock station that thumps through my car speakers.

It's a relief when I can get off the 80 and wind my way to the storage unit located on the outskirts of the city. I try to remember why we decided to store everything there—it makes no sense now that neither of us has a connection to the city—but I suppose we thought at some point we would come back together and what better place for that than the city we'd lived in? Chicago had been so exciting when I first came—strolling Navy Pier and Millennium Park in that unhurried way a local can do. We found a Vietnamese restaurant in West Ridge that became "our place" and went salsa dancing once with friends where we both laughed ourselves silly over our complete lack of coordination. We were treated to baseball games at Wrigley Field by Tyson's boss, visited the lighthouse in the harbor, took a camping trip to Kankakee—we had some happy times. But daring to remember the good memories brings the bad ones too. Throwing up on the L after my first round of hormone treatments, sitting on a bench in Maggie Daley Park and envying the innumerable families who walked past me while the ice in my drink melted in the staggering heat and humidity of summer. Fighting with Tyson over money while on our way to a wedding reception in Archer Heights. Tyson telling me over dinner in Little Italy that he wanted to take a job in London and put off our fertility treatments. "We've got to have a reset, Sienna. Otherwise what is this all for?"

What is this all for?

I feel as though I wasted all those years, wanting what I couldn't have—babies—while turning my back on what I did have—Tyson—and now I have neither one. Nor do I have the faith in my dad or knowledge of my mom or confidence in Grandma Dee that I took for granted. And now I'm missing part of my breast too. Have I gained anything? Cynicism, maybe. But strength too, I suppose. Empathy for the hard things people face that I'll never know about because, like me, they'll keep it under the surface and smile in all the right places and do their makeup every day without a hint of the vise tightening around their neck.

The radio announces that it's Easter Sunday. Growing up we always went to church on Easter and had a family dinner. After Tyson and I got married, we were either at the ranch or Tyson's parents'. Easter always felt different from other Sundays, and I would think about Jesus and what He taught and what I believed about His role in this life of mine. I don't know what to think about Him now, but I send up a little prayer—*Help me find my mother.*

No one answers, and Bon Jovi comes on the radio.

I stop the car at the gate to the storage unit and toggle to the text Tyson sent with the codes. The metal creaks as the gate raises. I pull forward and go up and down the aisles until I find number 348. Five minutes later, with the garage style door up and using my phone as a flashlight, I find my birth certificate— the exact same one Dad had. Not the long form. No answers.

I don't waste any emotion on it as I close everything up—not an easy feat with one arm and no strength left in the rest of me.

"So, did you get it?" Beck asks when I call her on my way to the airport. I'm early, but where else will I go?

I look at the birth certificate on the passenger seat. "It's another short form, just like the one in Dad's file." I now have both copies with me, having made sure to get Dad's before I left the ranch.

"You're kidding."

"I wish." My arm is killing me, throbbing and burning with equal intensity—worse than it's ever been. I change the position of the sling to ease it, but the improvement is minimal. I'm worried I've done something to my armpit incision. But maybe I'm just so tired that anything that hurts a little, hurts a lot.

"But you would have needed a long form for both your driver's license and your passport."

Beck had looked that up Saturday morning while I packed my duffel bag.

"Which means Dad has a long form somewhere." Beck had learned that every child born in Ontario got both a short form and long form, so Dad would have had to order an additional short form to give to me when I moved to Chicago and then stored the long form somewhere other than his files where he stores every other legal document. So much energy put into hiding information.

"How are you feeling?"

"Tired."

"I wish I could have come with you, even if I'd stayed on the States side of the border. I should have done that, huh?"

Yes, I think. It had seemed silly for her to come on only part of the trip and miss Easter with her kids. But I regretted not finding a way for her to have come. This driving was too much. "Of course not," I say out loud, trying to sound less tired so that Beck will be less worried. "I'm flying into Ontario tonight instead of driving."

"Oh, I'm glad to hear that," Beck said. "I didn't suggest it because of money and all that."

"Tyson suggested it."

"You guys talked, then?"

I love her for having so much hope in her voice. "No, he texted."

"He still cares about you."

I say nothing. Caring isn't enough. Love isn't even enough. I wish I knew what *would be* enough. "Thanks for all your support, Beck. I'll call you tomorrow."

27

Sienna

"Two days?" I repeat, staring across the counter that separates me from the tall blond woman who looks more like a cocktail waitress than a clerk for Service Ontario, the branch of the Canadian government that handles legal documents. I flew into Toronto last night, didn't sleep well, and Ubered here so that I was at the door when it opened. Despite that, it took forty-five minutes before I had my turn at the window and now I'm told that I have to wait two days to get the documents?

She doesn't look up from her computer as she speaks. "It takes that long for us to process the request, love." She finishes tapping on her keys and looks up at me.

"I didn't think it would take so long if I came in person," I say. "I came up from Wyoming."

She frowns prettily, yet sincerely too, I think. "I can mail your long form to an address in the States if you prefer." My short-form birth certificate is lying on the counter between us—proof enough for me to have ordered the long form.

"Doesn't that take longer?"

The woman frowns and nods. "And you pay for the shipping."

"Is there any way to get it rushed through this office so I can pick it up from you sooner? I can pay an express fee." I've already spent over a thousand dollars from our joint account on gas, plane ticket, food, and hotel. The dollar signs adds to the nausea churning in my stomach. Tyson was right about me having no way to pay it back.

The woman smiles the way you would right before you pat a child on the head. "You already paid for express service, love."

"Oh." I was so fired up about doing something and now I have two days to wait, which will cost hundreds of additional dollars. "So, Wednesday is the very soonest it will be ready?"

"Wednesday at nine a.m.," the clerk confirmed. "Is there anything else I can help you with?"

I shake my head, pick up my short form, and start to stand, but then lower myself back into the chair. "Actually, you handle all records here? Can I order my *mother's* birth certificate even though I don't have my long form yet?"

"Sure."

She says it so quick and easy that I pause an extra second to make sure I heard her right. "I can?"

"Sure thing. Any legal document. If you give me your mother's name and birth date, I can cross-check it with your records for verification of your authorization to order the document."

"Mable Gerrard Chadwick, Gerrard is her maiden name." I scoot forward in my chair and feel a trill in my chest. The computer this woman is typing into holds the answer to so many of my questions. What I wouldn't give for ten minutes to plumb the depths without having to go through this woman, helpful as she is.

"Spell her maiden name for me, love."

"G-E-R-R-A-R-D."

She types. Pauses. Reads. Turns to look at me. "Date of birth?"

"Um, February 23, 1969, I think."

I worry the woman will find it odd that I'm not certain, but she doesn't say anything. Blondie goes back to the typing and pausing and reading. Then types and pauses again. And again. She looks back at me. "Are you certain you have the right information?"

No, I'm not sure, I say in my mind. "My mom died when I

was very young, I don't have any documentation. That's why I came all the way up here."

"Let me try a back door—we'll go through the info on your birth certificate instead."

Type. Pause. Read. Type. Pause.

"Ah, I see," the woman said, nodding with satisfaction.

I scoot forward, barely perched on the plastic chair now.

"Her surname is Gérard—G-E-R-A-R-D. The French spelling, with an accent over the E." The G sound is soft and blends with the slight rolling of the Rs.

"Did you know your mother was French Canadian?" She smiles sweetly at me.

"No, I didn't know that." I hadn't questioned that the spelling was Gerrard because that was how Dad had always spelled it. Why spell it wrong? Was he trying to hide the fact that she was French Canadian?

"And then Mable is actually Maebelle." The name rolled off the woman's tongue like jelly—May-a-bell-a.

"May-a-bell-a?" I repeat, feeling the awkward cadence of a name I've never heard before. The names Mable and Maebelle are so similar and yet entirely different. One is old and sturdy, like a solid piece of furniture. The other is round and swirly, like a butterfly or a song.

"Maebelle Antonia Gérard, the birthday's right except for the year—she was born in 1976."

I slide back in my chair and let the lyrical name move slowly around my head, seeping in and casting out the sturdy name of Mable Gerrard. *Dad lied about Mom's name?* And her age. If she was born in 1976, she would have been only twenty years old when she died . . . and eighteen when I was born—by a *month*. The acknowledgment of these truths makes my chest feel shaky. She'd have gotten pregnant at the age of seventeen. Is that the reason behind all the missing information? Wait, how were they married if Mom was underage? Or is seventeen considered old enough to marry here in Ontario?

"She was born in Québec, so there's an additional fee to get a birth certificate since it's a different province. Is that okay?"

"Yeah," I say with a nod toward her computer. "Can you find my parents' marriage certificate?"

Blondie scans the screen in front of her, eyebrows pulled together in consternation. She turns to me with an apologetic look. "No marriage certificate under your mother's name."

"Are you sure?"

Her eyes narrow just enough for me to notice, and I backpedal. "I'm sorry. I don't mean to doubt you. I just . . . I thought my parents were married." Thought. Believed. Never doubted.

"They may have married in another province," Blondie says, her tone back to helpful. "Or gone over the border to Niagara. People love getting married with the falls in the background even though the preacher has to shout to be heard." She smiles, and I try to smile back for the sake of manners, but I know it can't look natural on my face right now. She adds, "There's a vital statistics office there that you could visit; it's only an hour or so away from here. If you want a fuller search here in Canada, it's fifteen dollars for each five-year period in each province and can take up to six weeks to complete. Would you like me to help you with that?"

"I think I'll wait to get these other documents first." They weren't married, were they? It's the third lie that's now proven—Mom didn't write me letters, my mother didn't die at the age of twenty-three, and my parents weren't married. Four, my mom's name was Maebelle Gérard. None of them were necessary lies, and they don't even support one another. I can see that maybe the age and marital status wouldn't be something Dad wanted to tell his young and impressionable daughter, but I'm twenty-five years old and my mother is dead—why not fess up? Maybe Grandma Dee didn't know and Dad was hiding this from his mother, who was conservative and hard to please. And then she coincidentally had her friend write letters to me? Hiding details from Grandma also didn't explain why there wasn't anything else about my mom in Dad's files.

I remember Blondie on the other side of the counter and meet her eyes—she's getting impatient. "S-sorry, this is a lot for me to take in." I can feel the prickle of sweat on my forehead but try to think through anything else this woman could help me with. She's the gatekeeper of public records; what else do I need? Beck's exclamation that night I told her everything: "Maybe she's not dead." We talked ourselves out of that because of the cancer but . . . did my mom even *have* cancer?

"Could I also order my mom's death certificate?" I say it fast, as if I might forget if I don't get the words out. Dad had said Mom died in October and he'd left Canada quickly because he was trying to outrun winter. Something knocks in my chest like a gong. Boom. Boom. Boom. Lies. Lies. Lies. I watch Blondie closely, imagining her eyebrows coming together as she tells me that there's no death certificate. The fantasy alone is enough to make it impossible for me to breathe.

Blondie nods and turns back to her computer. "Just one copy?"

The air rushes from my lungs. "So, there is a death certificate?"

Blondie looks a little concerned, but mostly sympathetic as she nods.

I swallow. I hadn't thought Mom was alive for more than a few seconds, but it still feels like a new loss. "One copy will be enough, thank you." I focus on my breathing and the temperature of the room—a little cool, but my chest is on fire and my mind is spinning. "Can you tell me the date of her death?"

"I can tell you it was in 1996."

That lines up with what I've been told. It's one of the only things that does.

It's another ten minutes before I insert the credit card into the little machine exactly like the one at McDonald's in Lusk. The total cost is nearly two hundred Canadian dollars, and Blondie frowns. "Sorry about the dent this makes in your wallet, love."

"It's fine," I say. The information is priceless. I only wish I could get the documents right now. "Thank you for all your help." The woman was an absolute angel. If she'd been a crank, I'm not sure I'd have managed to think of everything I needed.

She hands me my receipt and I stand, surprised that my legs don't wobble. Blondie's eyes rise with me. "When you come back on Wednesday, go to that desk over there and they'll have everything we ordered today."

I follow her arm pointing to a desk on the far side, with its own line.

"You won't need to wait in line like today. Just walk right up to the desk and show your ID and your receipt." She nods toward the paper in my hand, and I put it in the cash part of my wallet so I'm sure not to lose it.

Outside, I stop at a bench that flanks the sidewalk and look at the parking lot as though it's a beautiful vista that begs contemplation.

May-a-bell-a Gérard.

Twenty-three years ago the Internet wasn't what it is now and Facebook didn't exist. Dad could tell me anything he wanted because I had no way of knowing better.

I roll my bad shoulder, stiff and throbbing, and adjust it in the sling. The improvement is miniscule. The actual pain feels deep, as though something with its own heartbeat is burrowed inside. I've seen medical shows where sponges or even a clamp have been left inside surgical patients. Maybe the doctor left something behind, accounting for the pull I feel. Or maybe I'm not as healed as I want to believe. Then again, maybe this is what it feels like to everyone who has this procedure and I should stop being so dang sensitive. I consider going back to the hotel and taking a nap—my body relaxes just thinking about it, but my mind is still spinning. I've come all the way to Canada. Truths about my mother live in this town even if she doesn't.

I take ten deep breaths to settle what I've learned, then I pull my phone from my purse with my left hand. I Google libraries in Hamilton, Ontario. There's one not far from my hotel, but I continue sitting. Breathing. Trying to come to terms with what I've learned. In an envelope, in my purse, are the sixteen photos of my mother. I'm going to find her. I order an Uber—it's four minutes away. I stand up, adjust the strap of the sling that's starting to cut into my left shoulder, and head toward the entrance to the parking lot where I'll meet the car. I am both hoping and fearing that the library will give me the answers no one else will.

28

Mark

January 1995

Mark walked the five blocks from the bakery to their apartment with his hands deep in the pockets of his secondhand coat and a ski cap pulled down as low on his head as he could. He was still freezing, his toes tingling in his boots and his neck numb—he'd forgotten his scarf. He'd thought Wyoming winters were harsh, but they were nothing compared to January in Canada. It was three-thirty, and daylight was already fading, bringing on even colder temperatures, though that was difficult to imagine.

When he got home today they were going to bundle up Sienna and take a bus to the library here in Hamilton for family story hour—something the library did every Monday night. Mark had learned which bus to catch so they could get there by five, and he'd been looking forward to it all day—a normal, and free, family activity. More books and less TV would be a good step for all of them. Mae could spend hours watching all the TV talk shows—*Geraldo, The Ricki Lake Show, Jenny Jones*. Mark didn't think it was healthy.

Having a family was a lot harder than he'd thought it would be, but from talking to the guys at work, he didn't think he had it any worse than they did. All the guys argued with their wives and worried about money and felt at least as much frustration as they did joy in the hand-to-mouth lives they lived. It was good to know he wasn't alone, but he felt wary fear as he got closer to the apartment where they had lived for ten months, since Mae had been approved for housing assistance. He'd sworn to himself that *he* would take care of his family as soon as he could, but he didn't have a lot of job options even with his permanent residency, and a second job would mean never seeing his family. So they continued on the assistance and hadn't married because it would affect what Mae could get from the government.

Mark hurried up the concrete steps to the second-level apartment he would be embarrassed for anyone from his life in Lusk to see. It was such a dump. The paint was peeling around the doorways, and rust stains ran the length of the yellow painted cinderblock from the rain gutters on both ends of the building.

It will get better, he told himself. He only needed three classes to finish his degree. Then he could find better work. He used his key in the door—he'd never locked doors at the ranch. He wasn't even sure where the key to the front door would be should he need one. Here, people locked everything—one reason why the thrill the big city had once held for him had faded into acceptance combined with hope that he would not live this way forever. He'd told Mae about the ranch—miles of prairie, endless sky, and security he didn't think she'd ever known. She'd listened and then said it sounded boring. When he'd first learned she was five years younger than he—eighteen instead of twenty-one like she'd told him—he'd thought that wasn't too much of a gap. More and more, though, he felt like an old man trying to manage a teenager. Mom had always said that work was good for what ails ya, and Mark was seeing that more and more clearly. Mae didn't . . . do much, and that led to boredom, which led to dissatisfaction. He worried about what dissatisfaction would lead to.

"Hello, hello," he called cheerfully as he entered the apartment. Sienna squealed from where she sat on the floor playing with some Tupperware—poor man's play toys, Mae had called them—in front of the TV blasting out an afternoon cartoon. *He-Man,* he realized as Sienna flipped herself onto her hands and knees to crawl to him. She'd been crawling two whole weeks now and was getting fast. He scooped her up and blew a raspberry on her neck. She giggled with pure delight that lifted his mood. "How's my girl?" he said, pulling her back so he could take in every bit of her—feathery brown hair, blue eyes, grin that showed the tops of two tiny white teeth along her bottom gum. She threw her arms around his neck, and he hugged her all over again, filled to the brim with love and purpose and peace. A warm apartment and his daughter's arms around his neck made him reconsider going back out into the cold for the story hour, but they needed to do things outside of the apartment sometimes.

"Mae?" he called as he settled Sienna on his hip and crossed to turn off the TV. Sienna was still in her nightgown, but her diaper seemed fresh—that was good. Mae had never lived such a traditional life, and things like taking care of a house and child just didn't come to her automatically the way they did to Mark, who grew up with chores and rules and cousins and families. It was a tricky balance to be both supportive of the things Mae did while encouraging her to do a little bit more. Mae was always irritated at first when he gave her suggestions, but by the end of their conversation she usually said she would try to do better. Then she'd kiss him and he'd roll her beneath him and believe that everything would be all right. How he wished the feeling that lingered after their lovemaking would last longer than it did.

"Mae?" he called again when she didn't answer.

She wasn't in the kitchen, which had a sink full of dirty dishes he'd be washing before he went to bed. Again. The bathroom door was open, which meant he could expect to find her in the bedroom—the last of the four rooms. The bed was unmade, clothes in piles on the floor and spilling out of the plastic tubs they used in place of a dresser. Mae wasn't there, and he felt fire in his chest. This was the third time he'd come home to find Sienna alone in the apartment. On both of the other times, Mae had shown up within a couple of minutes and assured him that she'd only been gone for a quick errand. Sienna had been napping both of those other times, and Mae claimed that was why she'd run out "real fast." He'd still gotten mad and told her she couldn't do that again. Both times she'd promised she wouldn't.

Sienna had been awake and propped in front of the TV this time. There was no justification for that.

Mark changed Sienna's clothes and used a little pink clip to hold the hair off her face even though he suspected they weren't going to make it to the library. They'd have to catch the bus at 4:21 and it was already 4:02. Mae was supposed to have had Sienna ready by the time he got home. He was disappointed that they wouldn't be sitting in a room filled with other parents and young children listening to *The Very Hungry Caterpillar*. He ached for that life, a life he'd never thought to doubt before all this. He didn't want it because it was how he'd grown up— Mom ran the ranch and didn't cook much, and he had barely any memories of his dad—but he'd seen the life he wanted in Uncle Rich and Aunt Lottie's family and the families of his friends. He'd longed for that kind of security and comfort. There is still time, he told himself, but he worried he was kidding himself. He'd been raised to know that choices determine outcome—he'd chosen to fall for a free-spirited woman with a difficult past and limited view of the future. He'd chosen to sleep with her. He'd chosen to stay with her and their child no matter what. He also believed that they could build their life into something better than this, but he couldn't do that alone, and that's what scared him most. If he couldn't convince Mae that a traditional, secure, and family-oriented life was worth pursuing, he was in trouble.

Mark put Sienna in the high chair and found her some Cheerios to eat and drop and play with while he started the dishes. He tried to sing "The Wheels on the Bus" but struggled to make the tune sound like a happy one as ten minutes passed. Then twenty. What if he'd been held up at work and hadn't come home? How long had Sienna been alone before he'd arrived? At least the door had been locked, he told himself. She'd been safe in that respect, but there were still electrical cords she could mess with and corners she could bump her head on. She was nine months old, for heaven's sake. No one in their right mind leaves an infant alone for two minutes, let alone half an hour.

When Mark finally heard the front door, he was as near to

rage as he'd ever been. Even amid other arguments they'd had, he'd never yelled at Mae or felt this kind of anger. He wiped his hands off on a dishtowel and told Sienna he would be right back before taking long strides into the living room, arriving just as Mae closed the door behind her, her back to him.

"Where have you been?"

She startled and turned quickly to see him, her green eyes wide as she sucked in a breath of surprise. She immediately smiled at him. "Mark," she said, walking toward him while raising her arms to circle his neck. He caught both of her hands at the wrists and held her away from him. Her eyebrows came together on her freckled face that always gave her an air of innocence.

"Where have you been?" he asked again. "I've been home for half an hour, and Sienna was alone. Again. We talked about this."

"It was not 'alf an 'our," Mae said, smiling sweetly again. "I just ran down to Jill's to . . . borrow a cup of sugar." She laughed at this and then pulled her hands out of his, putting one in front of her mouth as though to hide the giggle. She swayed a little bit on her feet.

Mark narrowed his eyes and looked her over. She was wearing jeans and a sweatshirt with house slippers. It was freezing outside. "Are you . . . drunk?"

"No," she said, and laughed again. Sienna garbled something from the kitchen, and Mae's eyes went past him. "Where is my *bébé*?" she cooed. She tried to walk around him, but he stepped to the side to block her; she looked up at him in surprise.

"You cannot leave her in the apartment by herself," Mark said through gritted teeth. There was something languid about the way Mae pushed her hair behind her ears, as though she were moving through water. She'd gotten drunk at a friend's New Year's party a few weeks ago and had been like this, unsteady and silly. He didn't smell alcohol, though. A cup of sugar? He took a breath and swallowed. "Are you high, Mae?"

She laughed again and pushed past him. "I want to see my

bébé." Moments later she was singing in French to Sienna, who babbled and laughed back at her.

Mark stood where he was in the middle of the living room, staring at the front door while thinking about story time at the library; and Mom saying Mae was trouble; and Jill, the downstairs neighbor, who always smelled like weed and acted like a fourteen-year-old even though she had three kids. Mae had told him that Jill was a recovered addict, like Mae. She'd said they understood each other.

Mark had been worried about dirty dishes and Sienna wearing her pajamas at three o'clock in the afternoon. He didn't even know how to worry about *this*.

29

Sienna

I feel out of place and small when I walk into the library. In Lusk, the library is a hundred-year-old building with oak shelves and divided rooms. This building is bigger and brighter and . . . Canadian. Not that a modern Canadian library would be all the different from a modern American library, but everything that's happened today has come with a swirling amount of intimidation. Did Mom and Dad ever come to this library? Did Mom like to read? Did she bring baby Sienna here for story time before she got sick?

I have more questions now than when I crossed the border, and I'm anxious about the answers I'll find. The anxiety combined with my increasing exhaustion is almost enough to turn me around and push me back through the glass doors—but I am here, and somewhere in these walls is information. I have two days until the documents are ready; it would be stupid for me not to take advantage.

I adjust my sling, which doesn't ease the throbbing as much as I'd hoped, then walk toward the information desk, where I wait until a woman about my own age comes to the other side of the counter. "Can I help you?" the woman asks in a hushed voice. I clear my throat quietly before I speak. "I'm trying to find information about my mom who is from here but died when I was a baby. I don't know where to start."

"Oh, I'm sorry to hear that," she says, the vowels sounding

just different enough for me to notice. "Your best bet is probably the newspaper archives. Birth and death announcements and all that can be found there. Let me show you to the computers."

Ten minutes later, I am sitting in front of a flat-fronted monitor with a fresh screen that will take me through the archives of the *Hamilton Spectator*. Miriam, the librarian who helped me, has given me some basic instructions and provided me with some scratch paper and a half-sized pencil so I can take notes. She can make copies of anything I find for twenty-five cents a page and show me actual hard copies of some years of the paper if I want to see them. She also showed me how to access legal archives, for things like marriage, birth, and death records, but I don't need that anymore—I can't access actual copies of the certificates, just verify dates and things in the public domain.

I flex my fingers and then type "Maebelle Antonia Gérard" in the search field. A full page of hits comes up, and I catch my breath in surprise. The Google searches at the ranch had found nothing, which I understand now, but it's surreal to have all this information so quickly. I lean forward to review the titles of the individual links. I expect a death notice, obituary, or my own birth announcement, but the first link is for an arrest notice, and the title reads "Drug Raid Leads to Four Arrests." I let the mouse hover over the link for a few moments while I scan the other links scrolling down the page. One headline stands out above the others and I feel dizzy. "Woman Found Dead in the Grand Prompts Review of County Drug Enforcement Measures."

I pause. Gather courage. Take a breath. Move my mouse to that link. Click.

HAMILTON—Provincial Police have identified the body found by fishermen in the Grand River near Caledonia as that of Maebelle Antonia Gérard, who was reported missing on October 19,

1996. Gérard, a known drug user with substantial criminal history of drug-related crimes, disappeared from her home in Hamilton sometime between seven p.m. on October 18 and seven a.m. on October 19. After she did not return by evening on the 19th, the homeowner, David Vandersteen, contacted the police. The last people to see Gérard before her disappearance were the father of her child, Mark Chadwick, an American estranged from Gérard at the time of her disappearance, and his mother, Diane Chadwick, also an American citizen. According to police, extensive questioning has led to none of the three being implicated in her disappearance or her death. Vandersteen claimed to have argued with Gérard prior to his leaving to work his night shift job on the 18th.

A postmortem has confirmed that Gérard showed signs of recent drug use, which likely contributed to her death. Although foul play is a possibility, experts were unable to determine any proof of such due to the condition of the body. "It's impossible to know in a case like this what came first, the violence or the drug use. The shame is that but for different lifestyle choices, Gérard would likely have lived a long, full life."

Police suspect that Gérard overdosed in the company of other drug users and was dropped into the Grand so that her companions could avoid police involvement. "Sadly, we see more and more of this all the time. Users know they will face consequences for involvement in an overdose, so they simply get rid of the evidence. Gérard is yet one more example of how drugs are destroying lives. Her arrest record shows three separate arrests, each of which could have led to treatment but instead slapped her with minor penalties that obviously did nothing to change the course of her life. Now, we have one young life ended and a child who will grow up without her mother because we are not doing enough."

"She had been deeply troubled for a long time," Vandersteen said. "I did everything I could to help her, but ultimately her life was in her own hands."

30

Mark

June 1995

Mark was awakened by voices outside the bedroom window around two o'clock in the morning. People walked past all the time, but Mark recognized Mae's voice—he hadn't seen her in almost a week. He eased out of the bed so as not to wake Sienna curled up on the other side. It was finally warm enough that he didn't need to sleep in thick socks and flannel pajamas, but he still slept in the bottoms when Sienna was with him. He'd made it to the living room and flipped on the light just as the front the door opened. Mae was framed in the doorway, looking small and anxious.

Despite everything, all he wanted to do was pull her into his arms and tell her they could still make this work. They could be a family again. A hulking form stepped over the threshold behind her, and Mark's eyes went from Mae's thin face to the wide-shouldered man with a tattoo of some kind on his neck—an eagle, Mark realized, talons facing out and the wings wrapping around to the back. Mark's shoulders fell—the guy was huge with a shaved head and icy blue eyes that froze Mark to the spot. This must be David—she'd thrown him in Mark's face often enough—but Mark had pictured a scrawny addict like she'd become these last few months.

"I came to get some t'ings," Mae said, her chin lifted but her eyes nervous enough to trigger Mark's protective instincts.

She'd told Mark about David early in their relationship. She'd met him when she was sixteen years old. He had been married with kids but helped fuel her growing drug problems. Four months ago, she'd said his name again in an argument—asserting that David loved her unconditionally, whereas Mark had all these expectations. That was when Mark learned David had found her again and Mae had let him into their lives. It had to be the drugs that blinded Mae to the truth about this hard man. It was Mark who loved her.

Mark swallowed and focused his attention on Mae.

"Can we talk?"

"No," David said, his voice low and gravelly in his throat. "She needs to get her stuff."

All of it? Mark wondered. Did that mean she wasn't coming back this time? The thought made him dizzy. Not that they could go on living this way either, but held on to the hope that at some point Mae would sober up. He felt pathetic to still want her after all that had happened, but the Mae he loved was still in there somewhere, and he'd convinced himself that if he could just find her, he could bring her back and they could get married, leave Canada, and make a new start. He'd lived on that fantasy for months and didn't know what he'd do without it.

Mark pulled together his courage and kept his eyes on Mae. If he could still love her after everything she'd done, she must love him too. Down deep somewhere. His voice was calm when he spoke. "Mae, can we *please* talk?"

She looked at him with anxious eyes and shook her head. She'd cut her hair short about a month ago; it made her look even younger and more vulnerable than she had before. David had to be pulling the strings and keeping her sick so that she would stay with him. The guy had to be thirty years old at least. Mae moved to step around him. "I just need to get my t'ings."

Mark reached out to touch her arm, but a thick hand shoved him hard in the shoulder, sending him flying backward into the wall shared by the living room and the bedroom. Years of high school wrestling rushed to the surface, and Mark didn't hesitate to charge back, catching David full in the chest and sending *him* to the ground. Mae started yelling, part French, part English. Mark managed to straddle David's chest before David roared and rolled him off. Wrestling skills hadn't got Mark as far as he'd like, but he didn't give up—*couldn't* give up. This was his family he was fighting for; his everything. Frustration and heartbreak rose to the surface, sharp and flaming, adding fuel to his fury and his fists.

It took two police officers to split the men up some time later—the meager furnishings of the living room broken, torn, and scattered by then; both men were bleeding and winded. David was taken down to a police car amid curses and threats, while Mark was put into cuffs and pushed onto the couch. Blood dripped from his nose, and his left eye was nearly swollen shut. He began to cry, dropping his chin against his bloody chest as though that could give him some semblance of privacy. People came and went from the apartment, but he didn't look up, embarrassed to be the guy in this situation. He had ignored his better judgment from the start with Mae, and look at the mess that had caused. His mother's voice rang in his head. "You made your bed. Good luck sleeping easy in it now."

After a few minutes an officer sat next to him on the couch and undid the handcuffs. He handed Mark a wet paper towel that Mark used to wipe the worst of the blood from his face. The front door was closed, but Mark could see people moving outside the front window—he was certain the entire complex had been awakened by the brawl. He wanted to explain that he wasn't this kind of person, he was almost a college graduate, hardworking, and from a good family. This wasn't his fault, but then it *was* his fault, wasn't it?

"I need to ask you some questions, Mr. Chadwick."

Mark nodded sheepishly, unable to meet the officer's eyes and terrified that he was going to be arrested.

"Can you confirm that David Vandersteen arrived with Mae Gérard around two o'clock this morning?"

"Yes."

"And she used her own key to gain entry to the apartment?"

"Yes."

"And did you attempt to detain Ms. Gérard?"

Mark lifted his head to look at the officer, a man in his thirties. Probably a father himself, but with a wife who took care of the kids and kissed him when he got home from work every day. "I didn't try to detain her," Mark said, shaking his head. "I wanted to talk to her, that's all. She'd come to get her stuff, she said, but she seemed scared of that guy and I needed to talk to her. We have a daughter and—is Sienna okay?"

A new level of dread lashed through him like a prairie thunderstorm. He'd left Sienna asleep on the bed and hadn't thought about where she was since. He tried to stand, but the officer pulled him down. "Mae and your daughter have gone to a neighbor's apartment. The child *is* your daughter?"

Mark stiffened. "Of course she's my daughter."

"You're listed on the birth certificate?" the officer pressed.

"Yes," Mark said. "I can show it to you."

The officer let him go to the drawer in the bedroom where Mark kept all the important papers. He sifted through the papers until he found the longer birth certificate, the one with both his and Mae's names listed—the other birth certificate didn't have any parent information. He noticed blood on his shaking hands and hoped it was David's. The neighbor Mae had taken Sienna to wasn't Jill, was it? That woman would burn in hell for drawing Mae back into addiction. Mae had smoked weed with her in the beginning, and that seemed to spark the desire for speed and some other pills that Jill was no doubt dealing. It was when she needed something harder than what Jill had to offer that Mae had called David. He could burn in hell too. And Mae . . . Mark still wanted to hope that she could get over this.

The officer looked over the certificate and then up at Mark, concern in his eyes. "You're not married to Ms. Gérard?"

Mark shook his head, embarrassed all over again. Explaining that they weren't married so that Mae could get better government assistance did nothing to make him feel like a decent person.

"And you're American."

"I'm a permanent resident here. I have that paperwork too." He started to stand, but the officer waved him back to the couch.

"Mr. Chadwick," the officer said, handing the birth certificate back to him. "Do you understand the precarious nature of your situation?"

Mark swallowed. "Am I under arrest?" He couldn't go to jail . . . the very idea made his blood run cold.

"No," the officer said. "But Ms. Gérard has indicated that she has renewed a former relationship with Mr. Vandersteen and has every intention of severing ties with you."

Mark's stomach sank, and he blinked back the tears rising in his eyes. "What about Sienna?" Mark asked, once he had enough control to speak. When Mae had started disappearing for days at a time, first two, then three, then a week, she had left Sienna behind. He wanted Sienna with him, but he'd had to call in to work twice already when Jamie, an older woman on disability who lived two doors down, hadn't been able to babysit during the weird hours he worked—three a.m. to three p.m. He had been looking for a job with normal hours for a few weeks and had an interview at a meat-packing company tomorrow afternoon. Or, rather, today.

The officer continued, "You have a daughter together, but you are unmarried and Ms. Gérard is the mother and a Canadian citizen. Do you understand what that means?"

Mark looked up again and shook his head.

"You are not a citizen, Mr. Chadwick. If not for accounts from your neighbors, as well as Ms. Gérard, about what took place tonight, you would likely be in the backseat of a police car just like Mr. Vandersteen is right now. Were you to be convicted of assault, you would lose your residency and be kicked out of this country. Permanently."

He held Mark's eyes, and Mark stared back at him as the bitter knife of reality twisted in his gut. "What about my daughter?"

"That is precisely the point I am making, Mr. Chadwick. Your parental rights do not supersede the laws of this country." He paused, compassion softening his features. "Ms. Gérard's record is familiar to us, as is Mr. Vandersteen's, but at present we do not have cause to remove your daughter from her mother's care. The next time Ms. Gérard is arrested could be the time she does lose custody; you need to be ready for that by proving yourself a capable caretaker—if you can show you're committed to staying in Canada, all the better. Your daughter is going to need a stable influence, and you won't be much help to her back in the States."

31

Sienna

My whole body is throbbing when I let myself into the hotel room Tyson is paying for. I drop the scratch papers full of notes from the library on the dresser just inside the door. I've read every article linked to my mother and learned more truth in a couple of hours there than I had from a lifetime at home.

I am angry and hurt and confused and so very tired that I also feel dizzy and nauseated. It's a relief to focus on the physical pain right now instead of the grinding anxiety and dread I felt as I read about Maebelle Gérard—a stranger in every way except the face that stared back from different mug shots. I'll go through the notes when my head feels clearer—I want to put together a time line of her life. Once I have her birth certificate in a couple of days, I'll have her parents' names, and maybe I can use them to find other relatives who can help fill in the blanks— so many blanks. The woman Dad told me stories about and nudged me to emulate has been packed into a trunk like an item you can't throw out but have no use for—a cubic zirconia you thought was a real diamond, the handmade quilt you prized until you find a MADE IN CHINA tag.

I think of Dad and want to cry and scream and reach out to him all at the same time. I have as many questions about him now as I do about her. Did you know she was seventeen when you met her? Did you feel like a hypocrite every time you told me to save myself for marriage and always tell the truth? Yet it's his shoulder I can see myself crying on. And when I take him out of that image, because I can't turn to him the way I have in every other hardship I've ever faced, there is no one to take his place. No one has loved me the way Dad loves me. No one has betrayed me the way he has, either.

I brace the palm of my left hand on the counter in front of the sink and drop my chin to my chest. I'm flushed with heat, like I have the flu or something, and I'm holding my right arm tight in that broken wing position, trying to get some relief from the relentless pain. I must have forgotten to take ibuprofen this morning, and I didn't bring any in my purse this morning, because I hadn't expected I would be gone this long.

I take a breath and pull myself out of the mire that has been sucking at me for hours. I can't trust my thoughts, because I am at my physical and emotional limit. I need to focus on some short-term goals: I need food, a pain pill, and some sleep. Then I'm going to the house where Mae was living when she disappeared—David Vandersteen's house at the time. I need to *see* something tangible. Stand where she stood. Maybe the home owners will let me walk through it. If Mae lived there, I lived there too, right? What if I remember something about the house? The thought gives me goose bumps and makes me want to skip the nap, but I know that's not possible. I already feel as if I'm moving a few steps behind my body.

I eat a few chips left in the bag I bought at the front desk when I checked in yesterday. It would take only a few minutes to go back downstairs and buy something else from the little shelves of snack items—a protein bar would be a good choice—but it feels like a lot of work to leave this room and go down a flight of stairs and make a decision and go to the counter . . . not doing it. I open my pill bottle and tap one white pill into my hand, then stare at it for several seconds. Maebelle Gérard went to jail three times between her eighteenth birthday and being found in the Grand River a few months before she would turn twenty-one, twice for possession and once for . . . prostitution. She was nineteen when she was arrested for solicitation—I would have been thirteen months old—and she said she had done it to get money for drugs. A crack whore. My mother.

Had she left me with David when she went out that night? I'd seen his mug shots too—big, broad, hard, and with a huge eagle tattooed on his neck as though it was coming out of his skin, talons first. I wonder if the wings touch at the back of his head or if there's a space there. I wonder if he's still alive and if I have the guts to try to find him if he is. He knew my mother. He knew me. I think back to the imagining I've always had of meeting someone who knew her and hearing them say, "You look so much like your mother." That possibility is so different now. I'm scared of finding him—he doesn't seem like the kind of man I'd want anything to do with—but his is the only name connected to Maebelle's that I've found so far.

Or maybe I was with Dad the night my mom tried to sell herself for drugs. The article about her death said she and Dad were estranged. Would Dad have been in his apartment making dinner for me while my mother was looking to trade sex for money? Did he hate her? That thought frightens me as much as David Vandersteen and his eagle tattoo. I have always believed that my parents shared a tragic romance and that he still loved her after all these years—I've believed that's why he never married again, because he couldn't make room in a heart still so full of Mable. Remembering the lies I made up because of the lies I was told makes Dad feel like a stranger. A person I've never met before. The kind of man who shacks up with a seventeen-year-old girl and gets her pregnant. The kind who makes up a totally different woman to put on a pedestal for me. Was it embarrassment that made him do it? Shame? Fear?

I fill a glass with water from the bathroom sink and take the pill, then text Beck that all the travel has caught up with me and I'm going to take a nap. I should call and give her a fuller update but I'm too . . . embarrassed? Is that the right word? And what, exactly, am I embarrassed about? That Mom was an addict? A prostitute? That Dad made up a different mother for me to know? That I fell for it? Yes, I determine—all those reasons. My mother was not who I believed she was, so where does that leave me? I'm not genetically predisposed to law-abidingness or domesticity or all the other virtues I was led to believe my mother prized. What *am* I genetically predisposed to? Who was I supposed to be before I was told to live up to a very different expectation?

I climb between the starchy hotel sheets and pull the coverlet up under my chin, praying that I will wake up with a clearer head. The information I'm uncovering—the truth—is like one of those Russian nesting dolls; story hidden inside story hidden inside story hidden, except that each layer gets uglier, the images get darker, the faces drawn into more and more disturbing expressions that make me want to stop opening the next doll. But I won't stop. I deserve to know those layers even if they aren't pretty. I deserve to know all the dolls hiding inside me.

32

Mark

October 1996

"Mae," Mark said with his hands balled into fists at his sides and a lump in his throat. "It's my weekend."

She narrowed her eyes still smeared with yesterday's makeup and tucked her straight black hair behind her ears. Her hair was unwashed, as was the tank top she was wearing without a bra. Bright blue sweats hung on her boney hips. He barely recognized her as the woman he'd once thought he'd grow old with. "It's only your weekend because I said it was your bloody weekend and I've changed my mind, so it isn't your weekend anymore. You play nice, I play nice." She slammed the door. A few seconds later she slammed another door inside the house. The sound of her laughter came from the window to Mark's left, likely as she recounted what she'd just said to Mark—how she'd put him in his place. A man's voice laughed with her, and the tips of Marks ears burned.

Mark stared at the door and forced his hands to relax. *Be calm,* he told himself. *She wants to make you mad. Don't you dare give her what she wants.* There had been too much of her getting what she wanted already. It was killing him.

One.

Two.

Three.

Four.

Five.

Six.

Seven.

Eight.

Nine.

Ten.

He hadn't seen Sienna in a month because Mae had refused his previous weekend too. Why hadn't Sienna run to the door as she had the last time? He wasn't leaving without at least seeing his daughter. He knocked on the door again, softly this time as a way to test that they couldn't hear him. No one answered. He waited another minute. Then two. A gust of wind came around the side of the square little house where this guy used to live with his wife and kids. David wasn't even divorced and Mae was shacking up with him.

He waited several seconds, then knocked one more time. He could go to an ATM and get forty dollars as a peace offering—though she wanted one hundred—but he'd be broke until payday next week. He shouldn't have to pay more than the three hundred dollars they'd already agreed to when everything fell apart. But there was no court order that laid out the terms, and she was the mom and the citizen. Mark had tried to go about it the legal way, but she ducked and weaved and threatened until he put up his hands and took what he could get. The things the police officer had told him well over a year ago terrified him, so he clung to the idea that one of these days Mae would be arrested again, and this time Mark would be ready. He had Sienna's birth certificate, long and short version, his own residency papers, and pay stubs and rent receipts to prove he was upstanding. He'd gotten the job at the meat-packing plant, and though he hated it beyond what he'd thought possible, it wouldn't be forever. Just until. The police knew he was Sienna's dad, and if Mae went to jail, custody would revert to him. Then he'd leave Canada if he could. If he couldn't, he'd work toward citizenship and leave Hamilton, at least. There was a daycare center down the street that already took Sienna on the workdays when he had her. Sometimes Mae would drop her off for a week—thirteen days once—and each time he hoped that she wouldn't come back. But she always did. Sienna was two and half now, old enough that she was becoming accustomed to this chaos. He'd hoped he'd have custody before she started making memories. With each new understanding of the world and awareness of her place in it, the chance to give her the safe and happy life she deserved moved farther away. He looked ahead at her starting school with Mae as her primary parent, of being ten years old in this mess. A teenager surrounded by Mae's disgusting life. He was a fool to think his steady presence would protect her from anything if she stayed in Mae's care.

With the second knock unanswered, Mark took a breath and tried the knob. It turned, and he pushed the door open slowly, revealing, one inch at a time, the life Mae had chosen over the one he had begged her to live with him. The house was a wreck, mismatched furniture in the living room, green shag carpet, strewn clothes, kitschy crap, and a few toys mixed in—like an indoor yard sale. It smelled like smoke; cigarette and pot and something else he didn't know.

His daughter *lived* here.

He closed the door silently behind him, then stopped in the entryway in order to identify the sounds coming from down the hall. At first he thought the grunting and breathing was the TV, then wished it were when he realized what was happening on the other side of that door. He continued farther into the house, trying to ignore the breaking of his heart. Had Mae been different when they'd met, or had he just been too blinded by love and lust and freedom to see her for what she was? Even after all this time—she'd left him almost a year and a half ago—he did not know the answer.

Not my business . . . anymore.

Focus.

Where is Sienna?

He was determined to remain a part of Sienna's life no matter what it took out of him to deal with Mae. His dad hadn't given him the same consideration, but Mark was different. Sienna wouldn't wonder what it was about her that made her not worth sticking around for. She would know, every day, that she mattered. That he loved her. That she was worth any sacrifice.

"CC?" he whispered, scanning the living room to his left as he moved slowly toward the back of the house, the sex noises making him sick and the fear of being discovered inside David's house making his heart pound like hooves in a stampede. "Sienna?"

His heart rate picked up even more when she didn't answer. What if she wasn't here? Was Mae demanding money she knew Mark didn't have to disguise the fact that Sienna wasn't here for him to pick up? Where else would she be? With David's wife and kids?

Focus.

Look around.

Don't jump to conclusions.

With tentative steps, he moved past the living room and kitchen—an absolute disaster with dishes piled on the countertops and in the sink. Sienna wasn't in there. His mouth was so dry he felt as though he could spit sand. Why wasn't she answering his call? Could his daughter have been left with some druggy friends of Mae's?

There was a door across the hall from the noisy room; it had to be another bedroom. He turned the knob and pushed the door open. No crib. Just a twin-sized bed and a pink dresser with clothes overflowing the drawers. Sienna was asleep amid the pile of blankets on the mattress, and the vise in his chest released. A little. That she could sleep through Mae's yelling and slamming the front door in Mark's face and the noise coming from across the hall was proof of how ordinary this was to her.

"CC," he said as loud as he dared when he crossed the room and slid his arms underneath her. She stirred but didn't wake as he cradled her in his arms. He brushed the tangled dark hair from her face, covered in freckles like Mae's but sweet and bright where Mae's was growing more gray and gaunt each time he saw her. Sienna snuggled into him, and he adjusted her so that her head rested on his shoulder. He didn't even think about what he should do as he turned and left the room and then the house. He'd pawn his TV and get the hundred dollars Mae wanted if she freaked out over this, but maybe she'd get so shit-faced she wouldn't remember telling him that he couldn't take Sienna. It was his weekend after all—outlined on the schedule he'd typed up at the library months ago and made her sign—a copy for each of them. He kept vigilant records of his visits, when he paid his support, and the times Mae refused him his visits in case he ever needed to offer proof. He had to find a way to get the courts involved . . . only would they see things his way?

He pulled the front door closed softly, then all but ran for the car, afraid at any minute that David and his eagle neck tattoo would come charging after him. What would Mark do if that happened? The fear of it made him dizzy.

No one came, however, and within a minute Sienna was buckled into her car seat and he was on his way home.

That just happened, he told himself as he came to a halt at the first stop sign on his way out of the neighborhood. He'd walked right into that guy's house and *taken her,* just like that. There was something invigorating about the success, and he thought about driving back to Wyoming right now. What would Mae do? Could he do it? What if he couldn't cross the border without some kind of permission from Mae? What if he got arrested and they took Sienna away and it made this mess even messier?

He focused on taking deep breaths and being attentive to the cars around him so that the rush of adrenaline wouldn't over-take his other senses. If Mark were arrested or deported, he could lose Sienna forever, and yet he was risking exactly that by taking her this way.

He went through three lights, turned right at the Texaco onto Marlboro Street, then right onto Hutchins.

It wasn't until he parked in front of his apartment building and was taking Sienna out of the car seat that he wondered how she could still be asleep. It had worked in his favor that she hadn't been crying or babbling, but it was six o'clock. Even if she hadn't taken a nap today, a two-year-old shouldn't be so tired at this time of day.

He held her against him as they entered the apartment and flipped on the light. He locked the door behind him, and his heart spasmed to imagine what would happen if Mae called the cops on him. They'd be able to tell she was high, though, right? So that ought to protect him. But what if it didn't?

Focus.

"CC," he said in a soft voice once he was sitting on the couch. He laid her across his lap, supporting her head with his left arm while he finger-brushed her hair off her face, hoping to wake her up. "CC, sweetie."

She made a soft mewing sound and licked her lips as she snuggled closer into his chest. He could see her eyes moving behind her pale eyelids.

She smelled terrible, like Mae's place, but when he leaned in for a closer sniff, he recognized the tang of vomit and a medicinal smell he couldn't identify until he sniffed it a second, and then third time. Vodka?

Holy crap.

The spiral he'd been in got tighter, cinching around his chest as he blinked back tears. She'd given Sienna booze. So she'd sleep? So she wouldn't run for the door and cry when Mae wouldn't let her go with Mark?

Mark forced himself to remain calm and ran a bath so that he could wash his semiconscious daughter. The warm water roused her, and she woke up whimpering and a little panicked. He comforted her as best he could, crooning to her about black birds singing in the dead of night while he washed and rinsed her hair twice with the baby shampoo that smelled like strawberries. When the bath was finished and she smelled like his little girl again, he wrapped her in a towel, sat on the couch, and held her close as the sun went down on the other side of his window, turning the room to copper, while tears rolled down his cheeks. *Please,* he prayed, though he knew he didn't deserve much help from God. Sienna did, though. He could pray on her behalf, couldn't he? *Please help me save her from this.*

Sienna's whimpers turned to cries as she became more alert around nine o'clock. He made her eat some Cheerios, which she then threw up all over both of them. He bathed her again, dressed her in one of his T-shirts, wrapped her in a clean blanket, and got her to drink some grape juice that she didn't throw up. He gave her some children's Tylenol because she likely had a hangover headache. She was two. After she'd kept down a graham cracker, he bundled her up, put her in the stroller he'd gotten at Goodwill, and took her for a walk in the cold dark he hoped would clear both their heads. The crisp night seemed to wake her up even more, and it did his heart good when she started babbling. He began the game of "Do you see a tree? Do you see a house?" that they often played on walks, praising her when she pointed out what he'd told her to look for. When they got home, he gave her more grape juice and fixed her a peanut butter and honey sandwich. He wished he'd thought to get her some Gatorade when they passed the gas station at the corner. The few times he'd been drunk, he'd found the electrolytes helped him recover.

They watched the *Barney* episodes he'd recorded on the VCR, and finally Sienna was tired enough to go to sleep. He tucked her into his bed, sang "You Are My Sunshine" until she was snuggled up beneath the covers, then tiptoed out of the room.

He sat on the couch for what seemed like a really long time, with only the sound of other doors in the apartment complex and cars passing on the street breaking the silence. *I have to do something,* he told himself after going over everything a dozen times.

He didn't dare call the police. If Mae managed to turn the situation around and the emphasis came down on his sneaking Sienna out of the house, he could end up in more trouble than he could get himself out of.

Could he hire an attorney? He was an immigrant here and made only a dollar over minimum wage. Could he petition the court without an attorney? And what would his proof be that he was more fit than Mae? Mae had several arrests but nothing in the last thirteen months. She was the mom. She was the citizen.

He had a few friends here in Hamilton, but not the kind he could go to for help. What could they do anyway? Help him

WHATEVER IT TAKES 199

hire a lawyer? Would he spend a thousand bucks and end up with nothing? He'd heard stories.

Eventually he ruled out every option except one.

Mom answered on the third ring.

"Mark." The tone was concerned and careful—it was almost midnight, after all, and they hadn't talked for months—not since she'd told him to cut his losses and come back to Wyoming. "That woman's going to string you along for the rest of your life, holding that child like a damn carrot in front of your nose. Give it up," she'd said. But giving "it" up was giving Sienna up, and Mark couldn't do that. But he couldn't do this, either. Mom was tough and she was pissed about the choices he'd made, but she loved him fierce too, and at the end of the day, he didn't have anyone else.

"Hey, Mom." He tried to control the quiver in his voice so that he wouldn't come across as weak—she had no tolerance for tears. But he *was* weak. And he was sinking. He scrubbed a hand over his face in an attempt to get control of himself.

"Mark?" The increased concern made his insides feel melty. "What's going on?"

Emotion rose up in his throat despite his attempts to bank it, stinging his nose and breaking him down even more. "Things are a mess up here. I don't know what to do anymore."

33

Sienna

I dream about starfish and volcanos and cars weaving in and out of traffic. Tyson is chasing me in another car, and I'm looking for Grandma Dee, who wrote me a letter that told me she was sorry. I want to hear her say it, but I can't find her and the sun is going down. I wake up shivering beneath the covers. At first I think it's because of the dream, but then realize I must not have turned on the heat before I went to sleep. Canada was colder than Wyoming in April, and that is saying something, because it certainly wasn't warm in Wyoming.

I tell myself that my shoulder is feeling better, but I sit up slowly, holding my arm tight to my ribs. The digital clock next to the bed says it's 7:08 p.m., and I stare at it, confused. I slept for six hours? I'm disappointed not to feel renewed energy and motivation, but there's still time for me to see the house. In fact, maybe this time of day is perfect. Whoever owns the house now will likely be home in the evenings—will they let me walk through? All those times Grandma Dee talked about the timelessness of land and the stability of property, how energy and memory stay connected to places. Suddenly that has more impact.

By the time I've used the bathroom and finger-combed my hair—I can't manage a ponytail—I am breathing hard and feeling dizzy. I haven't eaten anything other than those chips, but the idea of food makes me even dizzier. My arm aches and the rest of my body throbs in time with the pulse I can feel in my neck. I promise myself a solid meal after I see the house—there's a burger joint on the corner. And then I'll take another pain pill so that I'll get a good night's sleep. That's all I need—food and rest. I'm tempted to take another pain pill now, but it won't do any good for me to show up on a stranger's doorstep slurring my words.

I order an Uber and sit under a light on the metal steps of the motel while I wait, shivering and telling myself a dozen times to wait inside and talking myself out of it a dozen times because I'm cold only on the outside. Inside I'm too hot. It crosses my mind that I might have a fever—I'll deal with that later too. I've decided not to wear the sling. I worry it will distract people, and it's weird enough already for me to show up on a stranger's porch. The car pulls up—a dark gray Hyundai—and I let myself into the backseat and hand over the paper where I've scribbled the address: 359 Ridley Way Drive. I'm glad I'm not driving— it's nearly dark, and I'm too overwhelmed to find my way.

The driver reads the address, then nods and puts the car into drive. "I know where it is." His words are lilty and choppy at the same time. Middle East. Maybe he is a terrorist. Maybe he has five kids and works full time in a call center, then drives Uber in the evenings to pay for the kids' dental work.

I imagine myself telling Dad that I'm going to the house he was at the night Mom disappeared. See how much I know? I want to tell him. See what I learned on my own because I couldn't come to you? My stomach burns with angry pain, and I shift to find a more comfortable position. I lean my head against the back of the seat and wish I would stop shivering. Instead, I fall asleep, waking up when the man staring at me in the rearview mirror asks if I'm all right.

The car has come to a stop on a suburban street. I blink and look around as though I might recognize something that will orient me to where I am. Then I remember I've come to the house where Mom lived. Where Mom *and* I lived.

"Miss?"

"Yes, I'm fine." I force a smile and reach automatically for the door with my right hand, sending a jolt of electric pain down my arm and side. I must have made a sound of some kind. Uber man turns in his seat so that he can look at me directly, his dark eyebrows pulled together in concern. He is wearing a Cubs hat and has a big, ugly mole the size of a nickel on the right side of his face.

"You are ill?"

"No, no, no, no, no, no." I stop the repetitive answer and shake my head. "My arm is hurt, that's all. I forgot."

He continues watching me as I reach across my body with my left hand and open the door. I swing my legs over the side of the seat and set my feet firmly on the ground before I stand, using the door to help me. I'm letting my nerves get the better of me. "Could you . . . stay?" I turn to look at him, suddenly afraid of doing this alone. What if the people don't let me in? What if they aren't home?

"You could order me a second time," he says, nodding toward the phone in my hand. "I drive around the block and come back."

It's a reasonable solution, and I lean my left side against the open door while I order a ride through the app. He looks on his phone, confirming the pickup, I assume. Once he's accepted the request, I put my full weight on my legs again, steadying myself with the car door. The drugs won't shake off, but wouldn't the pain be gone if that were the case?

Focus.

I shut the car door and watch my feet as I walk onto the curb and then the cracked cement of the sidewalk that leads to the house. I am halfway up the walk before I stop and look at the house. Squat. Square. Dingy red brick. With a metal roof and lights on inside. I look closely at things like the texture of the bricks and the railing on the porch, thinking maybe there's an infant's memory of this place hidden deep within me. No recognition comes forward, and I feel a tingle in my nose as disappointment tries to show itself in tears. I had hoped I'd remember something. I try to picture my mom playing with me in this front yard, but I don't know the woman in the memory. I don't know how to fit her in. The mother I've been told about all my life would have played with her toddler, but then that mother wouldn't have left my father and done drugs and lived with a married man. I don't know what kind of mother Maebelle Gérard was to me.

The flower beds around the house haven't been tended, for years maybe. The border made of bricks is uneven and missing a stone now and then like a set of bad teeth. There is a sagging chain-link fence surrounding the backyard, but the links have detached on one side, leaving a hole big enough for a Great Dane to fit through. Surely the house was in better shape twenty-three years ago, though. The mother I've been told about liked things neat and her favorite color was yellow—she wouldn't like a house like this.

Exhaustion and nausea seem to put their hands on my chest, holding me back and making me question why I have come to a crappy house in a dreary part of a city I do not know. The article said that Dad and Grandma Dee had picked me up for an overnight visit the night Maebelle Gérard disappeared. Dad had walked up this sidewalk. Stood on this porch.

The Uber pulls away from the curb, and I start walking toward the front door again, unsure how long I've been stopped in the middle of the sidewalk. The shivering is a continual little hum inside me that makes me feel as if I am powered by a small motor. Like a robot. Doing what I have to do without thinking about the why.

> *Who has seen the trembling?*
> *When the leaves hang wind?*

I reach into my jacket pocket to touch the Canadian twenty-dollar bill I plan to offer if I need to. "I lived here when I was a baby," I say in my mind, preparing to say it out loud to the homeowner. "Could I just walk around? For nostalgia's sake? You don't need to tidy up or anything." How weird is my request? Not too weird, I tell myself with conviction. I'd let someone walk around the ranch for twenty bucks. Grandma Dee wouldn't. She'd tell them to get the hell off her property.

There were three stairs leading up to the postage-stamp porch, with a wrought-iron railing on one side. If it had been on the left I'd have used the rail to help pull myself up the steps, but the railing is on my right and I have to keep that arm tight against my chest—it is absolutely screaming after the attempt to open the car door. I take the steps slow, matching the cadence to my breathing. One step. Two step. Three step.

I hear the sound of a TV and smell . . . spaghetti? I ring the doorbell despite a spike of nerves. Twenty bucks, I remind myself. Do Canadians use the term *bucks*? I'd better say twenty dollars just in case. Do they hate Americans up here?

The door is pulled open by a teenage girl who looks . . . familiar? Light brown hair. Narrow shoulders. Angst-ridden expression. This recognition freezes me for a moment and makes me wonder if I accidently *did* take another pain pill before I left the hotel. Or maybe she just looks like every teenage American girl I've ever met and I expected her to look different from them.

"Hey," the girl says, staring at me without a smile. Her hair is flat against her head, greasy near the part, and she's got acne spattered along her forehead and chin.

"Hi," I say back. I feel the prickle of sweat along my hairline even though I'm still shivering from the cold. "Is your mom or dad here?"

The girl looks at me another minute, then turns partway back to the house. "Mom!"

I hear a grumbled response, but then the girl turns to stare at me while we wait for her mom, and I watch as her expression begins to make me think I'm familiar to her, too. Do I look like the quintessential American the same way she looks like the quintessential teenage girl? Before I can puzzle it out, the teenager is replaced in the doorway by a larger silhouette, momentarily backlit by the lights from inside the house until the woman— presumably the mom—steps forward. I meet the woman's eyes, and something goes through me like lightning. The woman has light blue eyes with a thin black ring around the iris.

"Yeah?" the woman says in a punchy voice. She pulls the sides of her long sweater closed over a grayed-out black T-shirt and multicolored leggings that cling to her lumpy thighs. No shoes. Teal chipped nail polish on her toes. Her hair is a reddish blond, the kind you end up with when you use a cheap color kit on dark hair. There is half an inch of gray along the woman's part, and I doubt that lightning bolt I felt. She looks nothing like me except for those eyes that are uncomfortably similar to mine.

The woman raises her penciled eyebrows. "Can I help you?"

My thoughts have been shaken up like a box of Tic Tacs. Did I come to see this woman? No, I came to see the house. I have a Canadian twenty-dollar bill in my pocket. "Um, hi, my name is Sienna Chadwick. I, well, my mom lived here a long time ago, when I was a baby, and I . . ." This is weird. The woman is looking at me as if I'm a lunatic, and I'm not so sure she's wrong. I can feel my heart racing. My head is hot, and the dizziness is getting worse. I force myself to look away from her eyes. "Can I see your house?"

The woman's face puckers, and she pulls her head back, making a double chin out of the chub of her neck. "See my house?"

"Look around," I say quickly, trying to remember that this sounded reasonable when I left the hotel. "I want to know if I might remember something. I—I know it sounds weird. I just . . ."

The woman's expression changes in an instant. The lines soften as her eyes become more fixed. "Who are you?" the woman says in a low tone. I can feel something poised behind the question like a cat.

"Sienna. Sienna Chadwick."

"Your mom *lived* here? When?"

"Um, about twenty-three years ago." I don't know how much more to say.

The woman curses as though I've given the wrong answer. She takes a step backward into the house as though the physical strangeness I'm feeling might be contagious. "Get Grandpa," the woman says to her daughter, who had been hanging back throughout the conversation.

The teenage girl disappears.

Grandpa?

I blink at the woman, trying to make sense of her reaction until my eyes are drawn past her to the hallway with worn parquet flooring. I can see the threshold into another room with . . . green shag carpet like the carpet in that memory of me and Beck stacking cans when we were little. I look back at the woman in front of me. The memory is of *Beck*. But Beck had blue eyes in the memory. Same as me. Oh, my gosh!

A man suddenly blocks my view of this woman with eyes like mine, standing in a house with carpet from a childhood memory that no longer makes sense to me. Or makes more sense. The man steps forward until he fills the doorway. He has huge shoulders, a bald head, and a hideous tattoo on his neck. I stare at the tattoo and wonder if the wings touch at the back of his neck, or if there's a space there. I had wondered the same thing when I stared at a mugshot from more than twenty years ago when the lines of the tattoo were more crisp. They look blurry now, as though after finishing the artwork the artist brushed their hand over it, smearing the lines. I look up from the tattoo to meet his eyes and hear myself gasp as he stares me down, his gaze narrowed and searching, and then his face opening as though he's solved something.

"Tristin, get back to your dinner," he says without looking at the woman. He crosses his big, muscular arms over his chest and smiles at me in a way that makes me want to back up. "Well, whaddya know, you look just like her."

A breeze spins around the house, pulling at my hair. "You know me?"

"Sierra, right?"

"Sienna."

"Oh yeah, that's what *he* chose. She wanted Sierra."

He . . . Dad? She . . . Mom?

I can't remember what I've come here to ask—oh, yeah, to walk through the house. But that was because I thought the people living here would be strangers, maybe the second or third owners since Maebelle disappeared and was found in a river. My senses are popping, like wires shorting out. "You're . . . David Vandersteen?"

"Uh, yeah," he says as though that's obvious. Which it is. But still, I'm scrambling.

"You knew my mom, Mable—Maebelle Chadwick?"

"Chadwick?" He barks out the name, then sobers quickly, still staring at me in a way that makes me want to curl my shoulders in and try to hide. I resist taking a step backward in hopes that a few more inches could dilute this man's intensity. The hum in my chest has turned to a thrum, a tribal beat that feels like a warning I cannot heed. "*He* told you she married him?"

I nod, then shake my head. I know they didn't marry—it just came out wrong. I look past him into the house, remembering why I've come. I'm not sure I want to go inside anymore, though. I look over my shoulder; the gray Hyundai is at the curb, which makes me feel better. I swallow and draw up my courage as I look back at Mr. Vandersteen. I can't think of him as David, like we're friends. I remember that I considered looking for him while I was in Canada; it just happened differently than I was ready for. "My mom lived here before she died—with you, right?"

"*When* she died. I bet he didn't tell you anything about that, either, did he?"

I feel a snap in my head. "What?"

"How'd you find me?"

"An article, uh, from the night she died. This was where she'd been living before she disappeared."

"He didn't tell you anything, then?"

"He? My dad?"

He stares at me, and something sharp and prickly begins turning in my stomach. Dad had told me that Mom died of breast cancer, not a drug overdose. Dad had told me that Mom's name was Mable, not Maebelle. Gerrard not Gérard. Married. In love. Happy. "I don't know what you're talking about," I say.

"I'll bet you don't." He said the words in a slithery kind of way, part angry, part arrogant, part wanting to hurt me. Why?

"When he always said he wanted to take care of her, I thought he meant something different, but I guess you never can tell, can you?" The smug smile was gone, and the briefest wave of sorrow struck his eyes. Blue eyes. Light blue, with dark rings around the irises. He leans toward me, and I pull back. *This* is the kind of man who lies—I can't trust anything he says. Except Dad is apparently that kind of man too. A whooshing nausea upsets my balance when he speaks again, his voice low as though he's telling a secret. "Funny thing about needles—you never can tell who pushes the plunger. Mae knew her limit and she didn't waste a drop."

I feel as though my brain is blocking the information even as realization of what he's saying rises like the sun over the eastern plain. I wish in this moment that I'd never left the ranch. He's implying that . . . I can't say the words even to myself.

Popping lights at the edge of my vision herald the thrumming turning into a throbbing. I think back to one of a hundred memories of Dad drawing medicine of one kind or another into one of the thousands of syringes we use for the cattle on the ranch. I see the way he fluidly draws back the plunger, holds the needle to the sky, and flicks the shaft until the bubbles rise to the top so he can squeeze them out, sometimes spurting a drop or two of the serum in the process. Dad turns in this memory, holding the cow with one hand and using the other to drive in the tiny metal needle as smooth and as certain as an arrow cutting through water. A quick jolt on the cow's part and that was that. The needle goes into the sharps container. Dad goes on to the next animal.

The porch tilts beneath my feet, and another breeze grabs at my hair and the collar of my coat like hands trying to pull me away from here. From him. I'm nearly knocked off balance while the man with the neck tattoo who is named David Vandersteen stares at me with my eyes and smiles. "Yeah, it's coming together for you, isn't it? They took care of her, all right."

They.

Oh God, I say in my mind as a desperate prayer for Him to hold me up right now. I thought being lied to was the worst part. I thought nothing could be worse than learning who my mother really was. But this . . . Oh God, I plead again.

I finally take that step away from the intensity still pouring off David Vandersteen like copious sweat, pooling at my feet and sticking me in place. But there's nothing beneath my foot when I go to set it down. I realize the porch has run out at the same time I automatically reach for the railing with my right hand. Heat and pain rip through my side and chest, and the throbbing I've felt all day breaks open to a howl that goes deeper than the physical. David Vandersteen startles, and his arms, which have been crossed over his chest, drop. I snatch my right hand back to my chest, stumble for footing that is not to be found, and fall backward, twisting in the air so that I land hard on my left side against the pitted sidewalk. There's a crunch, the sounds of voices coming toward me, a moan from my own throat, and then silence.

34

Diane

October 1996

Dee resisted the desire to scowl at Mark over her shoulder as they got out of the car in front of the house where this woman was living. Tramp whore. Reckless boy. What an absolute mess.

He should have told her what was happening sooner. Months ago. *But he called you now,* a voice said in her head. She gave him credit for that; it hadn't been easy for him to admit that she'd been right about Mae. The trampy whore had been too eager to move in with him, she wouldn't get a job, and she'd lied to him about her age. Dee was glad to be here, though. It was time to get this figured out. Getting the custody arrangement into the court system was the first thing that had to be done. This leaving it all up to Mae was garbage. Dee impulsively reached behind her for Mark's hand as she started up the steps leading to the front door. She grabbed his wrist by accident instead and gave it a squeeze she hoped told him that everything would be okay. 'Cause it would be. One way or another, this would get fixed.

The door opened before they even knocked, and although Mark had told her about the man Mae was shacking up with, Diane couldn't fight the sudden panic completely. He was huge and had a hideous tattoo on his neck. This is what Satan would look like if he were a man, she thought, then pulled herself together. "We're here for Sienna."

The man looked from Dee to Mark standing a few inches behind her and smirked. "Ah, family reunion, huh?" He jerked his
head toward the inside of the house. "You might want to wait
for Mae to sober up a little—her party's just getting started."

He left the door open and pushed his way out between them,
giving Mark an extra bit of shoulder that nearly knocked him
off the porch. Equal to the flair of protectiveness that sparked in
her chest was irritation that Mark put his chin down and moved
out of the way. "Stand up for yourself," she wanted to yell at
him. At least this guy was leaving—it would be her and Mark
against Mae, and they would win. From what Mark said, this
guy didn't give Sienna a second thought. That would be on her
side too. Dee heard a car door slam behind them and looked
back just as the engine of a truck—as big and dumb as he was—
growled to life. He punched the gas and shot into the run-down
suburban street with a chirp of his tires and an explosion of
black exhaust. She was not impressed.

Dee led the way into the house, a sloppy square house with
an unimaginative layout and no personality. There was a big
blanket with a picture of a skull with roses in its eye sockets
pinned to the wall of the living room where mismatched furniture and just . . . crap was jumbled about. She saw a pink plastic
cell phone toy and felt a tug at her heart. This was where her
granddaughter was being raised? Mark said that this guy had
other kids, and a wife, too. Where were they? Where was Sienna?

Mark shut the door politely once they were inside. Dee gritted her teeth.

"Mae?" he called out, cautious and concerned. "We need to
talk."

Something clattered farther down the hall and they moved
toward it, then came to a stop in the entrance of the kitchen.
Dee wrinkled her nose. The room smelled like rotten milk, over-
ripe vegetables, and . . . vomit? She was still scanning the room
as Mark moved past her, suddenly intent.

Dee caught sight of the baby right before he blocked her view
on his way to the high chair where the child had been sitting,

silent as a bunny. Dee kept scanning the room, noting the over-turned bowl on the floor with milk seeping from beneath the edges. That must be what had caused the sound. There were dishes piled everywhere, boxes of food on the counter, and a pile of what looked like unopened bills next to an empty vodka bottle that added a medicinal smell to the room. She stepped onto the linoleum and felt her shoe stick to something on the floor. How did people live like this? How could Mark have fallen for a woman who could live this way?

Mark turned toward Dee, and she was pleased to see a little fire in his eyes. "She's got a dirty diaper," he said.

That wasn't the only thing dirty about the girl. Her face was smudged and sticky with food, and her T-shirt was stained. She had no shoes on, and the bottoms of her feet were black. This was the second time Dee had ever seen her only grandchild—the first time being a week after she was born. Dee had left Canada after a few days, grudgingly admitting that maybe Mark was going to make this work. He and Mae had seemed happy, and the baby was charming. Babies were always charming. But then, Sienna wasn't a baby anymore—she was two and a half years old, and she looked like a street urchin. There was a solid knot of feathery brown hair just over her ear. She sure had a lot of freckles for such a little girl. And she wasn't even a redhead.

The baby blinked huge blue eyes at Dee, then snuggled in under Mark's chin in a gesture of such love and trust that Dee forgot for a moment how irritated she was with her son. She crossed the room to them and reached out to stroke the little girl's arm. "Good morning, Sienna," she said. "I'm Dee . . . well, I guess I'm Grandma Dee, aren't I?" She looked up to share a smile with Mark.

Mark smiled back at her, looking taller for the pride in his eyes that sparked pride in Dee too. He was a good man despite the poor judgment that got them to this place. He was a good father, and she felt an infusion of protectiveness flush through her veins.

The little girl was part of Mark. Part of Dee. She deserved

someone to fight for her, and Dee had become pretty good at fighting.

Mark looked down at his little girl, kissed her snarly head, and then moved toward the kitchen doorway. "Mae?" he called out, his tone firmer than it had been. "We need to talk."

A mumble of words came from the bedroom. Dee turned and followed Mark out of the kitchen. They continued down the narrow hallway and came to a stop in the doorway. Mark swore and turned away. "Get dressed, Mae."

She said something obscene, but Mark was already moving back toward the living room. He met Dee's eyes, and she saw the pink in his cheeks. Was he still in love with her? After everything she'd done?

"I'm going to get Sienna cleaned up." Over his shoulder he added toward the bedroom, "Let's talk in the living room once you've got some clothes on."

Dee didn't follow him to the living room but moved into the bedroom doorway instead. The room was dark, with a sheet tacked over the window, and it took a few seconds for Diane's eyes to adjust. When they did, she saw a rail-thin version of the woman she'd met after Sienna was born stumbling around a bedroom just as disorganized and messy as the rest of the house. Mae had on purple panties, no bra, and could barely keep her balance as she leaned down to pick something up from the floor. Her hair was a mess, not much better than the baby's, and she had that hard, stretched look of an addict. This was the woman who had taken Mark's spine in her hands and twisted it into nothing? Mae finally looked up to see Dee standing there and had the decency to cross her arms over her chest. "Who are you?"

"Dee Chadwick, Mark's mother. We met after you had that baby girl." She pointed her thumb over her shoulder in the direction Mark and Sienna had disappeared.

Mae pulled back. "His mother."

"Everyone's got one," Dee said easy as you please. Did this girl not remember her? "Except maybe Sienna. This is pathetic." She waved her arm across the room.

Mae narrowed her eyes and put her hands on her hips, show-ing herself as a bony version of what had once been a woman. Dee turned around to leave but noted a section of dresser mostly cleared off that had a collection of half-full liquor bottles, a bag-gie of something, a syringe, a belt, a spoon, and a lighter. Mae shot up right here, with her daughter in the house? Was she high right now? Dee clenched her jaw as she walked back toward Mark and the baby. How on earth did he not know who this woman was when he took her to bed?

Mark was wiping down the baby's face in the kitchen, where Sienna sat on the edge of the sink. The smell of dirty diaper still hung in the air, but Dee could see the neatly folded disposable on top of the overfilled trash can in the corner. Mark made cutesy sounds at the baby and then kissed her nose. Even though Dee had come all this way to help, Mark would be stay-ing in Canada once things were settled. Sienna's pathetic excuse for a mother wasn't going anywhere, and much as Dee wanted Mark and his girl to come back to the ranch, it wouldn't hap-pen. Maybe Dee should take some pride in the fact that despite the gaps in her own parenting, her son was as devoted to his child as she was to hers. But it brought little comfort. She'd go back to Wyoming alone and maybe see this child once a year, if that.

Little Sienna laughed at Mark's antics, then threw herself for-ward when he put out his arms. Mark bounced her onto his hip and strode past Dee for the living room. Dee pivoted in place to watch as he sifted through the piles of clothes in that room until he found something cleaner than what the little girl had on al-ready. He whipped off the one shirt and threw on a different one that almost fit the tiny thing. Dee noted a dozen little bruises on the girl's legs, probably typical childhood stuff. But in a house like this, who knew what went on? Mark found a pair of black stretchy pants and had Sienna sit down so he could pull them over the bruised little legs.

"Where's his wife and kids?"

She didn't need to define who "he" was.

"She moved in with her mother."

Dee snorted. "They aren't divorced?"

"I don't know the details." He kept his attention focused on his little girl.

Dee was suddenly shoved from behind and stumbled forward, catching herself on the back of the recliner before turning stunned eyes on the mother of this poor child. Mae had put on a black sweater dress but still couldn't walk in a straight line to the couch. Disgusting. And dangerous. They should call the police, but Mark was against that. The police had been involved exactly once, and it had scared Mark half out of his head.

Mae fell onto the couch and looked at her daughter. "Come 'ere, CC," she crooned, though her words slurred. She put out her arms, but Mark picked the child up and made no move to hand her over.

"This isn't working, Mae," he said.

She blinked at him, slow and deliberate, as her hands fell into her lap and she slouched back against the couch. "What's not working?"

"This," Mark said, waving his hand around the house with its smoke-stained walls and green shag carpet. "And just . . . us."

She narrowed her dark eyes. "There's no us."

The room was silent, and Dee watched Mark wilt a bit. Idiot. She didn't intervene, because it would be better for all of them if Mark started the discussion. Still, her hands were clenched tightly at her sides.

"I mean our custody arrangement. You can't keep me from seeing her anymore."

"I don't." She yawned. "You see 'er. I mean, look, right now, you're seeing 'er."

"We're going to the family court tomorrow," Mark said. "If you come with me, we can file some papers together and make this a lot easier on all of us."

"I am not going to court."

"We need an official agreement, for Sienna's sake. I can make a petition on my own, but I would rather have us work together."

Mae sat up and glared at him. "I'm not going to court, and you are not taking my baby away."

Mark took a breath. "Mae," he said in a patient way that continued to grate on Dee's nerves. "I'm not trying to take her away. I want us to work together, but I need court-ordered visitation and child support that outlines my rights and responsibilities. I can't have you demanding more money or keeping Sienna from me when you're not in the mood to let me have my visits. When I agreed to the terms, I thought you would abide by them, but you pick and choose—"

Mae shot up from her chair and crossed the room so fast Dee barely noted the movement. She wrenched the baby out of Mark's arms, wrapping her arms around the stunned child.

"She is mine," Mae hissed, giving Dee chills. She stroked the girl's messy hair as though the child were a cat. "I am 'er mother—do you know what that means? It means that I am in charge. I make the decisions. And you coming 'ere and trying to bully me will be the worst mistake you ever made!"

After a short pause, Mark crossed to Mae almost as fast as she'd crossed to him seconds before. He grabbed Mae's hair and yanked it backward with one hand while pulling the baby back to him with the other. Mae screamed. Dee was stunned; she'd never seen Mark be violent with anyone—she didn't know he had it in him. Mae fell to the floor when Mark let go of her and moved away, looking as shocked by what he'd done as Dee was. As Mae was too. Dee motioned him into the hallway. He stepped behind Dee, bouncing from one foot to the other since the baby was crying now, though the cries were soft as she snuggled into Mark's chest. She knew she was safe with him.

With one hand on the back of her head, Mae sat up, glaring at them from her place in the center of the living room floor. And then she sprang up, like a cat or a demon. She surely expected Dee to fall back, but instead Dee grabbed her shoulder and pushed her to the side—the woman weighed nothing and was three sheets to the wind. She caught herself on the arm of the couch, regained her balance, and lunged again. Dee grabbed her wrist and twisted it painfully behind her back—all without having to move her feet.

Mae screamed, then started swearing a blue streak. Dee swallowed her rising panic, not daring to look at Mark for fear he was showing every thought on his face, which would help nothing.

Dee was as strong as any man from years of ranching and could snap this woman's arm without much effort or a moment's guilt. But she'd come here to help Mark and Sienna, and that meant doing this the right way. She pushed the woman forward, then glared at her glassy eyes once she'd turned to face them again. Mae's eyes flashed with something like angry excitement and in an instant Dee saw the future—Mark, a puppet on the end of this woman's string. Sienna, exploited and neglected. Mae in charge.

"Mark," Dee said, keeping her tone low and hard as she made the decision to take back Mark's power for him. "Take Sienna to the car. Don't come back inside."

Mark looked between the two of them, his eyes wide and his face slack. Dee all but glared at him. "Do it."

He glanced between them one more time and then took Sienna out. As soon as Dee heard the car door slam, she took a step into the room, and when Mae only lifted her chin defiantly, Dee slapped her hard enough that Mae spun back and then crumpled to the floor like a bag of sticks. She groaned and pulled her arms and legs into herself a moment, then turned back to glare at Dee, who had fire running through her veins now.

"You think this is going to 'elp, old woman?"

Dee pulled herself up straight. "He deserves that child, and you'll be fair to him or we'll turn you in for the state of that child and the state of this house. We *are* going to the courthouse tomorrow—all three of us—to present the case, and I'm not leaving until we have things sorted out, all good and legal. You understand?"

She laughed, a snorting, ugly sound that fit her as perfectly as any other sow. "I am the mother." She leaned forward, her eyes wild and her bony shoulders lifting as though they were bat wings and she was about to take flight. "I will do whatever I want, and your *son* will go along with me because 'e's still 'oping to get me back." She grinned, a wide and knowing grin that hit Dee full in the chest.

Mae used the wall to help her stand on spindly legs. "Keep Sienna tonight," she said, as though she were so very considerate. She pushed a hand through her uncombed hair. "But 'ave her back tomorrow."

"We're not bringing her back." Until Dee said it she hadn't realized she'd made that decision, but it set right with her. This woman had made Mark's life a living hell, and she wasn't ever going to be fair. Mark would jump as high as she wanted every time she issued the order. He'd have no choice. It would never end. He would never leave this place. He would never come back to the ranch.

Mae glared while she rubbed her wrist where Dee had grabbed her earlier. She raised it for Dee to see. "By tomorrow, this will be a bruise, and all it will take is a call to the cops to 'ave Mark arrested. So, bring Sienna back tomorrow, *oui?*"

"Mark is her father," Dee said through grinding teeth. "He has rights."

Mae's eyes almost sparkled as she leaned forward. "Oh, grandmother." She shook her head and laughed as though delighted. "Mark is *not* Sienna's father; 'e gets no rights that I don't let 'im 'ave."

Dee's heart hitched in her chest as the words settled like ash. A protest rose up in her throat that this was one more tactic to gain power. But absolute certainty was stamped into every element of this woman's face. Her grin got bigger, more menacing. "I've let 'im believe what 'e wants to believe because it suits me, but if you threaten me with judges and court cases, then I can just be done with all of it. You want me to tell 'im? David will take care of us now, I don't need—"

"Shut up," Dee said before the woman could say anything else. She felt sick. This woman was letting Mark believe he was Sienna's father for . . . money? Power? Control? Babysitting?

Mae laughed, a throaty sound that brought Dee's eyes back to hers. "Now, if you will excuse me *Madame* Chadwick, I have better t'ings to do." She walked past Dee, who was still standing frozen in the doorway, and went back to the bedroom. Dee stood where she was, staring at one of the roses in the eye socket of the skull on the wall, processing Mae's confession until her feet turned and made their way down the hall. She stood in the doorway and watched Mae hold a lighter underneath a spoon, like in the movies. Mae watched the contents of the spoon closely but then flicked her gaze up to see Dee and shut off the lighter. She attempted to put it all behind her back but was only mildly successful because she couldn't risk spilling the spoon. Dee looked at the section of dresser that had the other paraphernalia—the small belt, balled-up plastic wrap, another spoon, and a few syringes. That was like the movies too.

"Get out of 'ere," Mae hissed. "I 'ave better things to do than look at you."

"Glad to," Dee said, and turned to the front door. When she reached it, she pulled it open, then slammed it hard before stepping as quietly as she could into the living room. David had said Mae's party was just getting started, and if she'd only been drinking so far tonight . . . Dee pulled the drapes to the side and looked out the window to make sure Mark wasn't coming to check on her. Sienna was on his lap facing him, and they were looking at something in Mark's hands that he held open like a book.

She let the drapes fall back over the window and then stepped quietly out of the living room and back down the hall. Mae was sitting on the end of the bed, chin to her chest as though asleep, the belt wrapped three times around her upper arm. A syringe lay on the bed next to Mae's thigh, the plunger fully depressed. Dee had operated thousands of syringes just like this one. It would be nothing more than putting down a distressed animal. Survival of the fittest. Natural selection.

Dee's eyes moved to the spoon, the lighter, the crumbled plastic on the dresser. Five steps into the room, and she could confirm that within that crumpled plastic were three little crystals, like rock salt pellets. She picked up a T-shirt from the ground to use like a glove. It wasn't easy to manage the process with her hands covered, but she got the crystals into the spoon, added some water from the half-empty glass on the dresser, and flicked the lighter beneath it as she'd watched Mae do. Essentially, she was dissolving these crystals into a serum, right? Basic chemical conversion.

"Wha—wha?"

Dee looked over her shoulder to see Mae trying to focus her eyes on what Dee was doing. She lifted her right arm to fiddle with the belt on her left. Dee carefully put down the spoon and the lighter and dropped the T-shirt she was using in place of gloves. In two steps she had crossed to the woman, grabbed her by the shoulders, and spun her around. She smashed Mae hard against the door frame, held the woman's dilated eyes until they rolled back, and then dropped her to the floor. It would look as if Mae had overdosed and then hit her head on the jamb. Mae lay in a heap while Dee crossed back to the dresser to finish making the serum, encasing her hands in the T-shirt again to make sure she didn't leave any fingerprints. Her throat was dry, and her breath was shallow. *It's the right thing,* she said in her mind. It's the only way.

The water bubbled up again, turning from clear to yellow as the crystals melted. Dee retrieved the syringe Mae had used a few minutes earlier and drew it up until it was full. Then she stared at the woman lying on the floor, looking to the world as though she were asleep. The arm with the belt was paler than the rest of her.

Dee's heart felt as though it was going to burst out of her chest. She couldn't go back in time and make Mark stay at the ranch. She couldn't teach him about evil people who will use you and hurt you and kick you aside. There was no going back now, and yet a lump rose up in her throat all the same. This is a person, a human life. But why should Dee give that truth more consideration than Mae did?

Dee knelt next to Mae and pushed her onto her back. The woman moaned and kicked out one leg, but her eyelids barely fluttered open before they closed again. The arm with the belt still on it was turning blue. Dee's hand was shaking, and it was awkward to hold the syringe inside the T-shirt.

To protect Mark.

To save Sienna.

She took a breath and identified the speck of blood inside Mae's elbow that had been left by the prior injection.

No different from vaccinating a calf, Dee told herself as she looked at the vein bulging like an earthworm beneath the thin skin of Mae's arm.

35

Sienna

I can feel the difference when I wake up. My thoughts are . . . cleaner, and I'm not so cold and hot and cold and hot at the same time. I take a deep breath of sterile air and then let it out slowly as I look at the white ceiling and light green curtain set into tracks above me. The sound of beeps and feet and distant commands are taking place on the other side of the curtain. As my brain comes fully awake, the relief fades and the heaviness settles back into my chest. Time has warped in my memory, and I am pulled between wanting to move the pieces of memory into the right order and turning away from the bits and pieces I can recall; David Vandersteen's arms falling to his sides mix with a car speeding through the streets of Hamilton while I bleed all over the backseat. A fall. A woman with eyes like mine screaming. A teenage girl crying. The horn of the Uber car honking as it swerves through an intersection on a dark road. Lying on my back and looking at the leaves as the trees tremble in the wind.

I try to lift my left hand to my head. It doesn't necessarily hurt worse than the rest of me but the pain there seems important. My arm is encumbered with an IV and finger-pulse-taker-thing I recognize from the times I've woken up in recovery. I hear the zipping sound of the curtain being pulled back and look up to see a woman in purple scrubs.

"Ah, good, you're awake." Her teeth are really bright, and she's wearing lipstick that matches her scrubs.

"Am I?"

She smiles and lays a hand on my shoulder. "You're going to be okay," she says so soft and sweet that it makes me want to cry.

By the time the doctor comes a few minutes later, I know I am at Hamilton General Hospital—the same hospital where I was born. The doctor sits on a rolling stool and then pushes himself closer to the head of the bed. He meets my eyes and gives me a smile. "Good evening, Ms. Richardson, I'm Dr. Labrum. When did you have your lumpectomy and lymphadenectomy?"

Oh, right. I had breast cancer surgery. Funny how that had fallen down the list of things for me to worry about. "Uh, ten days or so ago."

He nods. "You came in for that bump on your head, but you were also septic. Do you know what that is?"

We have a septic tank at the ranch—no flushing hair combings or tampons—but that doesn't fit this conversation. I shake my head.

"It's also known as blood poisoning and can happen when there's an infection that gets into the bloodstream." He nods toward my right arm. "Did you notice your armpit incision feeling hot and tender the last few days?"

"I think so."

"Did you know you had a fever?"

I'd thought about it, but only for a second. The hot and cold and hot and cold makes more sense now. My mind flashes to the post-op instructions explaining the signs of infection. "Shit," I breathe, and close my eyes in self-disgust.

"Yeah," he says in a drawling tone. "You were 104.7 when you came in—that was your body trying to kill off the infection, but it wasn't making much progress." He stands and moves to the head of the bed, where he looks at the back of a fluid pouch connected by a tube to the IV in the back of my hand. I register for the first time that the area stings a little bit. "You were also severely dehydrated; have you been traveling? We know from your ID that you're from Wyoming—did you drive up here to Ontario?"

"I flew from Chicago, but I drove that first part."

He nodded. "Most people don't drink enough when they take road trips so that they can avoid having to take bathroom breaks."

I haven't thought about drinking enough water.

Dr. Labrum returns to the stool and smiles sympathetically. "If you'd gone back to your hotel and taken your pain pills, which I assume you are still using"—he pauses long enough for me to nod in confirmation—"and gone to sleep, you very likely would have gone into a coma as your organs shut down. You dodged one hell of a bullet by falling off that porch. You have two staples and some stitches on the back of your head as a reminder to thank your guardian angels."

A shiver goes through my chest. I picture David Vandersteen and the words I was backing away from that led to the fall.

"I would like to call your doctor and talk to him about what's going on up here."

"Her," I correct, even though I've been only half attentive to what he's saying. I remember that I have a follow-up on Thursday that I haven't thought about since I scheduled it. "Dr. Laura Sheffield in Cheyenne, Wyoming. She wasn't the surgeon, but she's the doctor who's been overseeing my . . . case."

He's writing down the information and nodding. "We're going to keep you a couple of days. Have you been staying in Hamilton?"

I nod. "In a hotel."

The documents I ordered will be ready on Wednesday—it's only Monday night. How am I going to get them?

"Ms. Richardson?"

My old name draws my attention back to the doctor, who looks as if he's waiting for me to answer a question I don't remember him asking. "We're working on getting you into a room; we need to keep you under observation for a few days and get this infection knocked down. Are you here in Hamilton alone?"

I nod.

"You're going to need help after you're released. We can call a family member or friend and explain the situation, but a call from a hospital often frightens people."

No kidding. "I can make my own calls, and I have Dr. Sheffield's number on my phone. Is my purse here?"

"The Uber driver brought it in, and we put it in a locker. I'll have someone bring it to you."

He leaves, and I relax my head back onto the pillow and stare at the white ceiling above me. There is something cold on the back of my head. Two staples and some stitches too, I guess.

I need to call someone to come to Hamilton. Check me out of the hotel. Be here when I get out. Help me get home. Take care of me. I'm too beaten by all of this to fall back on my usual determination to do things myself. I need help, and I know it.

Beck. The thought comes and goes just as quickly. I *will* call her and withstand her worry and her fear and maybe even a reprimand I deserve. But Beck doesn't have a passport.

Dad. Thinking about him makes my throat thick and tight. Up until the last few weeks, he'd have been the obvious choice, but now . . .

Tyson is the next name that comes to mind, and though my mind raises a protest, it settles quickly because there's no one else. He has a passport, and despite everything broken between us, he'll help me. Again. Because he's a good man. Because we made a promise that means something, at least for a little while longer.

36

Sienna

"CC!" Dad says on the other end of the phone call. His voice is plumb full of all the relief and gladness and happiness I expected. It's real, I can feel it, and I mourn how easy things once were between us and despair that we may never find our way back to that place.

Tears fill my eyes, and Tyson squeezes my hand. He got here a few hours ago and is managing the details like I knew he would. This detail, however, is mine to take care of. I pull my hand from his, smile, and then wave toward the door. He isn't offended by my asking him to leave. It was four a.m. in London when I called him, and he didn't even hesitate to catch the earliest flight he could. I've been in the hospital for twenty-four hours, talked to Beck three times and Dr. Sheffield twice. I can't put off calling Dad any longer.

"Gosh, I've been worried about you, kiddo," Dad says while Tyson pulls the door quietly closed, leaving me to the sterility of the room and the hums and beeps of the machinery around my bed. "Everything okay there in Chicago?"

"I'm not in Chicago, Dad." I pause for a breath. "I'm in Hamilton."

Dad is silent for six full seconds. I do not rescue him, and finally he repeats the single word. "Hamilton?" The anxiety in his voice is thick as paste.

I swallow and smooth the woven blanket over my legs. I'm shaking slightly, but I don't know if it's from nerves or meds or the lingering effects of last night. "There is a lot going on with me right now, Dad, and I'm going to explain that to you in a few minutes, but I have some questions first, and I need you to promise me that you'll tell me the truth."

"CC." He sounds so hurt and sad. I scrunch up my eyes against the sympathy rising in my chest, and the emotion making my nose burn. "Of course I'll tell you the truth. What's going on, sweetie?"

Of course. That helps strengthen my resolve.

"I need you to promise you'll tell me the truth about Mom even though you haven't told me the truth before now."

He's silent.

I open my eyes and take a breath. "I know Rachel wrote the letters, Dad. I know Mom's name is really Maebelle Gérard. I know you and Mom never married and she was only eighteen years old when I was born. I know she died of a drug overdose and that you and Grandma took me from David Vandersteen's house the last night anyone saw her alive."

The silence on the line is so deep and so heavy that I nearly hang up to be spared its intensity. Instead, I make it worse.

"Did you love my mother?"

A hushed beeping emanates from one of the machines pumping fluid and medication into my body, and a nurse laughs from the hallway.

"Oh, gosh, CC. I loved her so much." His voice breaks, and tears finally come to my eyes. I hadn't been lied to about that, then. It makes the story so much sadder, though. She did break his heart, and he never recovered. "I did everything I could, *everything,* to keep us together as a family. I wanted to marry her, I wanted—"

"Did you kill her?"

Every other sound has gone silent. I can picture Dad sitting in his favorite chair.

"CC, can you come home so we can—"

"Answer me." The words are pleading, and my voice shakes

as the emotional impact of what we are facing attaches itself to every syllable. "I deserve the truth, Dad." I hate that my voice is shaking. "The *real* truth, and if you can't tell me that, then I need to go. I came to Canada. I read the newspaper articles about Maebelle's arrests. I met David Vandersteen." I pause to take a shaky breath. "You and Grandma were the last people to see her alive. She was found in a river a few days after that. You have lied to me my whole life, but you *can't* lie to me about this, Dad, or I will never be able to believe *anything* you say. Did you kill my mother?"

He doesn't pause this time. "No."

I let out a breath and suck in another.

"Did Grandma Dee?"

A pause. A breath. "CC, we need to—"

"Tell me!" I shout, a sob rising in my chest. "Tell me or I'm hanging up." That I am saying these words to Dad is yet another knife wound in my belly. And in his.

Another pause. Another breath. Another prayer.

"Yes, CC, I think she did."

37

Mark

October 1996

Mark pulled up in front of Mae's house, or David's house, and got out of the driver's seat, eager and anxious about the inevitable confrontation but ready for it. He prayed Mae would agree to go with them to the Department of Justice and start the process of an official custody agreement—if she didn't, his mom had said they would do whatever it took to get his rights acknowledged. Mom couldn't afford a fight like that, but she'd offered it anyway. Because she loved him and because family was everything.

He flipped his seat forward and leaned in to unbuckle Sienna from her car seat. She grinned and kicked her feet, now clad in Dora the Explorer Velcro shoes. Mom had gone shopping that morning and come home with a week's worth of toddler clothes. Mark didn't have a lot for Sienna at the apartment because new things went always went back to Mae's and generally didn't return. A lot of what Mae dressed her in probably belonged to David's other kids; the clothes rarely fit well and always smelled like David's house.

Mom was still in the passenger seat when Mark came around to her side of the car with Sienna on his hip. He stopped by her door and smiled encouragingly through the window when she looked up and met his eyes. He'd rarely seen Mom so nervous, but then last night had been pretty horrible. He would make all this up to her, one day. His first responsibility was Sienna, but his second responsibility would be to get back to the ranch and take his place there. He'd wanted to see the world, and he'd seen more than he ever wanted to see again. Mom took off her seat belt while Mark let out a billowing breath that clouded in front of his face.

Mom got out of the car and glanced nervously at the front door of the house. She stretched out her hands, made a fist, and stretched out her hands again while looking around the neighborhood as though checking to see if anyone was watching them. She'd been eager to confront Mae yesterday, but today she had been in no hurry to return, coming up with all kinds of tasks and errands to do before coming here. If he didn't know better, he'd think she was stalling. It was already three o'clock and the office was only open until five. "Everything okay, Mom?"

She looked from the house to him and pulled her eyebrows together. "Of course I'm okay," she snapped.

"You just seem a little . . . never mind."

He turned toward the front of the house, his eagerness contrasting with Mom's hesitation. Something was going to happen, finally! They would get orders or papers or something drawn up so that he wasn't at Mae's mercy anymore. He turned his head and blew a raspberry on Sienna's freckled cheek. She giggled and tried to pull away. He spun around with her in his arms, her two little pigtails flying, and then blew another raspberry on her cheek. *After today I will have a chance to make things different,* he thought as her giggles filled him from top to bottom.

He was standing on the porch before Mom had reached the bottom step. He turned to look at her but bit his tongue to keep from asking again if everything was okay. Seeing Mae's life through Mom's eyes had showed Mark the depth of the ugliness that Sienna was subjected to every day. Would still be subjected to, but specific visitation rights would solidify his role as Sienna's dad. If Mae were arrested, he would for sure be contacted. If the neglect continued or if he ever found out that Mae had given their child vodka again, he would have something more than just a birth certificate to use in asserting his rights.

Mom finally joined him on the porch and made a "go ahead" motion with her hands and eyebrows as though he were the one taking his time. He knocked on the door and braced himself as he always did. He never knew what to expect from the other side of that door.

The door opened, and David filled the door frame. Mark didn't let himself shrink back even though he had *really* hoped David wouldn't be here.

"We're here to see Mae," Mark said, glad his voice sounded stronger today than it had yesterday. It was a little pathetic that it was because his mom was here, but whatever.

"She's not here."

Mark felt his face tingle. "She said she would come with us to the Department of Justice today, to start working on official visitation and stuff." He huffed out a breath and cursed in his mind. Mae always found a way to take the upper hand. Crap.

David pulled his eyebrows together. "She said she was going to go with you?"

Mark lifted his chin. "Yes, she said we could take Sienna last night and then come back today so we can go to the offices." He turned to his mother. "Mom, what exactly did she say?"

"Just that. She, uh, didn't want Sienna last night, but she said she would go with us today."

David was looking between the two of them. "So, when you left last night she was okay?"

"Well, she was high or drunk, I guess," Mark said in another show of bravery. Was David hiding her? "But that's kind of Mae's standard these days, right?"

David leaned against the door frame, as though he were feeling casual even though the tension was unchanged. He crossed his thick arms across his chest. "Ya know, one thing about Mae is, she knows her limits. All these years she's never OD'd 'cause she knows how much is too much. Last night she managed to take two days' worth of heroin—I wouldn't guess she could even stay conscious long enough after half that dose to take another one."

"She was blitzed when we got here," Mom said defensively. "You give her too much credit."

David's eyes seemed to zero in on Mom. "Do I?"

She returned his gaze with the same hardness. Seconds ticked by, and a car drove past on the street. Mark boosted Sienna farther up his hip. She was leaning against his shoulder, silent and tense. It was cold, but he wasn't about to ask David if they could go inside.

"So, what, she's too trashed to come with us today, David?" Mark asked, his frustration growing. "Is that what you're saying?" Crap. What if Mae found a way to keep this court stuff from happening until Mom had to leave? Mom had sounded so sure last night when she'd explained the conversation she and Mae had had after he went out to the car. He should have known Mae wouldn't keep her word. His neck started feeling hot, and his relief at having a solution on hand began to fade.

"Like I told you," David said in reply to Mark but with his eyes on Mom, "she's not here."

"When did you last see her?" Mom asked.

"Here's the thing." David's voice was low and menacing, and Mark swallowed. If this man wanted to, he could brush all three of them off the porch with one sweep of his beefy arm. Sienna snuggled in even closer. "Mae's gone, and I've got a *pretty* good feeling she's not coming back. I think you know why."

Mark was startled by the accusation, and then froze as two pink spots appeared on Mom's cheeks.

David continued. "I spent the day getting things together here." He nodded toward the house behind him, and Mark looked inside for the first time. The part of the living room he could see from here was . . . tidy. He could smell Pine-Sol. "I've been waiting for you guys to come so that I could see what you knew, but I need to call the police and file a missing person's report pretty soon. It would be better for all of us if our stories were straight. I don't want any trouble, and I'm betting you don't either."

"What?" Mark asked sharply. Sienna whimpered, and Mark automatically kissed her on the forehead and shifted her to his other hip. His feet were starting to tingle from the cold.

"That would be a good idea," Mom said.

Mark's head swiveled to look at her but words failed him. What was she talking about?

David nodded. "Mae and I had a fight about her drug use last night before I went to work, you guys arrived to pick up Sienna for an overnight visit just as I was leaving. When I got home, Mae was gone. I thought maybe she was with you guys working things out with the custody stuff." He included Mark with a glance. "She was wearing a black sweater dress and house slippers—not even a coat, which was weird. I went to sleep like I always do after working the night shift and expected her to be there when I woke up, but she wasn't. Now you guys have come back, so I know she's not with you and realize that I need to call the police."

Mark stared at David, and his heart raced. Why was he saying all of this?

"We talked to her after you left last night," Mom said, picking up the narrative. "We argued a little bit about us taking Sienna for the night, but she finally agreed. She was obviously high and—"

"No, she wasn't," David interrupted. "She'd been clean for a few weeks because I told her she couldn't stay here if she wasn't— my girls come every other weekend. So, yeah, maybe she'd been drinking before you came, but then she must have left to get a hit after arguing with me and sending Sienna with you guys. She hasn't been doing any drugs here, not in *my house*. The cops might want to search the house, and I'm gonna let them do it 'cause they won't find anything. Do you understand what I'm saying? They won't find *anything* that might interfere with me and my family. Mae and I had a fight yesterday afternoon because I told her that things weren't working out and I wanted to reconcile with my wife—I have a family, after all. She was upset when I left for work, but I expected her to calm down so we could talk things over this morning."

Mom nodded slowly. "You're right, she'd been drinking when we got here, but she was upset and agitated, probably from the fight you two'd had."

"Mom, what the hell are you—" Mom grabbed Mark's hand and held it tight enough that he jumped and shut up. She kept her eyes on David while her grip remained as tight as a vise.

"After you left, she told us we couldn't take Sienna, but then I sent Mark and the baby out to the car so I could talk to her a bit. She calmed down some and finally said we could take Sienna for the night and that today we would start work on the custody stuff. I was surprised that she gave in so easily but not about to argue. Then she said we had to go because she had someone to see." She paused, raising an eyebrow as though seeking approval.

David nodded.

Mom nodded too, let out a shaky breath, and continued. "Mark's name is on the birth certificate, and he is fully capable and willing to take responsibility for Sienna. We'll be fighting for that as things move forward."

Birth certificate? Responsibility? Sticky dread was beginning to settle into Mark's stomach. Mom and David were doing exactly what David had suggested, getting their stories straight. They would do that only if they both had something to hide and something to protect.

"That works," David said easily. "Sienna's all yours, and it sounds like our stories match up pretty well. So long as I don't get charged with nothin', I'm good to stick with it and move on with my life. Know what I mean?" He pushed himself away from the door frame and took hold of the knob. "Sienna should stay with you guys while things get sorted out. I imagine the police will be contacting you for your side of the story. I'll be telling them you came by tonight and we all talked. It won't surprise them that we both told the other person our side of things."

"We'll be ready," Mom said. "You have Mark's number to give the police?"

"Yeah."

"And then what?" Mom asked. "What about, uh, Mae?"

"Give it a few days. Junkies turn up in a bad way all the time—they get dumped, ya see, after partying too hard. The folks they're with don't want to take the heat so they get rid of the body." He looked at Mark, then at Sienna in a way that made Mark pull her closer and rub her back. David's light blue eyes came back to Mark's. "I think it'll all turn out okay in the end. Live and learn and all that, ya know."

He shut the door. Mark blinked and then turned his head slowly to look at Mom. "What was that?"

"Let's get that baby out of the cold." Mom turned around, going down the steps toward the car. Mark followed her. She let herself into the passenger side while Mark buckled Sienna into her car seat. He slid into the driver's seat and started the car but didn't shift into drive. He rested his hands on the steering wheel, took a breath, and stared straight ahead. "What happened after I took Sienna to the car last night?"

Mom took a breath of her own, then let it out. She swallowed and cleared her throat. "You love that baby, Mark?"

"Yes," he said, his hands tightening on the steering wheel as he braced himself.

"You'd do anything for her, right?"

"Yeah."

"Anything?"

He turned to look at her and was surprised to see tears in her eyes. He'd never, not once in his life, seen his mother cry.

"I'd do anything," he said.

"Don't forget that," she said, her voice catching. She laid her shaking hands in her lap. A tear rolled down her cheek. "You would do anything for that child, and I know this because I would do anything for mine."

38

Sienna

June

I stand on the front porch of the ranch house, watching Dad through the front window as he moves around the kitchen—he hasn't seen me. The buzz of insects and lowing of the herd are like music on the summer breeze around me, and I wish I could stay for a little while. I've been standing here long enough to watch Dad rinse his plate, wipe down the counters, and pull a beer out of the fridge—I better understand now why he never has more than one. He looks stronger now that he's working the ranch more, but tired. Lonely. It's been two months since that phone call when he told me what he knew and said how sorry he was over and over again until we were both crying. We have not spoken since. We've texted about ranch stuff—Where did I put the seat cover for the tractor? Do I know where the pin for the trailer hitch is?—but I told him I needed time and he has given me that. My dad has always done everything he could to help me—whatever it takes. I haven't forgiven him for that yet.

I am on my way to Chicago, where I'll be going through the storage unit for real this time. I need to bring my stuff back to Cheyenne, where some of it will go into another storage unit half a mile from my apartment I've been living bare-bones in for the last six weeks. My life in Chicago is over. My life on the ranch is . . . on hold. My new life in Cheyenne is just getting started. I had texted Dad this morning to see if I could stop on my way through town and say hi as though I'm a distant cousin who doesn't get this way very often. He was so excited to have me come that I almost changed my mind. Not because I don't want to be here but because I have missed him so much. It scares me to think we might try to go back to who we were. That can't happen, but I *am* ready to have him in my life again. One step at a time.

Dad disappears from view, probably heading into his office, where I couldn't find my mother. He's kept up his blog—I read every post—and he hired one of Uncle Rich's grandsons to help out for the summer. Beck said he sent a dozen yearlings to a feed lot to get quick money. I'm thinking about going to London after all or a folk-art school in the hill country of North Carolina where I can "major" in leatherwork. It's a whimsical idea, but I've worked out the numbers a dozen times all the same. An unexpected side effect of learning that the mother I idolized never existed is that I no longer feel as if I need to be her. Or Beck. Or the Sienna I thought was the only Sienna for me to become. I am just . . . me, and I'm okay with that for the first time in a really long time.

I let myself in through the front door of the house. "Hello?"

"CC," Dad calls from the study, his feet following his voice in my direction. His face lights up when he sees me. I wonder if David's other daughters have ever seen the kind of warmth I have taken for granted all my life. I haven't talked to David since I fell off his porch, and I'm not sure I ever will. I've learned enough from Tristin, my half sister, to know that he's not someone I want to know. Dad crosses the space between us but then stops before hugging me, insecurity entering his expression. I don't initiate a hug either, but I smile at him and feel those still-hard places soften as I look into his blue-blue eyes.

"You look good, CC."

"Thanks," I say. "So do you."

He grins proudly. "I'm doing more around the ranch and started going to the gym with Rod and the guys a few times a week. Stopped eating red meat too."

I smile at the irony of a cattle rancher who doesn't eat beef.

We continue standing there, looking at each other with every-thing between us. I wonder if he knows he's not my biological father, but I've decided that I will never ask—the day I realized that was a big step for me. He lied to me as a form of protecting me. I am doing the same thing for him, and that helps me better understand what he's done.

He half turns toward the kitchen, graying eyebrows lifted and thumb pointing over his shoulder. "Do you want me to make you some eggs?"

I laugh because it's such a Dad thing to say. He smiles again, and everything feels a little more . . . right. Good. Normal. "No, thanks. I'm not hungry."

"Can we sit?" Dad asks, waving toward the living room where I watched *60 Minutes* on Sundays and put together countless puz-zles with Grandma Dee, who isn't really my grandmother and en-gaged her friend to write letters because she thought that would make things better for me. Or maybe the fact that it made things better for *her* was a bigger factor. I wonder if her guilt was what stood between us all those years. I wonder if every time she looked at me, she saw my mother. Maybe it could have been dif-ferent between us if I'd known the truth, but maybe it would have been worse. I'm attending a breast cancer support group, and one of the women said, "I don't believe that everything hap-pens for a reason, but I think God can help us find purpose in the struggles." I've gone to her church a few times, and I like the way they talk about God. It's not Grandma Dee's church. It's not Beck's church either. But it might be mine, and it's helping me to forgive and look ahead and decide what I want to choose for myself.

I sit on the couch and Dad sits next to me. "How are you doing? How are the treatments going?"

"I've had the first two rounds of radiation. It makes me sick for a couple of days afterward, but overall I'm feeling pretty good. Two more rounds and then I'm done with that." No chemo, so I get to keep my hair.

"Radiation was worse than chemo for me," he says sympa-thetically, shaking his head.

I tell him about my part-time job at a sporting goods store and my tiny apartment that Tyson is paying for because working part-time doesn't pay the rent—Ty got a raise when he extended his contract and I've chosen not to feel like a leech for accepting his generosity. I've never lived alone before. I had asked Dad to set out my leatherwork kit—I need something to do with my hands when I'm home in the evenings all by myself. That same lady from my support group talks about how we are all creators and that making things—babies, food, crafts—puts us in touch with God. It's a little hippy-dippy, but I like it all the same. She taught me how to knit but all I've made are scarves so far. I'm missing my leathercraft.

"And where are things with Tyson?" Dad asks.

"Better." We talk on the phone at the end of his day and the start of mine a few times a week. Last night we talked about the embryos for the first time. Tyson said it would be a shame to waste them, and I laughed. Dr. Sheffield's given me the name of a specialist who's successfully helped cancer survivors conceive. I won't make a consultation appointment until I'm a year past treatments, but it's something to look toward. A possibility. It is no longer my whole life, and I feel more capable of dealing with what might come next. What doesn't kill you makes you stronger, I think, but I hope not to be bitter either.

"It seems like you're doing really good, CC. I can't tell you how glad I am for that."

I smile my thanks. He squeezes my hand, and his expression falls into regret.

"I've wanted to tell you, CC, how sorry I am for everything. I've always wanted to do right by you, and I . . ." He pauses and takes a shaky breath. "You have been the greatest gift of my life."

I breathe his words in and let them settle in my lungs and heart and mind.

Commitment.

Sacrifice.

Good.

Bad.

Wrong.

Right.

Struggle.

Fear.

Love.

What would life have been like with a father like David Vandersteen? Tristin and I have sketched out some things she's never fully understood before. Tristin's parents were together and apart and together and apart for years. The separations when they went to live with Tristin's grandmother started with Mae, Tristin thought, but there were other women too. And drugs. And fights. Her parents finally divorced when Tristin was ten—five years after Mae had been found in the Grand River. Tristin's mom overdosed six months later, and Tristin and her sisters moved in with their dad again. Tristin got pregnant at fifteen and went to prison for drug charges when she was twenty. She's been clean for six years now but can't make things work on her own even though David is verbally abusive and goes on binges a few times a year. One of Tristin's sisters moved to Alberta and is keeping herself together. The other sister died in a car accident three years ago; she'd been using since she was fourteen and had lost two children to social services. Tristin would like to get her sister's kids back, but she knows she can't take care of them. They're currently in an adoptive placement that could be final by the end of the year. Cancer isn't the disease that caught my biological family in its barbed fingers. Addiction and violence and emotional disconnection have proved more deadly.

"I've got something for you," Dad says, and pushes himself up from the couch. He goes to the kitchen table, and I recognize the plastic tub of my leatherwork stuff. Next to it is a banker's box—the kind with finger holds on the sides and a fitted lid. He picks it up, and I notice that the print label is faded as he brings it my way. Have I seen it before? I would have assumed it was old tax forms if I had.

He sets the box down on the couch between us, and I know that my mother is in this box. My long-form birth certificate must be in there. Maybe there are more photos. Maybe other things that Dad hasn't shared with me because it would inter-fere with the picture he and Grandma Dee had decided to paint instead.

"I wasn't sure whether to throw out the twenty-fifth birthday letter," he says with regret as he stares at the box. "I didn't give it to you because, I don't know, it didn't seem like a good time. There's also one in there for the day you become a mother, but . . . they're still yours and . . ." He trails off, swallows, take a breath. "I'm so . . . sorry." His voice catches, and I blink back tears. He takes another breath and waves at the box. "I'll let you decide what to do with all this stuff. It should have been yours a long time ago." He finally looks up to meet my eyes, layers of heartache and apology within his gaze.

Who would I have become if there had been no Mark Chad-wick?

What kind of life would I have had with Maebelle Gérard?

How would I have understood who my mother really was when I was young? When I was a teenager?

The anger and the hurt didn't go away when I started asking myself these questions a few weeks ago, but it moved aside on the bench, leaving room for something else. Something different. I wasn't sure what that space was for but maybe I do now. We will rebuild. We will come together. The knowing is as steady as a fence line disappearing into the horizon. I take a breath, let it out, and let it be. Picking out the old stitching of my life story has been hard. Now I'll need to sew in new, not so pretty panels. Dad can help me with that when the time comes, but too much pressure before I'm ready to open my heart as wide as it needs to be would shatter *this*. *This* that is left between us. *This* that can be a place to build from.

I pick up the box and set it at my feet—I'm going to look through it when I'm alone. I take Dad's hand and give it a squeeze. "I love you, Dad, and we're going to be okay."

"Promise?" he says, his eyes eager. Begging.

"Cross my heart," I say, making an X over my chest forever scared by the removal of the tumor that really was a one-in-a-million case. My cancer could have killed me, and yet it may have saved me too. Like growing up on the ranch. Like falling off a porch. Like having a father and grandmother who did whatever it took to keep me. Someday I'll ask Dad what their choices cost them.

Dad leans forward, and I duck my chin so he can kiss the top of my head. I feel the blessing of it as though he's poured cool water over me. "Cross your heart and hope for pie. I love you, CC."

I lift my head and look him in the eye. "I love you too."

> *Who has seen the wind?*
> *Neither I nor you.*
> *But when the leaves hang trembling,*
> *The wind is passing through.*

39

Mark

November 1996

Mark didn't think he'd breathed a full breath until he drove under the sign at the border crossing that said UNITED STATES OF AMERICA. Mom had gone home two weeks ago, he'd stayed until all the paperwork was finished and the immigration attorney he'd hired—he'd pay Mom back somehow—assured him he could legally take Sienna with him to the U.S.

Two days after crossing the border, Mark pulled to a stop in front of the ranch house and nearly cried. Acres of land and purpose. He would forget he'd ever wanted something more than this and raise his daughter to value all the things he now valued so much more than he once had: work, family, reaping, and sowing. Truth? He took a breath and let it out. Would the truth be a burden Sienna would carry for the rest of her life? Mark knew what it was like to have a parent you didn't know and couldn't trust. He knew was it was like to hear that parents disparaged and feel like those adults were accusing you of the same failings because you were a part of them. He wanted better for Sienna.

Mark turned to look into the backseat, then stretched his hand back to brush the feathery brown hair from the side of his daughter's sleeping face, letting his hand stay against her little girl skin an extra heartbeat.

"I love you, CC," he whispered, taking encouragement that

she was clean and safe and smelling like baby shampoo. "And I promise to do everything possible to give you the life you deserve."

He let himself out of the car and took a deep breath of the country air. Rhythm and purpose and seasons and life pulsed from the ranch, grounding him and welcoming him home. He would never leave again. Everything that mattered to him was here now.

He opened the back door to a blinking Sienna, her light blue eyes looking wider and bluer in the afternoon light. Not his eyes—he'd realized that after the night he first met David Vandersteen. But *she* was his. Would always be his. He couldn't save Mae from the course her life had taken due to the failures of the people who should have done better by her, but he would do everything he could to save Sienna from a similar course.

"We're home, CC," he said as he unfastened the straps of her car seat. "Everything is going to be okay. Whatever it takes."

WHATEVER IT TAKES

Jessica Pack

ABOUT THIS GUIDE

The suggested questions are included to enhance
your group's reading of Jessica Pack's
Whatever It Takes.

Discussion Questions

1. Have you ever had a secret in your family that came to light? How were members of the family affected?

2. Have you ever received a letter or note from someone who had already passed on? How did it make you feel?

3. Do you see a difference between the way Sienna "protected" her dad from learning about her cancer and the way he "protected" her from information about her mother?

4. How do you think Mark and Grandma Dee were affected by the lies they propagated in this story?

5. Does it feel reasonable to you that Sienna could forgive her dad?

6. Have you ever seen a relationship come together as strong or stronger after a betrayal?

7. Was there a particular scene in this story that stood out to you?

8. Sienna's portion of this story is written in first-person present tense, somewhat unusual for an adult novel like this. Did you like that perspective or did you find it difficult to get into?

9. Was there any part of this story or the relationships presented here that you thought should have been more developed?

Connect with U s

Visit us online at
KensingtonBooks.com
to read more from your favorite authors, see books
by series, view reading group guides, and more.

Join us on social media

for sneak peeks, chances to win books and prize packs,
and to share your thoughts with other readers.

facebook.com/kensingtonpublishing
twitter.com/kensingtonbooks

Tell us what you think!

To share your thoughts, submit a review,
or sign up for our eNewsletters, please visit:
KensingtonBooks.com/TellUs.